Thank God for quiet neighbors!

SINBAD

ROGUE OF MARS

A novel by John Garavaglia

Based on the graphic novel by
Greg Thompson, Scott Davis,
Jeff "Chamba" Cruz and
Kiatisak Piewkao

John C. Garavaglia

8-12-18

Published by Markosia Enterprises, PO BOX 3477, Barnet, Hertfordshire, EN5 9HN.

FIRST PRINTING, June 2018.
Harry Markos, Director.

Paperback: ISBN 978-1-911243-92-2
eBook: ISBN 978-1-911243-93-9

Book design by: Ian Sharman

www.markosia.com

First Edition

"A little body doth often harbor a great soul."
Arabian Proverb

ALSO BY JOHN GARAVAGLIA
AND PUBLISHED BY
MARKOSIA

DORIAN GRAY

PROLOGUE

An alien sun and a massive moon shone through a thick, dusty sky, at levels too bright for comfort. A blue skinned man and his two sons were standing in a barren wasteland.

The man known as Azrak was traveling through the desert with his children while they were on their way home from the marketplace. They had stopped in the middle of the desert for a water break, and Azrak was watching his two boys playing a very rigorous game of tag.

Then over the horizon, a light started to outshine the hot sun, adding to the feeling of intense heat.

Azrak knew something was coming.

He could sense it, feel it in the shaking of the surface under him. The air around the family rumbled louder and louder; the dust, swirling like a breeze, was kicking it up. Yet, the father could feel no wind against his face. Not even his fabrics moved in the high winds.

Something big was coming.

Huge.

But he didn't know what.

He just waited, facing it, wanting to turn and run; yet not doing so. He needed to know what it was.

He needed to face it.

The air swirled and the dust choked him. The surface under his feet shook, as the horizon got even brighter.

The unknown came closer.

And closer.

He shook off the feeling of dread and tried to calm his fast beating heart. He desperately needed to know what it meant. And what he was waiting for.

Azrak felt the earth move suddenly. Then he heard a loud rumble.

"Father, what is it?" said Sobek, his youngest son. "Is it a quake?"

"No," Azrak replied, "there are no fault lines anywhere near here."

"What's going on?" asked Matthias, Azrak's eldest child.

The rumbling deepened, growing into a deafening roar. The boys were frightened, but Azrak was just calmly looking over the horizon as if he couldn't be less concerned.

"Father?" Matthias called again, but Azrak wasn't paying him any attention.

He saw the sand from the dunes rose up like a violent sandstorm. It was impossible, but it appeared to him that it was the end of the days.

The children stood behind their father as the sand sprayed over to them. Then they all saw it. A meteor was streaking just above them, right over their heads. It was large and seemed to be made out of wood—not iron ore—and it was about to crash.

Azrak forced opened his eyes, the bright light was hurting them.

There was a sudden thunderous blast.

Then, for a moment, everything was silent.

"Is it over?" asked Sobek.

The answer came just a moment later with a deafening explosion that rattled the desert.

Azrak's heart was racing. He wasn't sure what happened. Then he shoved his fears aside.

"Follow me, boys," he said to his awestruck children. "No dawdling."

Azrak and his sons rushed over the dunes, and along the way they saw the charred trench, several hundred feet long. Rising from the superheated dunes far out in the desert as hot wind tickled the dune crests, spraying sand downslope in neat sire curves. It was not the cause of the eruption of sand that occurred near the center of one dune, however. Over the hill, they found it. It was still hot and smoking.

There was a deep crater in the middle of the desert. At the bottom of it the large wooden ship was cooling off from the heat of entry. He stretched out his foot to see how hot the ground was. The heat rushed up to his nose, and without meaning to, he pulled back instinctively. He could feel his pulse beating. It was loud and painful, but he braced himself and started again.

The craft was unlike anything Azrak had ever seen before. The ship wasn't built with metal and rivets. It was made of wood, and it had sails. This was certainly no spacecraft. It was a nautical vessel. The question running through Azrak's mind was what a ship of that purpose would be doing in the middle of the desert.

It looked like the ship had been through a terrible storm. The sails were ripped and tattered. The three masts were all entwine and cracked. The hull was damaged beyond repair. It was as if the entire ship had fallen from the sky.

"Over here, Father!" exclaimed Sobek.

Azrak followed his son to the starboard side of the ship to discover a humanoid alien life form. It had pink skin and also appeared to be male. It was wearing some sort of hat on its head, and the sun caught the glimmer of the golden medallion hung around its neck. The man's face was bruised and battered, more black and blue than anything else. One arm was bent in a way that told Azrak it was broken in at least two places. The outlander was suffering trauma from the crash. The foreigner was on the verge of dehydration and he was also starving. Azrak looked him over and faced his oldest son.

"I need my bag, now!" he ordered.

Matthias ran to his father and handed him the bag. Azrak ran through the contents and pulled out a small medical kit. He opened the case to reveal bandages, anti-toxins, rations, and disinfectants. He unlocked the rations compartment, and retrieved several morsels of food.

He placed his fingers on the stranger's neck to find a pulse. Azrak found a very faint trace of life in the strange visitor. Then the blue caregiver took a piece of food and placed it in the outlander's mouth.

Desperate for air, the man coughed violently. He hacked up plugs of putrid sand from his mouth and nose.

Matthias pointed to the stranger's face. "Its eyes are opening, Father!"

"Here," Azrak said to the pink life form, "take this. You have traveled a long way, my friend. It is my honor and privilege to have found you."

The man opened his eyes to discover the silhouettes of three oddly shaped strange beings standing over him in front of a blinding pink sky. Their eyes were much wider than any human being. Their skin was as blue as the sea itself and neither of them had any noses. He looked at the adult through half-closed eyes. His lips, dry and parched, quivered as he struggled to talk.

Azrak feared that the impact from the crash might have given the injured stranger a concussion. He had to keep him awake. It didn't matter what the subject of the conversation would be; as long as the Azurian man would keep the man awake.

"I know you must be in terrible pain, my friend," said Azrak, looking over the strange man's wounds. His attention was fully focused on the dislocated arm. "But can you move your arm?"

The man grunted with effort, and sucked his teeth in pain. Beads of sweat dripped through the pores of his forehead, and his face turned red.

"I think it's broken," he answered the tall blue man.

Azrak studied the severe ailment. "It's not broken, only dislocated."

"Can you put it back into place?"

"Yes, I can," Azrak replied, placing his hands on the man's shoulder. "I must warn you, the pain will be excruciating."

The man took a breath and looked at Azrak in a state of readiness. "Then do it."

Azrak gripped the man's shoulder. "Be still. I'm going to do it on the count of three."

The man closed his eyes and muttered a prayer in his native tongue.

"One..." the blue man began, and then a loud popping sound erupted inside the man's eardrum. The man howled in pain.

"I thought you were going to count to three!"

Azrak gave him a small smile. "I am very sorry. I thought you would back out at the last second."

He expected the bizarre pink man would be angry. But he was surprised to hear the sound of laughter.

"I would have too," the man laughed. "Well played, my friend. Well played."

Azrak laughed along with him, while he checked the arm, which was now placed back into its socket.

"Your arm looks better, but it's going to take some time to heal. What is your name, stranger?"

The adrenaline from the minor operation was wearing off, and the man had a feeling he could pass out at any moment. He mustered all the strength he had left to answer his savior's question.

"On the Isle of Kish, I am a hero," he began, forcing himself to keep his eyes open. "In the city of Abu Dhabi, I am a thief. And in Baghdad I am to be killed on sight."

Azrak leaned onto every word the man said. He had no recollection about the cities and countries that were mentioned. It was then Azrak learned that this man wasn't from around here at all.

"My friends call me a sailor. My enemies call me a pirate."

Pirate? Thought Azrak in fear. *Is he affiliated with the deadly pirate Rhadjan Vix?*

Then the man placed his hand onto Azrak's. "But you may call me Sinbad."

Sinbad the Sailor quickly surveyed his surroundings. Nothing was familiar to him. He had been all over the world, but he didn't remember anything about this place. Then he feared he wasn't in his beloved city of Baghdad anymore.

He finally gave into the shock and rolled his eyes inside his head. Azrak stood up in alarm and lifted Sinbad into his arms, and carried him off over the dunes.

CHAPTER ONE
IT'S ALL FATE AND CHANCE

Deep into the subterranean dungeon of the malevolent Emperor Akhdar Dadgar, the newly crowned monarch of the Dozhakian throne and ruler of the Thulian people; in the middle of the prison cell sat a man whose broad shoulders and sun-browned skin seemed out of place among these dismal surroundings. He seemed more a part of the sun and winds, and the high planes of the outlands. The legendary sailor Sinbad knelt on top of the red Martian dirt and began to greet the morning's dawn on this strange world he has been stranded since far back as he could remember by praying to Allah. The first of the five sessions he had to perform for the day. Salah is intended to focus on the mind of Allah, and seen as a personal communication with Him. Sinbad hoped the benevolent deity would hear His worshiper's prayers from all the way back to Earth. But Sinbad wasn't pleading for himself, but for those he had befriended on this planet.

Sinbad stood upright facing Qiblah and then proceeded to make Niyyah in his heart. He raised his hands to his ears and said softly, "Allah is the greatest." Sinbad placed his right hand on top of his left hand on his chest and looked downward to the ground. "O Allah, how perfect You are and praise be to You," the humble sailor silently began. "Blessed is Your name and exalted is Your majesty. There is no god but You. I seek shelter from the rejected Satan. In the name of Allah, the most Gracious and Merciful."

Sinbad took a breath to replenish himself before he could continue. He held onto his chest tightly and recited the first chapter of the Quran.

"All praises and thanks be to Allah, the Lord of the worlds, the most Gracious, the most Merciful; Master of the Day of Judgment. You alone we worship, from You alone we seek help. Guide us along the straight path, the path of those whom You favored, not of those who earned Your anger or went astray."

The Earth warrior bowed down and kept his head in line with his back, while he continued his vespers. Sinbad's turban rested on the ground in front of him, as the sun's rays poured in between the jail's bars. A luxury only the most fortunate of prisoners would ever receive in this broken down palace.

Sinbad prostrated on the floor with his forehead, nose, palms of both hands, his knees, and toes all touching the floor. Then he sat up with his knees and palms placed on them and said, "O my Lord! Forgive me." And he softly whispered "Allah, please grant me the strength and courage to face what is to come."

His fellow inmates had long since given up their attempts for any chance of escape. They have accepted their fates as gladiators for Zhar Akhdar's own personal amusement. The prisoners were native to Mars' soil. Their appearance was humanoid but they were much taller than average human height. Also much thinner, but muscular given the current diet the guards provided for them. Their skin was blue as if they were suffering a severe case of hypothermia. And their yellow eyes pierced through the darkness like a cat on the prowl. They all sat defeated waiting for the chilling sound of the guards opening the door. That only meant one thing for them: death.

This was no place for Sinbad. He felt more comfortable at the helm of his ship, *The Chimera*, sailing the seven seas with the sun on his back and the sea salt in his beard. But he was depraved of his true love of freedom in exchange to be the star attraction for the grisly entertainment of corrupt and malicious aristocrats. Sinbad couldn't remember the last time he ever enjoyed the majestic beauty of the ocean. He had been on land for so long he feared he had lost his sea legs. No matter what evil they had done to him, he will always carry his love for the sea and freedom in his heart.

He wore no ring or ornaments, except for the golden medallion that hung around his neck. Sinbad's pendant glimmered in the sunlight when he slipped it off his neck. Sinbad wrapped the chain around his hand so it wouldn't tangle, and placed it gently inside his turban for safekeeping. He didn't want its shimmer to catch any of the thieving guards' eyes. He knew the coming battle would be his most challenging yet. He couldn't afford to be distracted by his medallion jostling around in rapid combat. If it became taut around an obstacle Sinbad wouldn't have enough time or the flexibility to launch a counterstrike. He would need to consider every possible scenario on how this fight was going play out.

Ever since he was brought into the zhar's gladiator games, Sinbad was fighting for his own life. But this time he would fight for the sake of another.

"Do not go, Sinbad," said one of the blue men in the dark. "You will surely perish."

"I have no choice, Azrak," Sinbad replied, donning his turban. "Has the emperor not declared that if I refuse, he will have us all killed? As long as I fight, Akhdar has given his word that he will let you go, whether I am victorious or not." The Earthman took a breath and adjusted his turban for his medallion to sit still on the top of his head. "I already have the blood of your family on my hands," he continued, with sorrow in his voice. "I will not add yours to that, Azrak."

Azrak stood up from his spot on the ground and proceeded to his friend. Hoping he could talk some sense into him.

"Sinbad, that was—"

"Quiet, friend," interrupted another inmate. He was much older and the weakest prisoner in the whole cellblock. He placed his hand on Azrak's shoulder and pulled him away from Sinbad. "He has made his decision."

Azrak brushed the elder away; not caring for the way Sinbad has been acting. Azrak thought to himself how his otherworldly comrade can remain so calm and display such bravado. In addition how gullible he could be.

"Akhdar will kill us no matter what you do," Azrak sternly said to Sinbad. A worried look ran across his blue angular face. "His word is useless! Don't be foolish!"

Deep inside Sinbad's soul he knew his most trusted friend was right. There was no time to devise an alternative solution. Sinbad hoped this fight would buy his friend more time—time that was running out.

"The virtue of deeds lies in completing them, my friend," he said to Azrak, as he got up to his two feet. "I will keep my word, atone for your family's tragedy, and you shall live."

Azrak and his family showed Sinbad kindness when the mighty sailor came to this strange world. And for that kindness, all but Azrak was viciously murdered in cold blood on Zhar Akhdar's orders. On this day Sinbad still does not know why.

The loud click from the cell's lock filled the dungeon. Sinbad wasn't affected by the sound that filled the prisoners' hearts with fear. He stood ready, knowing his time has come. The guards, two burly green men, entered the grimy dark cell. They wore heavy plated armor, which covered most of their battle scars. One of them leered at Sinbad hardheartedly.

"Come, outlander," ordered the guard. "Your end is nigh. You must not keep the zhar and his guests waiting."

Before Sinbad could submit to his captors' demands Azrak held him back.

"Let me go with you. Two will fare better than one."

"No," Sinbad contested, "I must go this alone."

The other guard gave Sinbad a scornful smirk followed by a taunting chuckle. "Are you ready to die, outlander?"

Sinbad didn't dignify that with a response. His focus was completely set towards the arena. He clenched his fists and simply replied, "If Allah wills."

The trek to the coliseum was a long journey. The two heavily armed guards forced Sinbad to march ahead through the gulag's stone doorway. The passage was clearly the way *into* the prison. The way *out* was very different indeed, as a number of ill-fated captives learned by watching their fellow inmates fall in combat and succumb to disease and malnutrition.

Sinbad was greeted by the venomous harangues of jeering and catcalls from a gallery of murderers, marauders, and disgraced soldiers. Even the other guards didn't show the Earthman any respect at all. Sinbad didn't pay any attention to their coercions. He knew they were all trying to scare him. But they weren't trying hard enough. The sailor has seen almost everything in his world. From nature's wonders to the supernatural, there was nothing else that could frighten him. However, he was on another planet and he was the only human in this world. This made him the minority and an outsider to every society on Mars.

The equipped guards nudged Sinbad further with the tips of their sharp spears.

"Advance, outlander!" threatened the one on the right. "You do not have time to lavish in the company of your friends."

"What friends?" asked the other guard, as they both laughed cruelly.

When Sinbad proceeded down the passage he kept his eyes straight to the giant double doors that separated the prison and the arena. He blocked out the cruel hecklings, obscene gestures, and the rotted fruit and stones he was pelted with by the prisoners in neighboring cells. He would not give these vipers the satisfaction of retaliation or yield to their bullying. Even though more than half of the general population wanted to lynch him, they all knew Zhar Akhdar had something worse planned for the otherworldly stranger.

Sinbad made it all the way to the gateway of the arena. His escorts tended to each door and opened them to reveal Zhar Akhdar's coliseum. Without hesitation or being forced onward by his oppressors, Sinbad walked into the battleground.

The arena was impressive and filled with grandeur. However, no matter how magnificent it was for the dignitaries and spectators it was also terrifying. The entire structure was formed all over the caves. The viewing terraces resembled honeycombs in a buzzing beehive. The ground floor was surrounded by numerous doors and gates with at least two guards stationed in front of each and every one. Sinbad and the rest of the gladiators knew what was at the other side. Only a lucky few had survived to tell the horrifying tales of what savage beasts that been collected all over the planet. Only to be summoned again to encounter another bizarre monster again to gratify Akhdar's bloodlust.

Like a merciless child, Zhar Akhdar, treated his prisoners like insects trapped in a bell jar. Watching sadistically how long they could survive without any air. And how he relished pulling the wings off them in order to prolong their suffering.

Sinbad lifted his head to the royal balcony to see Zhar Akhdar accompanied by his lovely sister Aella, several alien notables, robed courtiers, advisers, and bodyguards stood in attendance. Akhdar was tall and slender with light green skin. He wore the traditional attire of his regal family, including many valuable golden rings adorned on his thin claw-like fingers. They were drinking wine and eating very rich delicacies native to the Thulian culture. Towering marble columns supported the high ceiling. Carved Martian hieroglyphs embellished the decorative cornice running along the tops of the walls.

Akhdar enjoyed being the center of attention. He just couldn't get enough of it. In all the evil he has done, his greatest sin would have to be vanity, followed by greed and pride.

His sister Aella wasn't as conceited. Her greed wasn't as equivalent because she had everything her heart desired. But all except for one: companionship. Aella's beauty was unlike all the other females in the kingdom. Many suitors were drawn by her loveliness and would give anything to run their fingers through her long, red luscious hair. Only to be rejected by her triviality. Aella didn't find politicians appealing with their big round bellies, their arrogant behavior, and of course the pungent stench of wine and smoke that stained their clothes and breath.

Akhdar found his sister's insincerities a thorn to his side. He continually evoked her to stop being such a child and finally consider marriage. Especially to a prince from a neighboring realm, so Akhdar would forge an alliance and expand his influence throughout Mars. Aella cared for her brother, but hated being treated as one of his subordinates. If she would marry someone it would be for love, not for her brother's personal gain.

Akhdar sat on his throne with his sister by his side. The young zhar looked down to the arena and saw the puny Earthman known as Sinbad meeting his eyes.

"I am here, Akhdar," Sinbad called up to him. "I have honored my half of our agreement. I trust you will honor yours."

Akhdar paused and briefly meditated on the subject. A look of confusion was on his face. It was as if he couldn't understand what language Sinbad was speaking. The zhar looked at his sister in misperception.

"'Trust,' dear sister?" he asked in bewilderment.

"A foreign concept, my brother," Aella replied, staring at Sinbad. A small lascivious smile crept on her delicate face. She couldn't take her eyes off this far-off creature's physique. Such strong arms and brightly tanned skin. "A rare quality his kind infrequently possesses."

"Ah," confirmed Akhdar, grinning savagely.

He signaled Tarkhun, his right hand man and loyal bodyguard, to bring Sinbad's confiscated scimitar from the armory. Tarkhun presented it to his lord and master. Akhdar merely waved it away for his majordomo to throw the sword out the balcony and landed several feet in front of Sinbad.

The sailor pulled his reliable sword out of the ground. He took several practice slashes and showed off some of his swordsmanship skills. Aella admiringly watched him from the royal terrace. She fantasied him as both her lover and her guardian. Even though he wasn't a natural inhabitant to this advanced civilization, this made her infatuation more taboo.

She stared at the handsome outlander and studied him with half lidded eyes at the fluidity of the way he moved. She had seen several of his fights and gathered enough evidence of his power and skill. Then she wondered if he had talents of similar magnitude in other areas of life.

In the corner of his eye Akhdar noticed her coarse ogling and followed her gaze to the human. *Disgusting*, he thought. Such an affair would damage his image to his faithful followers and his high-class peers.

Akhdar quickly rose from his throne and motioned to his guards on the combat zone.

"Release the moktar!" he yelled at the top of his lungs.

His bellowing gave his sister quite a jolt. She broke her fanatical gazing and turned her attention to the arena.

The two strong guards pulled the heavy chains under extreme duress. The sound of gigantic feet thundered behind the door and the vibrations shook the coliseum. Bits of rock shook loose and several stalactites fell into the arena. Sinbad and the guards maneuvered away from the debris. Then the sound of demonic trumpets and growls emerged through the door.

Massive and slow-moving, rapid movements sounded at the other side. Shadows obscured the light that had been pouring through the thin crack of the door.

Sinbad stood ready. Through everyone else's eyes, they all considered him lucky for staying alive for so long in his imprisonment. But Sinbad didn't believe in such a thing. He believed a man could control his own fate by the actions that define him. Not by playing as destiny's puppet. But he didn't argue with divine intervention. Sinbad believed Allah had kept him alive because this world needed him. The sailor had no qualms on that notion. All he cared about was the wellbeing of others.

Before the guards could fully open the door, the massive beast broke loose onto the arena. Its monstrous strength knocked the enormous door off its hinges and broke in two with its colossal feet. Two great eyes blazed from the wavering shadows. The moktar gave out a primal roar, with his small trunk swinging in the air with fierce rage. The hideousness of its face transcended more beastly.

Sinbad's hair rose up and he grasped his sword very tightly.

Cries of amazement rose amongst the assembled members of the audience and many scattered away from the creature.

He stared in the unknown at the creature, which sat with such uncanny patience before the closed door. He shuddered at the sight of the giant feet, thickly grown with hair that was almost fur-like. The body was thick, broad and bushy. It growled as it breathed.

To Sinbad, the creature resembled on what would happen if an elephant mated with a hippopotamus. This was far too horrific that even he could have imagined. The moktar's long inverted tusks were both dilapidated from when it was captured. Its left tusk was broken in half during the pursuit from Akhdar's elite hunters. Ever since it was first brought into captivity, the zhar made sure the beast was abused as much as possible. So it would be in the right mood for the games.

Azrak watched the rampage from his cell. His eyes widened in terror as he gripped the bars tightly.

"Run, Sinbad. Run!" he yelled at the top of his lungs.

The moktar raised its head in attention. Its wrinkled trunk waved hysterically on picking up Sinbad's scent. The moktar's head jerked swiftly and its black beady eyes caught the small man brandishing his sword.

The gargantuan quadruped dug its feet to the ground, like a bull ready to charge. Sinbad took a defensive stance with his sword in the air. With a loud, spit-spraying snort the moktar drove angrily towards the human gladiator on a gaudy snarl.

Various alien life forms from all over Mars and neighboring planets cheered chaotically for the well-awaited battle. Countless wagers were in favor of the monster. Some said Sinbad would fall as soon as the fight would start. But others were wary when they heard about the Earthman's extensive reputation.

There was something in the red murky eyes, its clumsy posture, and its whole appearance that set apart from the truly animal. That monstrous body housed a brain and soul that were just budding awfully into something vaguely human.

Sinbad stood his ground as the moktar boomed across the arena. He remained still as a statue. Just waiting to find his window of opportunity on when he should strike. He could hear the viewers' vicious barbs against him. How he had cheated death for the final time, and he had outlived their amusement. He seldom heard the very faint cheers from his very few admirers. He wasn't there for their entertainment. He was there to complete a task to save his friend Azrak's life.

The moktar made its move on a killing stroke to the right. Sinbad quickly dodged the slash and rolled aside. The beast turned around and saw Sinbad getting back to his feet. It stampeded toward the sailor again, but this time Sinbad made his attack. While the moktar jumped over him, Sinbad came at it like a charging bull. His head was down, his scimitar low for the disemboweling thrust. The moktar sprang to meet him, and all the outlander's strength went into the arm that swung the sword. The outlander moved in a blur of blinding speed. In a whistling arc the great blade flashed through the air and sliced through the monster's flesh. The blade scratched through the flesh like it was butter. Blood squirted through the large laceration on the moktar's hind leg, while it let out an awful wail.

The monster was dazed. It limped over to its right side, trying to find some support. But it wouldn't go down without a fight. Blood was in the moktar's eyes now. All it wanted was to impale its aggressor on its one good horn. With all its strength and fury, the moktar began its counterstrike.

Sinbad felt his blood freeze as he looked at the horror that seemed to be staring directly into his eyes. Involuntarily he recoiled, while Sinbad thrust his head truculently forward, till his jaws almost tended the surface, growling. It was some sort of threat or defiance in his own native tongue.

Sinbad found an opening and leapt upward into the air to deliver a swift slash to the moktar's throat. Hot red blood came gushing out and blemished the sands of the arena.

The crowd's cheering and applause abruptly ceased, and an eerie silence filled the air. It was as if people were trying to figure out whether they'd actually seen what they thought they saw. Not once in Akhdar's games they have seen a gladiator slay the fearsome moktar. The stillness carried from the first row, to the betting booths, to all the way to Zhar Akhdar's terrace.

* * *

The green-skinned ruler was appalled on this incredible feat. His sister Aella shared the same feeling. However, she was eager to see the striking warrior escape the ferocious tribulation.

"Impossible!" Akhdar bellowed. "How could this be? No one has ever bested the moktar—**NO ONE!**"

"Oh, hush now, brother dear," soothed Aella, taking his hand. "Don't you fret. This man—this Sinbad has proven to be quite the cunning warrior. Would you like to see him fight again?"

Akhdar heaved an irritating sigh and managed to squeeze out a patronizing smile. "Well, sister, perhaps you're right. This oddity might still prove promising."

One person shouted, "Sinbad!" and then "Sinbad! Sinbad!" over and over again.

The chant was picked up, resounding throughout the audience, and people were clapping and shouting. The guards who had arrived upon the scene, weapons at the ready began to lower them, and joined in the cheers and ovations from all around the arena.

Sinbad remained right where he was for a few moments. Akhdar surveyed the damage his prized beast had sustained. He saw all the wounds and huge lacerations in its body, and the rivulets of dark crimson blood.

Azrak smiled with joy inside his cell. "I-I can't believe it!" he exclaimed with glee.

"What? What happened?" the elderly Azurian beside him asked groggily

"Sinbad has slain the moktar!" Azrak replied in astonishment.

The old man heard the applause, the shouts, and as crazy as it seemed the name "Sinbad" being chanted over and over again.

He moved around a corner just in time to see Sinbad standing over the vanquished monster.

The ancient Azurian scratched his head, and had an epiphany. "Perhaps he is the one of whom the prophecy speaks."

Azrak looked at his elder in uncertainly. Before he could even reply, Azrak's attention was shifted back into the area as he saw Sinbad tower over the moktar with his sword in his hand.

The immense animal fell onto the bloodstained sand. It breathed heavily and then it became shallow. The crowd cheered in approval. They all go out of their seats and began to chant, "Kill, kill, kill!"

Sinbad took no joy in this victory. There was no thrill of battle. It was all about survival. Before he put the poor beast out of its misery, Sinbad silently prayed to Allah for forgiveness.

He grit his teeth and drove the sword deep. Blood streamed over the blade and his hand, and the monster started to convulse, and then lay back quite still. Sure that life had fled, at least what he understood of it, Sinbad set to work on his grisly task.

CHAPTER TWO
MISTRUST BEFORE YOU TRUST

Sinbad was brought back to his cell the usual way: thrown on his ear.

"Back to your cage, outlander!" said the guard. "Maybe after your next fight, your friend will have his freedom, eh?"

Sinbad met the ground with a harsh thud, followed by the slamming of the cell's door.

"Sinbad!" Azrak yelled in worry. He offered Sinbad his hand, but the sailor waved it away. "Let me help."

"I'm fine, Azrak," said Sinbad, slowly rising. "Just a little winded."

"There's no shame on showing humility, my friend," retorted Azrak. "You have fought a great battle. You must not strain yourself. You have to rest and keep up your strength."

"I cannot rest, Azrak. I have to be on my guard at all times. It has kept me alive so far."

Azrak gave him a dubious look. "You are making a dangerous habit on confusing bravery with arrogance, Sinbad. You will not make it through the next fight unless your wounds are treated and fully recuperated."

Sinbad knew his friend was right. He was not of use to anyone while being tired and bruised. He felt disappointed in himself for not fulfilling his promise to gain Azrak's freedom. Sinbad had achieved his share of the given terms, but Akhdar decided to renege on his part.

"You were right about Akhdar," Sinbad humbly admitted. "I tried playing his game and he decided to change the rules."

Azrak put his hand on Sinbad's shoulder. "You had no choice, Sinbad. You did what you had to do. You are not the one in blame. This is all on Akhdar."

Sinbad paused for a moment. He lifted his head to Azrak and gave him a smile.

"At least you did not say, 'I told you so.'"

The sound of the battle conch shell filled the arena. The spectators roared wildly as the primus was about to commence. Sinbad and Azrak turned around to look between the prison bars to see what the disturbance was about.

Sinbad could only make out a guard wrangling a horse. Sinbad had never seen any horses running through Mars before. When the horse advanced further into the arena, Sinbad discovered this creature wasn't what he thought it was. It wasn't a wild stallion at all. It was a man.

No, not a man—a centaur!

Sinbad couldn't believe his eyes. This creature had the upper body of a man and a horse's lower half. But he did not have the hooves of a horse, but three toes on each foot that resembled those similar of a gorilla. The centaur had a powerful frame. Broad heaving shoulders, massive chest, lean waist, and heavy arms. His skin was grey with a hue of purple, he had brown eyes, and a shock of tousled black hair crowned his balding forehead. Every time it swayed its head, its long ponytail would crack like a whip. The centaur was given a weapon from the guard, a kunai—a sharpened blade attached to a long piece of rope.

Astounded, Sinbad asked Azrak, "What is that?"

"A Kurwani," Azrak replied implausibly. "I thought they were all dead."

The elderly Azurian got off his perch and stared at the centaur.

"He is Kar-Tyr," he said, "the last of his people."

"Amazing," Sinbad softly said in awe. He hadn't seen a creature like that since his Golden Voyage years ago. But the one he encountered was a cyclops, and there wasn't a griffin to swoop in to attack him as well.

"Kar-Tyr's race, the Kurwani, valued combat over all things," continued the elder as Sinbad heeded to every word he said. "They lived to fight and fought to live. For years they were the personal guard of the Dozhakian zhar—never asking for more than to prove themselves in battle. When Akhdar gained power, he feared they would revolt." Then the elder's voice descended into despair, "He had them hunted and executed one by one. All except for Kar-Tyr. And now the once proud warrior merely serves as entertainment for Akhdar."

The conch of battle sounded again. The crowd gave out a laundry list of cheers and jeers when the guards pulled open the giant door under Zhar Akhdar's terrace. The thing that emerged was far greater in height and more horrendous than the moktar.

It was at least two stories tall and its body was transparent. The people in the viewing gallery and Kar-Tyr could see the creature emitting some sort of electric charge inside its body. Its arms were two very lengthy tentacles with hundreds of suction cups on them. And enough force to pull a man's face clean off. Unless its long ragged teeth would gnash them first. The jellyfish-like monster had an extensive jaw that could swallow a man whole, bones and all. Fangs, the size of swords, protruded through its receding gums. It had no legs, but it got around with six small tentacles on the bottom of its bulbous base. The strangest thing was it had no eyes. It relied mainly on some sort of radar sense, which was being produced by sound. It was receiving a clear view from all those cheering spectators.

Kar-Tyr speedily galloped towards the monster, whirling his kunai in coercion. The giant monstrosity screeched and began to flay its stretched appendages at him. Kar-Tyr dodged its devastating blows, while the aftershock sprayed sand all over the fighting circle. Kar-Tyr was trying to find the beast's weakness. He knew the rope attached to the end of his kunai wouldn't be long enough to reach around its swollen neck. He had to find another way to take this enormous fiend down.

Kar-Tyr was biding his time. Allowing the monster to make attacks so he could catch it off guard. It lashed its tentacles, now crackling with electricity and the centaur barely evaded the assault. But several guards weren't as prompt as the gladiator. A tentacle shot down from above, clamped around one guard's torso, and lifted him off his feet. With a casual flip, the tentacle tossed him aside as if he were a rag doll.

With growing dread, Kar-Tyr watched as the airborne guard came crashing down to the ground clear on to the other side of the arena. He didn't move.

The monster grabbed the other Thulian guard with its suction cups and with all its might it backhanded the captive's partner across the arena.

The doomed guard saw the bioelectric energy surging through the bulk of the gigantic creature. A beast-like snarl was the last thing he heard in his life, as the monster pulled him in closer to its mouth.

The monster shocked its prisoner with an electric impulse. The guard gave one gasping cry, and slumped down limply in the creature's tentacle, and then was eaten voraciously. Bits of flesh and chinks of the deceased's armor flew out of its mouth while some of the bloody bits had gotten stuck between the beast's teeth. The crowd gave an outburst of merriment, knowing anything can happen in this fight.

Kar-Tyr kept his bottom four legs steady. Then he noticed the creature's small tentacles on its lower body. Kar-Tyr unraveled his kunai and spun it to distract the beast. The monster's use of echolocation could see the small parasite of a life form. It gave a wrathful shriek and brandished its massive limbs in rage.

Kar-Tyr threw his kunai around the creature's forelegs and felt the blade latched itself on the other end of the cable. The beast felt its limbs locked together and frustratingly tried to keep itself balanced. With a powerful tug, Kar-Tyr sent the monster to the ground followed by a thunderous thud.

The crowd erupted in a roaring applause. Back in the dungeon, Sinbad was amazed by the centaur's abilities. He wondered how such a bulky specimen like him could have performed such daring feats. What really caught Sinbad's eye was the weapon Kar-Tyr was using. Small but practical. It probably took a lifetime to master.

The spectators were imparting the "kill" chant. Kar-Tyr moved with the supple ease of a jungle cat, his steely muscles rippling under his grey skin. He slowly approached the beast, which was flat on its back, unknotting his kunai. The monster angrily screeched as its foe pulled his weapon apart. The rope attached to the blade was straightened and it snapped all together to form a spear. The monster showed its teeth to Kar-Tyr before the gladiator shoved the blade into its mouth.

The crowd chanted Kar-Tyr's name in celebration. Another victory for the last of the Kurwani. The beast took its last breath and succumbed to its wounds. Kar-Tyr retracted his weapon and basked in the approval of the court holding his bloodstained spear aloft. He caught a glimpse between the dungeon's barred windows and saw Sinbad. Their eyes met and said nothing to each other. Sinbad was impressed with this creature, and thought to himself Kar-Tyr would be a powerful ally. All Kar-Tyr saw in Sinbad was another victim met at the end of his kunai.

Night had fallen; Sinbad is knelt beside Azrak as the sailor said his evening prayers. Azrak stares at his friend as he silently mediates and inaudibly beseeched to his idol.

"Does your god watch over you even *here*, Sinbad?" asked Azrak.

Sinbad opened his eyes and casually said, "Allah is everywhere, and in all things, my friend. He begetteth not, nor is He begotten; and there is none like unto Him"

"Is that why you pray so much during the day?"

"Praying five times a day is considered the second most important of my religion's five pillars, after professing that there is no god worthy of worship but Allah and that the Prophet Mohammed is Allah's messenger," explained Sinbad. "It reminds me about Allah throughout my day. At fixated intervals, no matter how busy you are, all of a sudden you have to take out a few minutes and you are remembering why we a really here."

"In prison?" asked Azrak.

"No," said Sinbad, "the true reason we are in existence, my friend."

Azrak stared perplexed at him. "Why do you move so much when you pray?"

"Each prayer includes a series of movements, supplications, and recitations from the Quran—a sacred text for my people," replied Sinbad. "We consider prayer to be both spiritual and physical. The various standing and bending symbolize my devotion to Allah. My entire being is involved in my prayer, and it is in service to my creator."

"I have something I must tell you," began Azrak, trying to find the right words. "There is a prophecy amongst my people. It is written that a stranger from a foreign land will free the Azurians."

Sinbad broke out of his worship. What Azrak said took him unaware. Something about that last part really alarmed him.

"What—what are you saying?" Sinbad was stunned.

Azrak took Sinbad's hand as if he was going to reading the palm.

"I believe yours is the hand that will one day slay Akhdar and reunite the Azurians and the Thulians. That's why I took you in, and that is why you are a prisoner." Azrak's face was filled with remorse. His voice was breaking and he hung his head in shame. "I am sorry."

"There is no need for an apology, Azrak," assured Sinbad. "You saved my life and treated me as if I were a member of your family. For that I am eternally grateful. I fear, however, I am merely a sailor, not a savior. I am not of whom your prophecy speaks."

The Azurian priest shivered, it was very windy and cold. He pulled his robe's collar tighter around his neck and scanned his environment. There was a temple far off in the distance, and the holy blue man set off in its direction. He walked for a very long time, and eventually he found himself in the foothills of the mountains, a hazy mist filled the atmosphere. He trudged to the foot of the nearest slope and began the hike upward.

The moon was almost directly above, and the wind had increased in pitch by the time he found a steep, twisting trail and saw a cluster of huts a few hundred yards away. The clouds had completely covered the luminous moon and the mountainside was colder and windier. The priest was panting as he climbed to the top of a stone ridge. The rest of the mountain was covered in clouds and mist. The priest clamped his teeth together to stop their chattering, but he could not control the shivers that racked his body. Wind howled down the slope, driving gusts of dirt into his face and eyes. He blinked, wiped his face on his sleeve, and struggled on.

At the next level clearing, the priest stopped and rested for a moment. The sky grew darker and the wind felt like a razor slicing his face but he did nothing to shield himself. He was completely exhausted.

The priest glanced at the stark outlines of the mountains all about them and shuddered. His soul shrank from their gaunt brutality. This was a grim, naked land where anything might happen.

A remote mountain village was in front of him. It was cut off from the world by sky-high peaks. There was a temple that overlooked a small enclave of thatch-roofed huts. Wooly yaks were tethered outside the dwellings.

Something was visible through the mist, the silhouette of a temple. Prayer flags fluttered in the breeze, which carried the chiming of wind-bells down from the looming place of worship. Through the cold, blustery night the temple gongs boomed and the conchs roared. Their clamor was a faint echo from within the temple while the priest struggled on his journey. Beads of sweat glistened on his dark blue skin. His fingers twisted the hem of the rich fabric beneath him.

He proceeded to the stone walkway and up a small flight of wide steps to a tall marble door. The priest cautiously made sure he wasn't followed, and opened the huge door while it gave a creaking and grinding sound.

The priest pulled himself inside. He was in a huge, vaulted hall lit by torches set into iron brackets on the stone floor, forming pools of flickering firelight that melted into surrounding shadows. There were thick, supporting pillars every few yards.

The door creaked and scraped and thudded shut. He locked the doors and took a tour of the temple. He walked down the center aisle past the rows of empty pews. The waning moonlight filtered through the windows overlooking the interior of the building.

The priest squinted, adjusting his sight to the semidarkness. At the far end of the hall there was a raised platform. Numerous candles glowed brightly on the altar, with the scent of incense filled the air. By it stood a robed figure, a person whose features, in the dim glow of the torches, seemed vaguely feminine, but only vaguely.

Despite the freezing temperature outside, the main chamber was warm and humid. The priest felt his body recovering from its ordeal as it warmed. He unclasped his robe and shuffled forward.

He hoped his contact didn't have second thoughts on joining him.

He was startled by the swift loud flutter of his contact's moving cloak. Before he could realize what was going on, or could draw a breath, a small green hand was placed over his mouth. Then he felt someone's mouth closing in on his ear.

"I'm going to move my hand away from your mouth," she instructed him, "and you are not going to scream. Is that understood?"

The priest narrowed his eyes, puzzled. If this was a nefarious plot from one of Akhdar's most ruthless assassins, he would be dead by now. He could see his breath coming from his mouth. At first he feared a vindictive specter had risen from the dead and wanted to claim the old man's soul for its own. But he recognized the soft female voice to be an ally. The priest slowly nodded his head, and the unseen attacker removed her hand.

"Qani!" the priest gasped, feeling his heart had skipped a beat. "This was most unwise! Akhdar has eyes and ears everywhere. I am risking so much to be here."

"I wasn't followed," she replied. "Ankhara made sure of that. And my men are stationed around the temple so we won't be interrupted. They're outside waiting for my return."

"You do not understand the peril, Qani. Akhdar's spies make a profession on murder. Women have been stolen and men stabbed between here and the city. This is not like your home province."

"But I am here, and unharmed," she interrupted with a trace of impatience. "Now let us not waste any more time. Now tell me what you know, father."

"We have located the Earthman, Qani," he said, his voice level, conversational. The echo bounced off the walls and it was sent back right at him. He proceeded down the aisle, looking behind each and every pillar. "He has been taken prisoner by Akhdar. It will be a most dangerous undertaking."

The priest was at the end of the corridor. In the corner of his eye he could see a dark figure swiftly scurrying beside him. He sensed instinctively that he was in grave danger. He quickly turned his head to the side to see it had vanished. He knew she was there. He could feel her presence.

"You need not go. We are not sure he is the one."

Suddenly the light went out and someone very close behind him said, "What if he truly is? We cannot take the risk. I will go."

"Then may Daizha protect you, my child," blessed the priest, his voice sunk into a whisper.

He waited for a reply. Finally, he turned around and he found that the temple was empty.

CHAPTER THREE
JUDGE A MAN BY THE REPUTATION OF HIS ENEMIES

Every battle won was a step closer to Azrak's freedom. It was a weak justification for Sinbad's deeds in the arena. With each victory he felt less than a man and more of a beast. Sinbad prayed to Allah that this will end soon, and that Sinbad will once again taste the salty air of the sea.

No matter how many bloodthirsty rogues and nefarious monsters Sinbad killed in the pits, it wasn't enough to sway Emperor Akhdar's decision to release Azrak. He was starting to believe the blood on his hands were all in vain. But he had no place to argue for his friend's freedom.

While he was fighting in the arena, Sinbad could feel he was being watched. Not just by Akhdar and his royal court and the thousands of observers in the stands, but by someone who aimed to kill him.

Kar-Tyr watched Sinbad from cell. Studying the outlander's technique, and running the upcoming battle through his mind. Taking in every detail and thinking of every possible situation the Earthman would be capable of. However, this human proved to be quite unpredictable in his last several matches. He had been fighting as if he had a death wish. He proved to be reckless and did not waste any time to try to end his fights as quickly as possible. Kar-Tyr wouldn't accept such an informal victory. He was in dire need of a worthy opponent. All the past combatants have been mediocre to the least. After Kar-Tyr saw Sinbad vanquish the moktar, he believed the outlander would be a commendable adversary. But after his last fight, Kar-Tyr began to have his doubts.

To Sinbad's surprise and horror his next challenger was none other than Kasson Bay, the Thulian inmate who gave him a hard time when he first arrived in the dungeon. With a burst of confidence he felt he could hold his own against the marauder now.

As Sinbad watched, Kasson pulled out a huge burnish iron sword with a flourish. He gave it a nonchalant spin, letting it catch the light. Then he touched the tip to the floor in front of him.

A challenge.

"Are you ready to die, outlander?" Kasson called out to him. His voice was low and sibilant, like the purr of a leopard, and yet it seemed to fill the entire arena, echoing off the walls and raising strange harmonics in the air.

Sinbad glanced at his opponent. "If Allah wills."

Kasson smiled. "I'll tell him you're on your way."

Sinbad's breathing was steady and his gaze was clear.

A muscle twitched in Kasson's leg as a bruised tendon complained. Sinbad saw the marauder's attention waiver for a split second.

He attacked.

Sinbad felt the movement of Kasson's sword before his eye had even registered that it had begun to move. Sinbad deflected the blisteringly fast swing with a powerful upward strike that made the muscles in his arms quiver. The two swords met in the middle in a blinding shower of sparks.

The battle was joined.

Grunting with effort, Sinbad twisted his sword away from Kasson's with a squeal of metal on metal. The joints in his wrist and elbow stinging from the aftereffects of the mammoth blow sweeping around, he advanced to Kasson, his eyes glinting with anticipation.

Sinbad parried a second deadly blow, then another, and another, his sword moving faster and faster, until it was clanging and singing like a blacksmith's hammer on sheet metal. Sinbad's body became a blur of kinetic motion, as he cut, slashed and stabbed at the prison's toughest inmate, driving him back. Kasson was fast, but Sinbad had fought his ilk before. His mind hummed as he parried Kasson's fast strikes, glorying in the strength of his muscles, the steely power of his limbs as they whipped and cracked around him. He concentrated every fiber of his being on beating Kasson back, using an entire lifetime of determination to fuel his attack. An electric adrenaline sure drove him to attack again and again, not allowing Kasson a single instant to recover.

Kasson spun away and snarled at Sinbad, defensively swinging his sword up in a spinning strike that should have impaled the outlander through the heart. But Sinbad anticipated the blow even before it came and blocked it with a blindingly fast diagonal slash that almost knocked Kasson's sword from his hand. Kasson had to duck to avoid being decapitated as Sinbad carried the blow through with a shout. His scimitar struck the side of the arena.

Kasson straightened up behind him, growling. Recovering from Sinbad's onslaught in seconds, he whirled his sword downwards with inhuman speed, aiming to slice the outlander's hands from his body.

At the last possible second, Sinbad whipped his blade in a sweeping arc, blocking Kasson's strike and locking swords with him at close range. For a heartbeat, the pair was face-to-face.

Sinbad's body thrummed with tension as he struggled to hold off Kasson. His arms were shaking with the effort as he felt the insane strength behind his opponent's sword. He glared into Kasson's bloodshot eyes and saw the conviction lurking there, as though he were an insect that had to be crushed.

In an instant, Sinbad realized what that frightening look meant.

This devil dog thought that he was going to win.

Sinbad bared his teeth at Kasson and snarled at him like a wild animal. Then he savagely twisted his sword free with a powerful upward jerk, deliberately slicing open Kasson's cheek in the process.

The wound was insufficient, but it stung in more ways than one. Kasson touched his fingers to the cut and licked mournfully at the lost blood.

Then he swiveled his head towards Sinbad, his face contorting into a rictus of hate. Kasson regained control of himself with an effort.

With a growl, Kasson threw his fist to Sinbad's face. Before the outlander could defend himself, Kasson whipped around and knocked him sprawling across the arena with a savage, pile-driver blow. As Sinbad struggled to right himself, Kasson crossed the pit in a single bound and grabbed him by the throat, his fingers digging into Sinbad's windpipe.

As Sinbad fought to free himself, Kasson brought his blade to his captive's throat. He pressed the razor edge hard enough to break the skin and trickle blood.

Sinbad grimaced in pain.

He wrestled with Kasson, unable to break his hold on him. Gasping, Sinbad reached into his sash with his free hand and felt for the wooden spoon he pilfered from the guards when they had served him his meal the day before.

Kasson gave him a cruel smile. "Do you have any last words, outlander?"

Gripping the spoon, Sinbad replied, "Yes…if you can't win, CHEAT!"

And with all his strength, Sinbad stabbed Kasson in the side of his right leg.

Kasson gave an ungodly shriek and released him. Sinbad rolled to one side and clapped a hand to his neck to stem the blood flow.

Kasson tore the wooden spoon from his leg with a howl and threw it across the arena. Then he came at Sinbad full bore, swinging his fist towards the outlander's head in a murderous blow.

Somehow, Sinbad managed to duck. Kasson's fist went straight at the wall behind Sinbad. Blood spurted out of his broken hand. Kasson gave out a guttural cry of rage, and held his hand in pain. Driven into a berserker rage, Kasson grabbed his sword with his one good hand in a blind fury. Aiming to crush the outlander to a bloody pulp.

Even Aella, from up in the royal terrace, thought it was clear that the outlander was still living. She watched as he dived out of Kasson's way. Blood loss and exhaustion slowed the Earthman's movements. But he kept moving, ducking and dodging so he could wind Kasson into a greater and greater frenzy as Kasson screamed in fury when he missed Sinbad for the tenth time in a row.

Despite the outlander's best efforts, Kasson was throwing him around the arena. Sinbad's senses blazed as the shock of the impact, whiting out the pain of his bruised and torn flesh. His body felt out of place, and a deadly exhaustion clouded his mind. It made it difficult for him to think, but he knew he had to keep moving.

Groaning, Sinbad gathered what little strength, he had left and tried to roll over onto his side. His body rebelled; a powerful quiver of exhaustion ran through him as his abused muscles complained. He felt like his body was moving through thick, clinging tar.

Sinbad knew he couldn't take much more of this.

As he struggled to rise, Kasson pounced on him, dragging him to his feet and slamming him back against a wall. The force of the impact knocked Sinbad's breath out of him. He was unable to muster the strength to defend himself as Kasson hammered a punch into his stomach and then a second at his face, bouncing his head off the wall. Sinbad's vision filed with blinding flashes as Kasson hit him again and again, venting his fury on the struggling outlander.

In desperation, Sinbad lashed out and dug his fingers into Kasson's eyes. The marauder roared in pain and threw up his hands, knocking Sinbad away.

Sinbad saw stars as his head hit the ground. Despite his agony, Sinbad's mind was floating, disengaged from the pain, and he realized an odd sense of calm that he was going into shock. Black speckles flooded the edge of his dimming vision as darkness threatened to steal what little consciousness he still had left.

Sinbad took a shuddering breath. He was fighting to stay awake, as Kasson's stepped towards him, wielding his sword.

Snarling, he pulled Sinbad up. With a savage grin, the outlander head-butted Kasson, breaking his nose. Blood spurted and Sinbad howled in triumph.

Kasson's eyes glinted as he swung his sword at Sinbad in a savage blow, which clearly meant to slice him in half. This time, Sinbad wasn't quick enough. The sword caught him in a glancing blow in the ribs and sliced cleanly through his bare flesh, sending blood into the air. The force of the blow spun Sinbad around, knocking him off balance. He fell heavily to his knees, blood pouring from his side in a shady stream.

Up above, Aella's heart pounded faster as she watched Kasson slaughtering Sinbad. She tried to look away, but she could not. She held on to every hope she had for the outlander, but she was well aware of Kasson Bay's reputation. How he led a revolt against the slave traders in the dark mountains, the exact number of the many men he had murdered in cold blood, and how he savagely abused their widows.

Aella gasped loudly as Kasson kept on attacking without displaying any shred of mercy. It was amazing on how Sinbad took all that brutality, but a chill ran through the very ventricles of her heart.

He was going to kill Sinbad.

Kasson's eyes narrowed to see the puny outlander was still alive. Crawling weakly towards him. Smirking, Kasson swung his sword high above his head, preparing to finish the fallen Earthman off. His sword sparkled as it sung upwards through the air, catching a thousand glimmering reflected on its polished surface.

Sinbad pitched his body and threw Sinbad in Kasson's eyes. His attacker was blinded. Lunging forward, Sinbad crossed the few steps that separated them and plunged his sword so deeply into Kasson's chest that its tip pointed out through his back in a spray of dark crimson blood.

Kasson staggered backwards, furious. Snarling at Sinbad, he tried to rip the sword out.

The he stopped.

Total shock registered on his face as he felt death was taking him.

Sinbad sagged to the ground, exhausted beyond measure.

Kasson dropped his sword with a clang and turned towards the outlander, outraged. He clutched at his chest, and spat out blood. He staggered forward and reached out toward Sinbad. Then he slowly sank to his knees. His eyes flickered open, glaring with a feeble internal light.

He wiped the blood from his chin as realization crept over him. Sinbad had beaten him. And he was going to die.

With an effort, Kasson turned his head to face Sinbad. The outlander got back to his feet with numerous promises his body would be aching the next morning.

A tide of darkness flooded Kasson's synapses and to framed, blinking hard as his vision briefly wasted out in a sea of sparkled grey. Physical weakness was not something that he was used to, and how the murderous inmate was experiencing all kinds of strange sensations. Not all of them were pleasant.

Kasson gasped as a lifetime of bright images were shown in front of him. He gazed at them with wonder. He had once heard that one's life flashed before one's eyes as death approached. Of course he had never thought he would have the opportunity to find out, yet here he was. He laid back and readied himself.

Villages burning, women screaming, and the smell of death were in the air as his enemies broke ranks and charged at him.

Kasson smiled, enjoying the show as it washed over him, filling his mind with a thousand gory images. He had slaughtered indiscriminately, the young, the old, the sick, and the wounded—all held fallen beneath his sword, or else by his hands. And in the end, he had no regrets. He had enjoyed every last moment of it.

He coughed weakly, blood trickled from his wounds. A very special part of him, had always known that the day would come when he would lose. Then he frowned. The person to vanquish him was a lowly pink outlander.

Where had he come from?

What circumstances had led him to become what he was?

It all didn't matter. Sinbad had succeeded where all others had failed.He turned his head stiffly to the side so he could look closely at Sinbad's face. "Well done, outlander," he whispered. "Well done."

There was no reply. Then a moment later, Kasson died.

From atop Zhar Akhdar's private terrace, his sister Aella watched Sinbad delivered the killing stroke to the unfavorable gladiator. She looked at her brother, who was enjoying the show, and gave him a smile.

"The outlander fights well, dear brother," she said, twirling a lock of her long red hair with her finger.

"That he does, sister," Akhdar replied with a smirk on his face. "That he does. Although I suspect you admire him for things other than his combat ability."

Aella's green cheeks blushed red, and laughed off her brother's ridiculous concept.

"Akhdar, whatever do you mean?"

"Do not play such childish games with me, Aella. I've seen the way you look at him. If you wanted a private audience with this Sinbad, all you had to do is simply ask."

Aella admitted her feelings for Sinbad, and held her brother's head. She couldn't keep a straight face to acknowledge Akhdar's offer. She merely nodded in response. Akhdar gave her a half smile and snapped his skeletal fingers. Tarkuhn, his trusted advisor rushed to Akhdar's side, waiting for his master's orders.

"Bring me the outlander, Tarkuhn," said Akhdar. "I wish to speak with him."

Sinbad looked down upon his fallen challenger with Kasson's blood sprayed all over his bare chest. The champion looked up to the skylight where the sun and the moon were almost aligned. He silently prayed to Allah to give him a sign. As Sinbad watched the sky, the moon united with the moon and caused a solar eclipse.

"Praise be to Allah," Sinbad said softly.

He heard heavy footsteps on the sound from behind him. Sinbad didn't bother to turn around to see who the messenger was.

"His majesty wishes to see you, outlander," said Tarkuhn.

Sinbad knew his time had come to bargain once again for Azrak's freedom. He was relieved all the fighting wasn't for nothing.

CHAPTER FOUR
AN UNJUST KING IS LIKE A RIVER WITHOUT WATER

Sinbad walked behind Tarkhun, flanked by several armed guards. Entering the throne room, the guards split apart, opening a path for Sinbad to walk alone. He strode with a purposeful gait, not breaking pace, and proceeded to the center.

The chamber was vast and was filled with interesting antiquities throughout the far reaches of the universe. It was decorated with Martian sigils, galleries and other trappings of the court. There were plenty of candles and lanterns, but they were not illuminated. But if they were, the bright ember would create a large circle of light in the enormous space. There were also rich tapestries on the polished paneled walls, deep rugs on the ivory floor, and with the lofty ceiling adorned with intricate carvings and silver scrollwork. The floor, ceiling and walls were highly polished and gleamed dully, and they were carved with the figures of Akhdar's ancestors and half-forgotten gods.

Whoever designed this room like this must have an eye for beauty of Allah Himself, thought Sinbad.

What stood out the most was a mammoth jade statue of the six-armed Kali that loomed over Akhdar and Aella.

Sinbad looked wary at the giant idol. It stared back at him ominously, as if it were to spring to life at any second.

There she was standing before him.

Kali, the Black One.

The consort of Lord Shiva.

Hindu goddess of time and change, but mostly death.

Sinbad hadn't seen the accursed idol since his journey through Marabia. He and his crew had to engage in combat against a reanimated statue of Kali. And they also had to contend with a one-eyed centaur.

Sinbad was very familiar of Kali's background. She, Durga and her assistants, the Matrikas, wounded the demon Raktabija with a variety of weapons in an attempt to destroy him. Actually, they only worsened the situation for every drop of blood that was spilt from Raktabija and he created a clone of himself. The battlefield was consumed of his many duplicates. Durga summoned Kali for help to combat the demons.

Then Kali destroyed Raktabija by sucking the blood from his body and putting the many clones in her gaping mouth. Pleased with her victory, Kali danced on the field of battle, stepping on the corpses of the slain. Her consort Shiva lied among the dead beneath her feet. She became drunk on the blood of her victims, and as a sign of shame at having disrespected her husband by sticking out her tongue.

If Sinbad had a choice to fight the goddess of death again or the Kurwani warrior, he would gladly choose the latter.

Why would Akhdar and his followers worship Kali? thought Sinbad. *Could it be possible that Kali was a native of Mars and found her way to Earth? If she had some sort of transportation, maybe I could find a way home.*

Massive stone columns, engraved with intricate markings, supported the ceiling. An imposing black onyx desk rested in one corner, beneath a large framed map of Mars. The view was spectacular. The sunset was beautiful with the sky being filled with pink, red, and purple.

At the far edge of the circle was Emperor Akhdar. He was seated on a well-worn throne. Beside him was a slightly smaller chair, which Aella gracefully resided. They sat side-by-side, comfortable with one another's company.

The doors to the vast chamber closed and Sinbad was brought into the center of the throne room. He was forced on his knees and handcuffed. Tarkhun and the guards fanned out, taking their assigned places.

Tarkhun turned to face Akhdar and adjusted his voice to be heard. "Sinbad the Sailor, lord of the Sindth River, and outlander of Earth."

Sinbad reluctantly bowed his head lowly to the young emperor.

"Does he please you, sister?" asked Akhdar.

"He is quite handsome," she replied, "for an alien."

"You find favor in my sister's eyes, Sinbad, and I admire your ability in combat. What have you to say in return?"

Sinbad stared blankly at the ruler of the Dozhakian Empire.

"I am reminded of a proverb," he said to Akhdar. "'Beware of one who flatters unduly; he will also censure unjustly.'"

"How quaint...and disappointing," said Akhdar, feeling disillusioned. "I think there may be hope for him yet, dear sister. But first I think a story is in order." Akhdar rose from his throne and advanced toward a full-scale model of his kingdom. "Listen, Earthman, as I tell you of my rise to power. After the unfortunate death of my beloved uncle Dadgar, the former zhar, and the disappearance of his only child, I assume the throne. Soon after Dozhak fell into civil war.

"While I might have stopped it, I've always thought the Azurians inferior and a bit impure. The outcome was inevitable. The Azurians are philosophers, farmers, and theologians, not warriors like we Thulians. Those few that did not become slaves fled to the badlands.

"Of course, there was still the problem of the Kurwani. They were a great possible threat to my reign," Akhdar gave Sinbad a cruel smile. "I offered a hundred slaves to anyone who brought me one of their heads. Of course, slaves that have no hope become lazy and complacent, so I started a rumor. I believe they now refer to it as the prophecy."

Akhdar walked across the room and stopped to admire the immense green statue.

"And all was fine. That is, until *you* showed up. You see, your being here gives the Azurians a bit too much hope. So much, in fact, that I've heard there are some rebel Thulians that have joined their movement," Akhdar approached Sinbad slowly. "While I will surely have their pitiful rebellion crushed, it would make me happier if you were to join me. With you by my side, the Azurians will believe that their gods favor me and act accordingly.

"So what is it to be, Sinbad? Join me and have your every wish be a command, or refuse me and die in the arena?"

"What you are planning to do is a blasphemy to your gods," answered Sinbad. "I will take my chances in the arena."

Akhdar gave his prisoner a dissatisfied look. He signaled his guards to seize Sinbad. The green brawny sentinels hoisted the Earthman to his feet with brute force.

"I knew you were going to say that," said Akhdar, looking at Sinbad contemptuously. "Still, the offer stands. At least until your next battle, or until you cease to entertain me."

The guards removed Sinbad from Akhdar's royal court and he was on his way back to his dingy old cell. Before they could begin their trek, a young attractive Thulian woman stopped the guards.

"Move aside, girl," said the guard impatiently. "We have a prisoner to escort."

"A thousand pardons, sir," pleaded the girl. "I am Kori, handmaiden to Princess Aella. I have come on her behalf to grant the outlander a private audience with her." Then she handed the guards a sealed envelope with the Dadgar family crest embossed on the seal. "I believe you will find everything is in order."

The guard took the envelope and studied the seal. The Dadgar family crest was very hard to duplicate, making it impossible for any forgery. Then he opened the envelope and read the letter. He came to the conclusion that the letter is indeed authentic and it did come from the princess.

"Very well," said the guard, "we shall take the outlander to the baths."

"There will be no need for that, sir," said the girl. "We can take it from here."

Behind her there were the rest of Aella's handmaidens. Their eyes were lowered on the floor and they covered their mouths to hide their giggles.

"Lucky dog," muttered the guard. Then he and his partner left Sinbad in the care of all those beautiful women.

The girl took Sinbad's hand and looked at him with kind eyes. "It is all right, outlander. Come, let us take care of you."

Aella watched from the shadows as the slave girls guided Sinbad into the marble basin filled with steaming water. She allowed her gaze to linger on the outlander's naked body. Searching his sun-kissed flesh for any bruise or blemish. No imperfection marred the alien's beauty as he sank into the water and the slaves began to wash him.

On the request of Princess Aella, Kori had clipped a lock of the man's hair, and sniffed it. Sweat and grime, and even the foul lather of the beasts he had fought in the arena. But beneath that was something more earthy, musky, and strong.

As Sinbad bathed, other slaves brought platters of fruit and viands, delicious from throughout Mars. Sinbad, sedated, ate mechanically, as he was bidden, and sloppily drank wine. The bathers washed spills from him, then took him from the bath and dried him with scarlet towels. Once they dried him off, the handmaidens took him to a couch and then left the room in an orderly fashion.

As soon as the women were out of sight, Sinbad was off the decorative couch and on his feet facing the arched door, all in one instant. He stood ready and took a defensive stance, and then checked the movement.

It was a woman who had entered unannounced; a woman whose gossamer robes did not conceal the rich garments beneath any more than they covered the suppleness and beauty of her tall, slender figure. A filmy veil fell below her breasts, supported by a flowing headdress bound about with a triple gold braid and adorned with a golden crescent. Her dark eyes regarded the astonished Earthman over the veil, and then with an imperious gesture of her green hand, she revealed her face.

Sinbad rose in attention to discover it was none other than Akhdar's sister, Princess Aella.

She was beautiful, and it was hard to imagine there was a time he hadn't noticed. Had she changed so much? He took her in, as though for the first time. Aella's hair was the color of a garden of roses, and the candlelight gave her fair green skin a heavenly glow. Her movements were supple, graceful, her body been but curved in the right places. Curves accentuated by the colorful silks tied around her body. As she looked at him and smiled, her sapphire blue eyes twinkled with mischief. He knew that any of the noblemen on Mars would have given all their riches for one night with her.

She stepped up and put her hands softly on his shoulders.

Sinbad started to speak, without the slightest idea of what he wanted to say, but she stopped him with a finger against his lips.

"You've fought valiantly, Sinbad of Earth." Her eyes were laughing with anticipation and delight as she leaned in closer to him. "Now it's time for you to claim your reward."

Then, unable to restrain herself, she embraced him tightly.

Sinbad could smell the spicy, complex scent of the finest berries and juices in her hair. So different from the flowery fragrances preferred by the maidens back home. The touch of her was electric; he was intoxicated by her heavenly scent as Aella's hands ran across his chest. Then she went up to the thick column of his throat to take hold of him along the line of his jaw and brought his lips to hers.

The kiss was intense and it fulfilled all of Aella's expectations. She trembled against him, catching her breath with the sparkling overload of physical sensation. She danced with danger, as it gave spice and meaning.

She bit him tenderly on his lobe, hard and sexy. Then she sat straight up before him and shifted her position a little bit so she could make her intentions and desires unmistakable.

She held the embrace for a moment, and then he slowly started to reluctantly pull her away.

He hadn't been with a woman since Princess Farah—his betrothed. Then he wondered if she and her brother King Kassim were well. Sinbad was ready to marry Farah, but a spell was cast on Kassim by their evil stepmother Zenobia turning him into a baboon just as he was going to be crowned caliph.

Then Sinbad and Farah had to set off in search of the Greek alchemist Melanthius who had the cure that could break the spell. They eventually found the wise man and his daughter Dione, who agreed to help them with their quest. Then Metlanthius told Sinbad and his crew that they must travel to Hyperboria where an ancient civilization once existed, to find an ancient pyramid where Kassim can be restored to his original state.

But Zenobia and her equally wicked son Rafi pursued them by unleashing hordes of monsters, including a bronze golem called a Minaton that resembled a minotaur. However, Sinbad and his crew were able to turn the tide with the unlikely help of a friendly troglodyte. In the end, Zenobia and her son were slain, Kassim is restored by the magic of Hyperborea and is crowned King upon his return.

Sinbad was gone for a very long time.

Had it been weeks?

Months?

Has it been over a year since he crash-landed on Mars?

He feared his disappearance might have made her feel jilted. He shook it off his mind, knowing Farah wouldn't misconstrue this predicament. She probably had Kassim sent fleets of ships in search for him.

If only those ships could fly into the stars.

Then Sinbad wondered if the search had been called off and he had been pronounced legally dead.

How long did Farah mourn for him?

How many tears had she wept?

How lonely and cold she felt when she laid in her bed at night.

Then he realized she might have taken a lover to fill the void in her heart. Did he really expect her to wait for him forever? All he wanted was her to be happy. Even if it meant for her to run into another man's arms to comfort her. Although it granted such sadness in the fiber of Sinbad's soul.

With that thought, he broke off Aella's kiss. She sat there confused, wondering if she did anything to upset him.

"What's wrong, darling?" she asked, breathlessly. "Do I not please you?"

"No," Sinbad sighed, "it's not that. You are very beautiful, your highness. But my heart belongs to another."

Aella looked at him as if he was uttering nonsense. "What do you mean?"

"I am betrothed."

Aella's face became twisted with anger. "Who is she? I'll have her killed!"

Sinbad backed away, taken by surprise on Aella's sudden change of character. "Calm yourself, please."

Aella didn't abide by Sinbad's plea. "What makes her better than me? If she really cared about you, Sinbad, she would have found you by now. I would not be surprised if she is carousing with a fine young Earthman as we speak."

"You don't know anything, vile woman!" Sinbad snapped at her, as he got off the couch. "I don't know what you were hoping to get out of this, but you don't own me."

Aella's eyes narrowed at him, but she managed to squeeze out a warm smile. "Maybe the promise of half the Dozhakian kingdom and my dowry might change your mind, beloved. Be my consort and all of this can be yours."

"What about your brother?"

"Well, *accidents* do happen," she chuckled.

"My answer is still no."

Aella pouted and held back tears. "What a pity."

Then she quickly ripped the seams of her dress into tatters and threw herself off the couch. Sinbad tried to help her up, but she swatted his hand away and began to back up against the wall.

"Guards, guards!" she cried. "Your princess needs help!"

The door slammed open as two guards entered the room.

"Help me, please!" Aella screamed, with tears running down her cheeks. "The outlander attacked me and he was going to rape me!"

The guards looked at Sinbad, who towered over the princess. He raised his arms in defense.

"It's not what it looks like!" said Sinbad. "You're being duped. She's lying!"

"Step away, defiler!" said one of the guards. "Lay not another hand on the princess!" The man's voice boomed. The two guards vaulted from the doorway.

They were gaunt giants of men, no bigger in girth than Sinbad but several inches taller. Their skin was a darker shade of chartreuse. In their hands, they each carried very heavy swords.

One of them grabbed Sinbad by the throat and slammed him against the wall. The other sentinel helped Aella to her feet and covered her with a blanket.

"Are you all right, your highness?" he asked her. "Did this animal hurt you?"

"He came in here trying to escape," Aella sobbed, "then he saw me coming out of my bath and threw me down, and got on top of me like a wild animal."

"Lies! All lies!" Sinbad shouted.

"Silence, you cur!" said his captor, delivering a punch to Sinbad's stomach. "What do you wish us to do, my princess? Kill him…or worse." The guard's sword ran from Sinbad's chest to all the way to his groin.

Aella held on to the blanket tightly. "No. He shall die in the arena like the dog he is tomorrow by the hands of the Kurwani. Now take him away!"

The guards bowed to her. "At once, your highness," they both said in unison and dragged Sinbad out of the room.

As the guards were out of sight, Aella's tears dried up and a sinister smile appeared on her cruel face.

The loutish guards brought Sinbad back to his cell. The sailor could see Azrak's face leaning against the door. Sinbad had a lot to talk about with Azrak, concerning Akhdar's devious plans he had for both the Azurians and the Thulians.

"Azrak?" Sinbad called out.

There was no response.

Sinbad spoke up, "Azrak? How..."

Then he realized something wasn't right.

Azrak wasn't reacting to his calls. His face was frozen and his eyes were wide open. He didn't blink, not even once.

The guards opened the door and something rolled out of the cell. It was the size of a melon, but it was blue and it had something sticking out of the bottom. Sinbad fell to his knees in alarm. His eyes were watery and his complexion was cleansed of all color.

It was Azrak's head that just rolled past him. Part of his friend's spinal cord was sticking out of the neck area. Azrak's head was being held on a pike inside his cell and it was propped up against the door.

Sinbad tried to break the chains with all his might, but it was no use. He got up and tried to get past the guards so he could personally kill Akhdar.

He didn't care what would happen to him. Already he had lost everything—his home, his ship, and now his one and only friend. He had nothing else to live for.

"Akhdar!" Sinbad cried out in anguish. "Akhdar! Show yourself, you bastard!"

The guards caught Sinbad before he could make through the passageway. They held him down, and one of them took Sinbad at the back of the head.

"Enough, outlander!" said the guard at his right. The other guard slammed Sinbad's face to the ground, and the sailor lost consciousness.

CHAPTER FIVE
HOW TIGHT CAN LIFE BE WITHOUT THE SPACE OF HOPE

Sinbad awoke hours later in his dark and damp cell, praying to Almighty Allah it was all a nightmare. But to his dismay it wasn't. He squinted his eyes to adjust to the darkness and used the faint moonbeams to look at the other side of the cell. He could see only the trace of small drops of Azrak's blood on his cot and on the floor. Sinbad was guilt ridden and he felt truly alone.

Time weighed heavily upon him. Plans were in motion, but there was little for him to do at the present. A long, lonely evening awaited him. He took this opportunity to pray.

"How many an unfortunate, who has no rest,
Comes later to enjoy the pleasant shade.
But as for me, my drudgery grows worse,
And so, remarkably, my burdens now increase.
They live in comfort all their days,
With ease and honor, food and drink.
I'm like the next man and he is like me,
But oh how different are lives we lead!
How different is wine from vinegar.
I do not say this as a calumny;
Allah is All-Wise and His degrees are just."

He had been in control of his life for as long as he could remember. He was convinced that his life was going to be ending in short order and there was nothing he could do about it.

His passing thoughts of taking revenge were replaced by finding a way to escape the prison. Then they had given way to self-pity and a bleak conviction that even mattered.

"It was my responsibility," he said out loud. "I should have sided with Akhdar."

"That would have made no difference, Sinbad," said a voice in the darkness. It was the elderly Azurian. His heart was full of sympathy and quail. "Akhdar would have had Azrak killed regardless of your decision, and he would have died a thousand deaths for his belief in the prophecy. You know that."

Sinbad sighed and decided it was time to spread the truth about the foresight. Even though it would crush whatever hope the prisoners had.

"The prophecy is a lie," replied Sinbad. "A rumor started by Akhdar to give the Azurians hope and keep them in use."

"Truth can be hidden within a rumor, Sinbad," said the elder, sitting up straight against the wall. "Azrak, believed in you. As do I."

Sinbad shook his head, trying to assemble his scattered wits. Now the weight of this world rested on Sinbad's shoulders. He could not picture himself as the savior of this alien planet. How could he save an entire civilization if he couldn't save the ones he cared about the most?

At least he knew Azrak is now with his family in the next life. Before Sinbad went to sleep, he made a vow to Allah to see that Akhdar and all his minions will pay dearly. Not just for the injustice that was done to him, but for the downtrodden to both Azurians and Thulians alike.

CHAPTER SIX
DISCORD BETWEEN THE POWERFUL IS A FORTUNE FOR THE POOR

Sinbad watched as another ill-fated prisoner had been killed in the arena. The gladiator cried out at first, but his feeble protests were quickly replaced by the sounds of crunching bones and the thud of heavy fists and boots against tender flesh. Sinbad couldn't even see the man beneath the pack of homicidal maniacs satisfying their never-ending thirst for bloodlust.

They piled onto the doomed Azurian man. The poor soul was fighting back sobs and screams. The audience either stared at the grisly scene with horror, or else buried their heads in their hands, trying unsuccessfully to hide from the awful sights and sounds.

The beating lasted less than five minutes, but seemed to go on forever. Just when Sinbad thought he couldn't possibly stand another moment, however, the gang of murderers stepped back from their victim. The prisoner's pulped body lay face down in a puddle of dark, venous blood. His limbs were twisted at unnatural angles that made Sinbad's joints hurt just looking at them.

The guards took hold of the man's limp arms and dragged his lifeless body into the catacombs as it left a trail of blood across the arena. The remaining guards left their posts and began to purify the ring before the next match could commence.

Sinbad looked at the Azurian elder, "I am set to fight the centaur."

"Kar-Tyr of the Kurwani," the old man corrected him. "He is Akhdar's recent favored fighter, since you lost face to the insufferable whelp."

"What is the hearsay within the prison walls?"

The elder hesitated to reply. "They all are placing wagers with odds against you."

"Perhaps I could reason with Kar-Tyr."

"I think you will be wasting your time, Sinbad. You have seen him fight. He would not lay down his weapon to have a friendly conversation with you."

"Akhdar had all his people slaughtered," Sinbad clarified. "We all share a common enemy and goals."

"Indeed. You, me, him, and the rest of the inmates here," retorted the elder. "If you are planning a prison revolt, do you think you are the only person here whoever thought of it? Akhdar's followers would crumble that plot before you could even execute the first stage."

"It is at least better than fighting in the arena until we are all dead."

The old Azurian wiped his oily brow and gave Sinbad a smile. "We all wear the stripes of Akhdar's whip on our backs, and we are likely to continue to wear them. But your lashes are carved in your heart." Then the elder gave out a heaving sigh. "Despite of everything that has happened, you still retained your optimism. Maybe if I had your sanguinity I would have gotten out of here years ago."

The Azurian man had been watching Sinbad, his face inscrutable. Perhaps he had been waiting for the Earthman to come out of the depression that had paralyzed him all on his own, but it didn't appear to be happening.

"Hoping to hold out, are you, Sinbad?"

Sinbad's gaze flickered toward the old man, a mildly questioning look in his eyes.

"You're figuring that if you simply shut down, refuse to cooperate they won't kill you because they need you, and perhaps it will provide enough time for your friends to come rescue you."

The old man could not have been more wrong. Sinbad wasn't thinking of anybody like that. He was, first, convinced that they wouldn't find him, and further influenced his captors would indeed kill him if they decided that he wasn't going to cooperate. There was no grand stalling tactic involved here. Sinbad was simply positive that there was no way out.

Unaware of that, the old man continued, "I'm sure they're looking for you, Sinbad, but they will never find you here." He approached Sinbad and crowded so that they were on eye level. His voice became soft, even understanding. "You don't like fighting."

Sinbad shook his head, despondent.

"I didn't like it either when I was leading Akhdar's army."

Sinbad's eyes widened and stared at the old man.

"You were a soldier?"

"I was sergeant-at-arms, until I was ordered to lay waste to an entire village."

"Did you carry out the order?"

The Azurian shook his head, "No, I couldn't go through with it. It was occupied with innocent civilians. I've killed several members of my battalion in order to save as many people as I could." He buried his face in his hands.

"Then what happened?" Sinbad carefully asked.

"On the planet you are from, Sinbad, do they have the saying, 'no good deed goes unpunished'?"

"What did Akhdar do to you?"

"He took everything from me," the old man replied. "Not only he stripped me of my rank, he seized my home, my land, and had my entire family slaughtered before my own eyes. He even made me choose in which order they would die in…all my sons are dead. My lineage ends with me when I go into the next world. I begged him to kill me as well, but he said I wasn't worthy of death. So he casted me here in the dungeon to be with all the scum I brought to justice. Worst of all, Akhdar even took my name away from me."

"He took your name?"

"He replaced it with 'traitor.' So everybody I would meet will know the crime I committed against the crown."

"You don't deserve that," said Sinbad, "*nobody* does. You should be treated as a hero."

"Not in the eyes of Akhdar and his minions. I can still hear the villagers' screams," the Azurian confessed. "A vision of a little boy, who had to be no older than five years old, was running through the street. One of my soldiers appeared behind him and raised his weapon. And then all at once, the boy wasn't running anymore. He was flying through the air, and the top half of his head was missing. I saw his eyes widened, and he made a gagging noise in his throat.

"It still haunts me in my dreams."

Sinbad gave out a desolate sigh. "Why should I do anything? They're going to kill me, and if they don't I'll be dead in a week."

"Then, this is a very important week for you."

Slowly Sinbad looked at the old man as if truly focusing upon him for the first time. "Why do you care what happens to me?"

The old man shrugged, "Someone has to."

Sinbad leaned back against the wall. For the first time in ages, it seemed, his thoughts moved away from his own predicament, spurred by what the old man had just said.

If he died here, now, forgotten in some abyss—*would* anyone care? He had no friends on this world and nobody on Earth knew if he was even alive.

All of that went through Sinbad's head, and as it did so, the sheer anger that it generated began to energize him, to scrape away the misery and self-pity like barnacles being scraped from the hull of a vessel.

Slowly he eased himself from the wall. He said, "The next time Tarkhun shows up, I'm willingly to cooperate." The Azurian looked surprised at the sudden turnaround in Sinbad's demeanor.

"You're giving in to them?" asked the old man. "You have the most spirit in this prison and suddenly you're abandoning your beliefs. What would Azrak think of this? If you are going to honor your friend's memory you shouldn't devote the remainder of your life to senseless bloodshed and violence. I don't know if it was luck or divine intervention that you're not buried with the rest of the bodies. It sure wasn't the training I had given you."

Sinbad spoke very softly. "I should be dead already. But I'm not, and I have to think that the fact that I'm not…I have to think it's for a reason."

He left it there.

Zhar Akhdar escorted his sister Aella to her spot next him on the royal terrace. Aella noticed the somber look on her brother's face. She had been accustomed to it for many years. Even though they weren't twin siblings, Aella knew what really goes on inside her brother's twisted mind.

"You never cease to amaze me, Aella," Akhdar said to her sarcastically.

"I know how you feel, brother; but it had to be done."

"You were in no place to carry out the order," Akhdar scowled at her. "*I am* zhar! If I wanted to have the Azurian executed I would have said so. I hope your little romantic fiasco was worth it, Aella. Because I no longer have any leverage on the outlander."

Aella silently rolled her eyes at him, and gave out an irritated sigh. "I admit my actions were quite rash and maybe perhaps foolish, but now the outlander doesn't have any reason to fight back. By committing this horrible act, I've broken his spirit. Even as we speak, he's probably racked with guilt and sorrow he can't even focus. In which he will be prone to commit costly mistakes—mistakes that would cost him his life."

Akhdar looked at her with a puzzled expression, "I thought you fancied him."

Aella turned away and watched as Sinbad the arena half-heartedly, as a guard handed him his sword. Her eyes didn't usually light up with excitement or amorous intent as they once had. She didn't even give a smile, but instead she had a small sneer of hatred and repulse.

"I have outgrown him," she said scornfully. "He just bores me now."

Akhdar's face lit up with contentment.

Tarkhun approached Akhdar with a scheming grin on his hyena-like face. "I think you will find this battle most pleasing, sire," he said, wringing his hands maliciously.

"I hope so, Tarkhun," replied Akhdar, as both he and Aella took their places. "I grow weary of this tedium."

Akhdar looked downward into the arena to see Sinbad being given his scimitar, and at the opposing side was Kar-Tyr obtaining his prized kunai.

"Tarkhun, Remind me to reward you handsomely."

"Oh, yes, sire," Tarkhun said with the sound of delight in his voice.

Kar-Tyr gave Sinbad an expression of regret. "I was hoping it would not come to this, Earthman," he said, while untangling the rope to his kunai.

"As was I, Kar-Tyr, last of the Kurwani," Sinbad replied, polishing his sword. He noticed the Kurwani's intricate tattoos on his right arm. "Interesting design. What does it mean?"

"For every man I kill, I tattoo his name on my body," Kar-Tyr grimly replied.

"What happens if you run out of room; do you stop killing?" joked the outlander.

But the huge centaur didn't give any reply, except for the cold stare that pierced Sinbad's soul.

The crowd grew silent as Akhdar rose from his throne. Both Kar-Tyr and Sinbad brought their attention to the wicked ruler. This was a first, they both thought. Usually Akhdar didn't say anything before a fight. He always let his guards blow the horn of battle, but this time he had plotted something. Sinbad could feel it in his bones. Whatever Akhdar had planned, it wasn't good.

"If this show pleases me, I promise the victor a quick and painless death," the young zhar announced.

Then he signaled to his guards at the other side of the arena. "Sound the horn of battle!"

The horn was blown but it was deafened by the loud bombardment of explosive blue energy that destroyed the northeast wall of the arena. Huge chunks of rock and blue fire filled the ring. The coliseum was in pandemonium with all the spectators and dignitaries getting caught in the crossfire and trying to escape the carnage. The blast took Kar-Tyr and Sinbad off their feet. When they both got their bearings, they looked at each and both nodded in agreement that this was the perfect time to make their escape.

The explosion shook the arena and flaming debris landed near the gladiators.

Sinbad's eyes stung and he coughed uncontrollably. He could barely see Kar-Tyr through the smoke. He was aware of men running past him, scrambling toward the doors. But he dared not joined them. The moment he would turn his back, he knew Akhdar would signal for his guards to eliminate him.

The back of the arena was a warzone. Sinbad ran for the front, jumping over chunks of stone that littered the floor. The crowd's uncertainty was replied with screams of panic as debris showered down upon them, nearly crushing several terrorized spectators.

Kar-Tyr lay directing in his path, between him and the exit.

Sinbad readied himself for a fight, but the huge centaur lowered his weapon.

"What are you waiting for?" Kar-Tyr asked the Earthman. "Now's the time to escape."

Sinbad gave him a smile and followed the last son of the Kurwani race across the arena.

The royal terrace rocked with a frightening deep rumbling. Tarkhun and the rest of the guards hurried over to Akhdar and Aella with frantic looks on their faces.

"Cover yourself, sire!" cried Tarkhun, rushing to his lord and master's side.

Aella shielded her head from any fallen wreckage. She was so afraid she started to cry hysterically. Akhdar pulled his sister in and held her tightly. Terrified, she began to mutter nonsense, which was made unintelligent to the human ear as it was being broken up by the gasps of her sobs.

"Do not worry about me!" Akhdar said to his loyal bodyguard, as he pointed to the gladiators. "Stop them!"

With a yell from Tarkhun on the royal terrace, the guards flooded the arena. Sinbad and Kar-Tyr almost reached the exit into the passageway until a Thulian guard armed with a crossbow ambushed them.

"Halt!" The armored sentinel ordered. "Move and you die!"

The two rogue fighters stayed where they were, but it turned out the guard had gotten excited and then fired. The flying arrow was going straight to Kar-Tyr's face. Sinbad took his sword and hoped he wasn't too late.

"Kar-Tyr! Look out!" he warned his fellow fugitive. With all his might, he threw his sword as fast as he could and it the swirling blade cut the zooming arrow into two and deflected off Kar-Tyr's path.

"Amazing!" yelled Kar-Tyr, while being stricken by awe by the impossible feat that just happened right in front of his face. He turned to Sinbad, who was running after his sword. "Thank you."

"Save your gratitude when we get out of here," Sinbad interjected. "Now run!"

Kar-Tyr made a beeline to the opposite doorway that was sealed off by a pile of giant rocks, as five more archers joined their comrade in the pursuit. They aimed their bows at Sinbad and Kar-Tyr.

Caught in the crossfire Sinbad faced the incoming guards. He was no defensive fighter; even in the teeth of overwhelming odds he always carried the war to the enemy. Any other man would have already died there, and Sinbad himself did not hope to survive. But he did ferociously wished to inflict as much damage as he could before he fell.

"Kar-Tyr, what are you doing?" Sinbad yelled across the arena.

The Kurwani man cracked his kunai and whipped it at the biggest rock on top of the sealed entry.

"Behind the rocks there is a canal," he said, latching onto the rock and holding the rope with both hands. "If I can get this wall down it would provide us with the distraction we need to escape."

The archers fired their arrows at Sinbad and Kar-Tyr. The sailor deflected each and every one with lightning fast swipes with his sword. The archers quickly reloaded and began shooting at different directions, waiting for a chance the escapee would slip up. But Sinbad was onto their plan and repelled the arrows as fast as humanly possible.

He should have been terrified, and immediately killed, and if he had taken even a second to think about his situation, he would have been. But he did not. No, he merely did as, without knowing it, he had been learning to do all these years. He became fully in the moment and became vastly quicker than thought to guide his movements.

He could feel his muscles strain from exertion. He was losing his breath and also his concentration.

"I can't hold them off forever, Kar-Tyr!" he panted.

"Almost done!" Kar-Tyr replied, pulling on his rope with determination.

As Sinbad deterred another arrow, a sudden pain stupefied him in his arm. He let out a cry of pain and discovered he had been shot. The arrow didn't hit the bone, but it made Sinbad feel ill. He gritted his teeth and pulled the arrow out, as a spurt of blood shot out of the wound.

Sinbad noticed some sort of discolored liquid besides his own blood was smeared on the arrowhead. He pulled it up to his nose and discovered it gave out some peculiar odor. Then Sinbad felt his left arm getting heavy and slowly going numb.

"There's something on the arrow tip," he said to Kar-Tyr, holding his arm in pain.

"Poison!" Kar-Tyr gasped. "We've got to get you out of here."

The world was spinning around him, and Sinbad fought off a wave of nausea as he staggered to his feet. The arena was suddenly miles long and the doorway was receding into the horizon. Sinbad staggered, shook his head. He had to make the vision go away somehow.

With a powerful yank the Kurwani claimed the rock, while a makeshift waterfall flowed immensely into the arena. The sealed door crumbled, unleashing a deluge of water on the guards. Pure spring water sprayed down upon the arena, starting the attackers who lifted their heads in confusion. The force of the water sent the archers off their feet. While their pursuers were abstracted by their waterlogged impediment, Kar-Tyr grabbed Sinbad and placed him over his shoulder.

"Let me carry you," he said to his infected comrade. "It will be much faster."

Kar-Tyr checked to see if the coast was clear and progressed through the impromptu exit, which led them outside. The afternoon sky was a beautiful palette of strawberry pink with heavy mauve overtones.

Sinbad couldn't turn his head to witness it himself. He was busy staring vacantly into his reflection on the water's surface. His face was becoming awfully pale—almost as white as a ghost. His eyes were sunken and there was also a pattern of black complex veins were outlined beneath him. He could feel his body getting weaker and his heartbeat growing faint.

"Allah, protect me," he said hazily, feeling his eyelids getting heavy. He had the sudden urge to sleep. He had never been so tired in his whole life.

Kar-Tyr incessantly fled, losing the guards. He looked over his back to see if there were any more after them, but was thrown at ease to see they were in the clear. He held on to Sinbad tightly and knew the first thing on the centaur's mind was to find a healer.

Kar-Tyr turned past a pillar only to be stopped by a gang of five Thulians. Two females and the rest were males. They were all armed with swords, daggers, and battleaxes. Kar-Tyr cursed in his native tongue. This was far any prisoner in Akhdar's dungeon has ever escaped. But something about this group didn't sit quite right with Kar-Tyr. They didn't wear the official garb of the royal guard. He glared, puzzled as to their identity. Then a single thought ran through the Kurwani's mind.

Mercenaries.

Out of the group came a petite Thulian female. She was young with long, smooth brown hair with the eyes to match. Her hair was kept under a purple bandana and she also had a long shimmering purple cloak of fine fabric. She gave off an imposing demeanor to Kar-Tyr. She stood in front of the group where she waited, silent but seen before the mighty centaur.

Kar-Tyr stared at them as a shiver ran down his spine.

"Stop there, Kurwani," said the green woman with confidence. "I am Qani, leader of the resistance against Akhdar's forces. If you value your life you must come with us." She gestured to two long boats that were berthed at the side of the canal.

Kar-Tyr looked at her with obscurity. *Who is she to give orders? She is merely a child.*

He could have easily set her aside. But her friends wouldn't take too kindly to that. They provided her with enough cover and their weapons were at the ready.

The woman held herself perfectly still, giving away nothing. The epitome of graceful control, and with a single glance, she caused every hackle to rise on the back of Kar-Tyr's neck.

Her top was cut high and tight, showing off her superbly toned dancer's body to the best effect she could. Kar-Tyr thought she was just asking for trouble. Especially being dressed as a common harlot in the company of these rogues.

With a firm and bold tone in her voice, she gave Kar-Tyr another command. "This is not open to debate, Kurwani. Give us the Earthman."

Kar-Tyr saw scant reason in this, and a faint suspicion of these strange and dangerous people.

CHAPTER SEVEN
IF MAN BE A RIVER, THEN WOMAN WILL BE A BRIDGE

Akhdar was furious. He had never seen such incompetence. How was it possible two prisoners escaped from his impenetrable fortress? This was more insult than injury. No one ever made a fool out of Zhar Akhdar and lived to boast about it. Akhdar stormed out of his terrace with Aella by his arm.

Tarkhun caught up to his master's quickened pace.

"Thulian dogs!" he spat. "I'll have their heads for this."

"You're lucky yours is still attached, Tarkhun," scolded Akhdar. The fiendish hatred of the young emperor glittered for an instant redly in his eyes. "I could have been injured." Akhdar pointed down to the guards in the arena who were recovering from Kar-Tyr's diversion. "Seize those bunglers and have them executed for their utter stupidity."

"Yes, sire, at once," replied Tarkhun in trepidation. "They will be severely punished."

"Fortunately for you, Tarkhun, I have other ways of dealing with the Earthman Sinbad," snapped Akhdar, sweating at the mere thoughts of failure.

Aella suddenly stopped and pulled her arm away from her brother's. Akhdar reacted fretfully by his sister's unexpected tremor.

"Sister, are you all right?" he asked, full of dread. "Are you hurt?"

"Yes, brother, I am," she replied. "That filthy human has played us for fools, and he humiliated me in the sanctity in our own house. I want his head, Akhdar! Do you hear me?"

Her voice thrummed with hate as she uttered the last words, and her hands clenched at her sides. The knuckles of her compressed hands were showing white. She looked like an image of passion incarnate as she stood there with her head thrown high and her bosom heaving.

Akhdar's eyes narrowed. For all his iron-willed self-control, he was near bursting with long pent-up shame, hate and rage, ready to take any sort of a desperate chance. His worrisome face turned into a disdainful scowl. He held his sister's hand with care.

"And you shall get, dear sister. This I promise you."

Then he turned his head over to Tarkhun, who was already carrying out his master's first command. Akhdar stormed towards his most faithful bodyguard and majordomo.

"Tarkhun, summon Doctor Panhek and Sardeth Rex."

Tarkhun was surprised to hear this. "Forgive me, sire, but you cannot be serious about calling those heretics. Panhek has been known to use forbidden knowledge, and has fused Rex with that perversion to his own arcane arts. Technology and sorcery is highly dangerous."

"Desperate times call for desperate measures," Akhdar replied, rubbing his temples. "We are not dealing with an ordinary man. And now he is with the rebels. Tell Panhek he has my authority to commence his Mortis Trooper program, and to start production at once starting with those imbeciles who let the Earthman escape."

"But you denied him that proposition because it was unnatural," argued Tarkhun. "Re-animating corpses into mindless automations is wrong. Do you remember what he did to one of your harem girls? He shrank her to nearly a foot tall, and he *still* doesn't know how to get her back to her original size!"

Akhdar fumed at his closest confidant. "Tarkhun, you will do as you are told, or I'm going to persuade the good doctor to make you the chief Mortis Trooper. Are we on the same page?"

Tarkhun's face went ashen. Sweat was beading down his forehead.

"As you wish, my lord," he said, before taking off to fulfill the emperor's request.

"That's a good dog," said Akhdar, looking over the damage that had wrecked over to his beloved arena.

He will have Sinbad's head on a pike for this.

Qani and her band of Thulian rebels took Sinbad's comatose body and laid him on the deck of the first ferry. Qani held the outlander and supported his head. He was barely breathing and he was running a fever. The toxin was going into effect. Time was of the essence.

"Be strong, Sinbad," Qani said to him.

The world swam in and out of focus before Sinbad's eyes. The poison had rendered him largely senseless during the ride.

Sinbad opened his eyes for a brief moment and looked at the beautiful green woman. She was unrecognizable to him. He squinted his eyes and barely made out the shape of her face. He couldn't hear her; he was once again slipping in and out of consciousness.

Sinbad could feel Death coming for him. Finally the grim entity will claim his soul. Long enough the sailor had eluded the black angel. No longer would the great soul collector be cheated from his prestigious prize. Sinbad the Sailor's essence will be the pride of his entire menagerie of lost and damned souls.

Death believed in only one thing:

Everything dies, it all matters to when.

As Sinbad twitched in agony, he was visited by ghostly images of his past. He was sweating profusely more than ever as a mixture of fear and guilt coursed through his veins. He tried to open his eyes, but he could not. It was as if they were sewn shut, and he was being forced by someone to watch all these horrific scenes.

Right before him stood the figure of a very gaunt and frail young man. As he came into the light, Sinbad lost his breath to see the man's face.

"Harufa!" he gasped, seeing that his former first mate was alive and well.

But something was terribly wrong.

Harufa's skin was dreadfully pale as if he had just risen from the grave. His eyes were sunken and the life in them had long since gone out.

There was also a huge red stain on his shirt. The blood in the fabric had seeped in and dried over time. The puncture wound above his heart had never healed. He made no effort on concealing the affliction.

He wanted everyone to notice it.

Especially Sinbad.

The most disturbing feature on his old friend was the rotting and festering flesh that was peeling off his body. Huge chunks of hair were missing from the top of his head, and most of Harufa's facial tissue was severely decayed. The open lacerations on his face and body were crawling with uncountable maggots scuttling in and out of his rotting skin.

The stench was unbearable for Sinbad. He thought he was going to be sick. He could feel his stomach churn just by the sight of Harufa.

"Hello, Sinbad," the ghastly figure finally spoke, "I see you're looking well. Me on the other hand…not so much."

"I am truly sorry on what happened to you, my friend," said Sinbad, trying to look away from the gruesome sight.

"Don't you dare patronize me!" Harufa shouted. "You left me to die on the godforsaken island! In the hands of that mad wizard."

"I didn't kill you. It was Sokurah! He's the one who buried that dagger into your heart. But I slayed him and avenged your death, Harufa. You should be at rest under Allah's beauty and grace."

"And *that* is supposed to make me feel better?" Harufa tearfully replied. "I was your best friend and second-in-command. You and I have been friends, sailors, and brothers-in-arms for most of our adult life. You once swore to me you were going to watch my back and I agreed to do the same for you. But you betrayed my trust when you brought Sokurah to our expedition, and you were stupid enough to trust him. And looked what he did to me!"

Harufa opened his shirt enough to show Sinbad the stab wound above his heart. He had been dead for several years, but by some kind of black magic Sinbad could see the blood oozing out of the gash.

Sinbad tried to find the words to fight back and defend his innocence, but he was feeling the horrid sting of the painful truth.

Then Harufa quickly transformed into a beautiful young woman, wearing fine fabrics and on her head rested a golden tiara with several diamonds encrusted all over the band.

It was Farah—Sinbad's betrothed—and she was frowning.

"Why have you left me, Sinbad?" she asked. "I thought you loved me."

"Farah, I was going to come back to you, but I ran into some trouble."

"Am I not enough for you?" she immediately dismissed him. "All you care about is sailing and looking for treasure."

"Farah, darling, you *are* worth more than all the riches in the world."

"Liar," she scowled at him.

She lifted her left hand to show Sinbad a ring around her finger. On the gold band there was a generously sized diamond that glittered in the sunlight. It was as if she wielded a miniaturized sun encased in an array of precious prisms.

It was more than any man would ever give to a woman.

It was far more than Sinbad had to offer.

Farah gave Sinbad a cruel smile. "You didn't expect me to wait forever, did you, Sinbad?"

"Farah…" he exhaustingly moaned.

Qani was puzzled. He was delirious and experiencing such vivid hallucinations. Whoever this Farah was Qani could tell that her and Sinbad had a history. She wondered if this Farah was his lover, friend, or a relative of his. Qani didn't have time to contemplate. She was aware Akhdar would send reinforcements to come after her group.

She signaled the rest of her crew to make haste with Kar-Tyr dashing by the port side of her small vessel. The water was shallow and only two feet deep. The current was quick and it was proven to be a quick getaway. Kar-Tyr looked over to Qani's boat and noticed Sinbad bobbing in and out of consciousness.

"How is the Earthman?" he asked Qani.

"Weak and getting much worse," she replied, feeling Sinbad's heated forehead. Sweat and poison dripped from his pores and seeped into the soft cloak. "We have to get him to shelter."

Sinbad wondered if he were already dead.

Qani pulled out a telescope from the satchel she kept under the seat. She peered through the lenses toward the bright pink horizon. Her jaw dropped in revulsion, and her heart began to race.

"What?" she gulped, when she saw a ship filled with three angry Thulian guards that Akhdar had dispatched.

Two of them were armed with axes and the other one had a crossbow. The shooter was reaching into his quiver for a poisoned projectile. Qani's eyes were broadened with terror. "Kar!" she shouted over to the Kurwani warrior. "A ship up ahead!"

Kar-Tyr looked forward and saw the incoming threat. He straightened his kunai rope and ran up ahead at full speed on his robust horse legs.

"I've got it!" he replied, watching the guards tremble at the very sight of him.

The archer was so invoked with fear he had difficulty loading his arrow. His chartreuse cohorts were begging for him to calm down and shoot the imminent invader.

Kar-Tyr cracked his whip as the kunai's metal tip was buried into the hull of the long boat. With all of his unearthly might, Kar-Tyr pulled the boat into the water. The guards went airborne flying off in three different directions. Each of them made an enormous splash one after another.

"Well done, Kar!" said Qani in gratitude. The victorious centaur nodded in response and rolled up his weapon.

"Qani!" exclaimed one of her comrades in the boat behind her. "We've got company!"

Qani turned her head to see another Dozhakian guard infested ship tailing them from behind. She looked over to Sinbad who was looking much frailer. She removed her long purple cloak and made it into a provisional pillow. She placed it under his head and carefully stood up.

"Lay still," she instructed the ailing sailor. He couldn't find the strength to answer her or give her a bodily response. He just lay there, staring emptily into space.

His breathing continued to be erratic.

"Breathe slowly," Qani told him. "Close your eyes."

But it made the pain and vertigo worse.

He was silently praying to Allah for forgiveness.

Praise be to You, my Lord, Creator and Provider,
Who sustains those when You wish beyond all reckoning.
I ask You to forgive all my sins,
And I repent of my faults to You.
My Lord, none can oppose Your judgment or power,
Or question Your acts, for You are omnipotent,
praise be to You.
You make one man rich and another poor, as You choose;
You exalt some and humble others in accordanc
with Your will.
And there is no other god but You,

How great You are!
How strong is Your power,
And how excellent is Your governance!
You show favor to those of Your servants whom You choose,
For here is the owner of this house living in
the greatest prosperity.
Enjoying pleasant scents, delicious food and all kinds
of splendid wines,
You have decreed what You wish with regard.
To Your servants in accordance with Your power,
Some are worn out and others live at ease.
Some are fortunate while others, like me,
Live laborious and humble lives.

With supernatural grace and agility, the nimble green woman performed a death-defying backflip from the bow of her long boat over the rampaging waters and onto her friends' craft. Before she could lose her momentum and engrossed all her power into one titanic handspring that sent her on top of the mast on the guards' boat.

The armored sentinels stood there flabbergasted at the very sight of her. There was a collective shout, gasps, the guards pointed upward. Despite the fact they were all armed, they abruptly became of secondary interest compared to the sight that presented before them on the bow. Qani rose fully erect on the post, stretching her arms far apart. She looked over to the starboard side and saw a cluster of jagged rocks. She shifted her weight to the right, countering the helmsman's steering.

"Get her off!" he ordered his friends, trying his best to regain control of the rudder. "She's steering us into the rocks!"

The two guards attempted to grab Qani, but she was too far away. She remained perched on the small summit of the mast. Beads of sweet ran down her brow and she felt the tremendous strain in her legs.

"Can't reach her!" said one of the unscrupulous Thulians.

The helmsman crossly groaned. "Then shoot her, you imbeciles!"

Before one of them could reach for their slings and arrows, the boat crashed into the rocks. The tail of the small ship tilted upward, sending all of the guards into the water. Qani hovered into the beautiful pink and magenta sky with both her arms out, as if she was being transcended into heaven.

Kar-Tyr saw his new friend flowing through the smooth pastel atmosphere. She was losing altitude and was heading for the sharp rocks. Kar-Tyr threw his arm back, with the handle of his kunai in his bulky hand.

"Grab on, Qani!" he called out, snapping his kunai to the falling lady.

Qani saw the metal tip coming straight at her. She stretched her left hand forward and grabbed the rope. Then Kar-Tyr hurled her back to the boat where Sinbad laid there unattended. The long rope gave a whooshing sound throughout the air. Qani landed softly in the galley and held Sinbad. His health hadn't improved since she left for her assault on the enemy ship.

"Not too much farther, Sinbad," she said to him.

The sailor did not now much because he could not discern the real from the poison-induced dreams and Sinbad knew he could not. Whatever was on that arrow's tip was much stronger than all the opium in every back alley death den put together back on Earth. But he was about to die. Of that he was certain.

The convoy was heading towards a dark cavern, which made Kar-Tyr very nervous. He had heard tales about this cave. Especially the ones where no one had ever made it through the other side alive.

"Sheol's Cavern?" the anxious Kurwani asked the crazy Thulian girl. "Surely you don't mean for us to enter it?"

Qani flashed the edgy centaur a sly grin. "That's exactly what we're going to do, Kar."

The two boats entered the nightmarish cavern with courageous endeavors. The uneasy centaur reluctantly followed suit, wondering if these strangers were indeed his friends.

"Even Akhdar's reach cannot overcome generations of superstition," she assured Kar-Tyr when he finally decided to join them.

Back at the dungeon, Tarkhun opened the door to the cell where the old Azurian rested on the cot. Through the threshold, Zhar Akhdar entered the cell with his arms behind his back at ease.

The elder Azurian showed no sign of surprise or agitation. He had none of the fear or respect for authority that civilization instills in men.

"Greetings, oh wise one," he insincerely addressed the old man. The ancient Azurian crossed his arms in sedition. "Your zhar has need of your clairvoyance yet again."

"I know what you have come to ask, Akhdar," the blue elder replied. His voice was gravelly and his tone overly abhorred.

Akhdar came over to the Azurian's bunk. He placed his left foot at the edge of the bed and rested his left arm in a casual manner. He looked at the small decrepit blue man as if they were old friends.

"Well, that should make it all the more easy, old man."

"I will no longer betray my people," said the elder. He looked at the boy prince with disgust in his eyes. "Your end is near."

"*My* end?" questioned Akhdar, with concealed bitterness. "You would dare speak to your zhar in that manner?"

The hot-tempered emperor started up and struck the old Azurian heavily across the mouth. The elder reeled back, blood starting from his lips.

"You don't deserve to rule," muttered the elder, wiping the blood from his mouth. "You are nothing but a usurper.

Just a cruel little boy pretending to be something he is not. Your uncle would be ashamed of you."

Akhdar started to reply, then stiffened suddenly. All he could think of was the nerve the old codger had. This was the greatest insult that anyone had ever thrown at the malevolent tyrant. The older Azurian did not speak, but the intentness of his gaze answered for him.

"I don't think he's going to talk, sire," said Tarkhun, breaking the silence.

Akhdar clenched his teeth and grabbed Tarkhun by the collar of his tunic.

"You don't think, Tarkhun?" the young and impatient zhar jeered. His dark eyes flickered with menacing lights and shadows. "I am zhar! He will do as he is instructed."

Akhdar let out a heavy sigh and released his second-in-command. Tarkhun felt around his neck if there were any contusions.

"As will you. I tire of this senile old thing, Tarkhun. Please deal with it in the same manner as all things that exhaust me."

Akhdar left the dingy cell as Tarkhun unsheathed the dagger from his belt. Halfway down the corridor he could hear the elder Azurian sway and the parting of his lips, but only a dry rattle burst from his throat.

The old blue man stared up to his killer with dilated, gazing eyes that somehow held a terrible bewilderment. His lips slobbered and gurgled, and then suddenly he stiffened.

Akhdar grinned bleakly when he heard a sudden thud on the floor.

CHAPTER EIGHT
A FABLE IS A BRIDGE WHICH LEADS TO THE TRUTH

The rebels' hideout was located up in the East Mountains outside of the badlands, well hidden from Akhdar's forces. Inside the main chamber, Qani is mixing herbs and juices in order to develop an anti-toxin to Sinbad's poisoned blood.

Could this pale pink Earthman truly be the one of whom the prophecy speaks? She thought, looking at the pathetic human, who was twitching in his sleep. The putrid stench of the medicine filled her nostrils and she nearly gagged.

"*Ewwww,*" she muttered repulsively. "I'm glad you're the one who's about to eat this." She joked, feeding him the antidote. "Are you really our savior, or are you an imposter, like Akhdar?" she said, with a somber look of doubt shadowing her eyes.

On what she was waiting for an answer, all she got was a single word from the ambiguous redeemer.

"Azrak."

An alien sun and a massive moon shone through a thick, dusty sky, at levels too bright for comfort. A blue skinned man and his two sons were standing in a barren wasteland.

Several months ago, Azrak his two boys were traveling through the desert on their way home from the marketplace. They stopped for a water break and Azrak was watching his two boys playing a very rigorous game of tag.

Then over the horizon, a light started to outshine the hot sun, adding to the feeling of intense heat.

Azrak knew something was coming.

He could sense it, feel it in the shaking of the surface under him. The air around the family rumbled louder and louder; the dust, swirling like a breeze, was kicking it up.

Yet, Azrak could feel no wind against his face. Not even his fabrics moved in the high winds.

Something big was coming.

Huge.

But he didn't know what.

He just waited, facing it, wanting to turn and run, but yet not doing so. He needed to know what it was.

He needed to face it.

The air swirled and the dust choked him. The surface under his feet shook, as the horizon got even brighter.

The unknown came closer.

And closer.

He shook off the feeling of dread and tried to calm his fast beating heart. He desperately needed to know what it meant. And what he was waiting for.

Azrak felt the earth move suddenly. Then he heard a loud rumble.

"Father, what is it?" said Sobek, his youngest son. "Is it a quake?"

"No," Azrak replied, "there are no fault lines anywhere near here."

"What's going on?" asked Matthias, Azrak's eldest child.

The rumbling deepened, growing into a deafening roar. The boys were frightened, but Azrak was just calmly looking over the horizon as if he couldn't be less concerned.

"Father?" Matthias called again, but Azrak wasn't paying him any attention.

He saw the sand from the dunes rose up like a violent sandstorm. It was impossible, but it appeared to him that it was the end of the days.

The children stood behind their father as the sand sprayed over to them. Then they all saw it. A meteor was streaking just above them, right over their heads. It was large and seemed to be made out of wood—not iron ore—and it was about to crash.

Azrak forced opened his eyes, the bright light was hurting them.

There was a sudden thunderous blast.

Then, for a moment, everything was silent.

"Is it over?" asked Sobek.

The answer came just a moment later with a deafening explosion that rattled the desert.

Azrak's heart was racing. He wasn't sure what happened. Then he shoved his fears aside.

"Follow me, boys," he said to his awestruck children. "No dawdling."

Azrak and his sons rushed over the dunes, and along the way they saw the charred trench, several hundred feet long. Rising from the superheated dunes far out in the desert as hot wind tickled the dune crests, spraying sand downslope in neat sire curves. It was not the cause of the eruption of sand that occurred near the center of one dune, however. Over the hill, they found it. It was still hot and smoking.

There was a deep crater in the middle of the desert. At the bottom of it the large wooden ship was cooling off from the heat of entry. He stretched out his foot to see how hot the ground was. The heat rushed up to his nose, and without meaning to, he pulled back instinctively. He could feel his pulse beating. It was loud and painful, but he braced himself and started again.

"Father, Father!" Sobek cried, running to Azrak.

"What is it, child?" Azrak asked, holding his youngest offspring in alarm.

"This ship is nothing I have ever seen before," the boy rapidly explained. "Father, I think it might be from another world."

"What makes you say that, my son?"

"Because I see a man over at the other side," the boy replied in panic. "He does not look either Azurian or Thulian. He's pink!"

"Don't listen to him, Father," said Matthias. "He's telling you another one of his wild stories."

"No, I'm not!" Sobek argued. "It's there. I saw it!"

"Like the time you saw a monster in your room and it turned out to be your coat?"

"Enough!" Azrak told his eldest son. He could tell by Sobek's quick breaths and his wide eyes he was telling the truth.

Azrak put his hand on his son's shoulder and showed him the urgency in his eyes.

"Take me to him," he ordered Sobek.

"Father," said Matthias. "Don't tell me you're actually going to—"

"Stow that talk, Matthias," warned Azrak. "Fetch me my bag. If what your brother is telling me is true, there may be an injured man out there. And he would need some remedies. Now hurry!"

Matthias did what he was told and collected his father's bag, and followed him behind the canyon. Sobek led the way, holding his father's hand with eagerness. Azrak was amazed to see the ship his son told him all about. It was indeed unlike anything he had ever seen in his entire lifetime. This ship wasn't built with metal and rivets. It was made of wood, and it had sails. This was certainly no spacecraft. It was a nautical vessel. The question running through Azrak's mind was why a ship would be in the middle of a desert.

It looked like the vessel had been through a terrible storm. The sails were ripped and tattered. The three masts were all entwine and cracked. The hull was damaged beyond impair. It was like the entire ship had fallen from the sky.

"Over here, Father!" exclaimed Sobek.

Azrak followed his son to the starboard side of the ship to discover a humanoid alien life form. It definitely had pink skin and it also appeared to be male. It was wearing some sort of hat on its head, and the sun caught the glimmer of the golden medallion hanging around its neck. The man's face was bruised and battered, more black and blue than anything else. One arm was bent in a way that told Azrak it was broken in at least two places. The outlander had passed out from the trauma of the crash. This foreigner was on the verge of dehydration and the man was starving. Azrak looked him over and faced his oldest son.

"I need my bag, now!" he ordered.

Matthias ran to his father and handed him the bag. Azrak ran through the contents and pulled out a small medical kit. He opened the case to reveal bandages, antitoxins, rations, and disinfectants. He unlocked the rations compartment, and retrieved several morsels of food.

He placed his fingers on the stranger's neck to find a pulse. Azrak found a very faint trace of life in the strange visitor.

Desperate for air, the man coughed violently. He hacked up plugs of putrid sand from his mouth and nose.

Then the blue caregiver took a piece of food and placed it in the outlander's mouth.

Matthias pointed to the stranger's face. "Its eyes are opening, Father!"

"Here," Azrak said to the pink life form, "take this. You have traveled a long way, my friend. It is my honor and privilege to have found you."

Sinbad opened his eyes to discover the silhouettes of three oddly shaped strange beings standing over him in front of a blinding pink sky. Their eyes were much wider than any human being. Their skin was as blue as the sea itself and they neither of them had any noses. He looked at the adult through half-closed eyes. His lips, dry and parched, quivered as he struggled to talk.

Something told him he wasn't on Earth anymore.

Azrak feared that the impact from the crash might have given the injured stranger a concussion. He had to keep Sinbad awake. It didn't matter what the subject of the conversation would be; as long as the Azurian man would keep the man awake.

"I know you must be in terrible pain, my friend," said Azrak, looking over the strange man's wounds. His attention was fully focused on the dislocated arm. "But can you move your arm?"

Sinbad grunted with effort, and sucked his teeth in pain. Beads of sweat dripped through the pores of his forehead, and his face turned red.

"I think it's broken," he answered the tall blue man.

Azrak studied the severe ailment. "It's not broken, only dislocated."

"Can you put it back into place?"

"Yes, I can," Azrak replied, placing his hands on Sinbad's shoulder. "I must warn you, the pain will be excruciating."

The Earthman took a breath and looked at Azrak in a state of readiness. "Then do it."

Azrak gripped the man's shoulder. "Be still. I'm going to do it on the count of three."

Sinbad closed his eyes and muttered a prayer in his native tongue.

"One…" the blue man began, and then a loud popping sound erupted inside Sinbad's eardrum. The man howled in pain.

"I thought you were going to count to three!"

Azrak gave him a small smile. "I am very sorry. I thought you would back out at the last second."

He expected the bizarre pink man would be angry. But he was surprised to hear the sound of laughter.

"I would have too," Sinbad laughed. "Well played, my friend. Well played."

Azrak laughed along with him, while he checked the arm, which was now placed back into its socket.

"Your arm looks better, but it's going to take some time to heal. What is your name, stranger?"

The adrenaline from the minor operation was wearing off, and the otherworldly visitor had a feeling he could pass out at any moment. He mustered all the strength he had left to answer his savior's question.

"On the Isle of Kish, I am a hero," he began, forcing himself to keep his eyes open. "In the city of Abu Dhabi, I am a thief. And in Baghdad I am to be killed on sight."

Azrak leaned onto every word the outlander said. He had no recollection about the cities and countries that were mentioned. It was then Azrak learned that this man wasn't from around here at all.

"My friends call me a sailor. My enemies call me a pirate."

Pirate? Thought Azrak in fear. *Is he affiliated with the deadly pirate Rhadjan Vix?*

Then the man placed his hand onto Azrak's. "But you may call me Sinbad."

Sinbad the Sailor quickly surveyed his surroundings. Nothing was familiar to him. He had been all over the world, but he didn't remember anything about this place. Then he feared he wasn't in his beloved city of Baghdad anymore.

Azrak saw the man's eyes roll up into his head. He stood up in alarm and lifted Sinbad into his arms, and carried him off over the dunes, with his two sons following him to the horizon.

CHAPTER NINE
A GOOD MAN IS ONE WHO REJOICES IN THE WELL-BEING OF OTHERS

Sinbad dreamed of sand and nothingness that stretched around him in all the directions, with not a shred of shelter to be had. Sinbad started moving. It was slow going. The sand kept shifting beneath his feet so that in a very short order, the muscles in his legs were screaming at him for rest. He didn't dare to accommodate them. Instead he had to keep moving, if for no other reason than that—should he be captured and killed.

His lips were parched. He tried to lick them but he had no spit or any moisture in his tongue. In short order his tongue acknowledged the absence, swelling so that it felt as it were taking up the entirely of his mouth. Automatically he reached up to wipe the sweat from his brow, but there was no moisture there either. Several times he had to stop and take slow, measured deep breaths to force air down his throat because he was having problems swallowing.

Sand managed to work its way into just about every orifice he had. He was blinking sand from his eyes, scooping it from his ears. It was in his teeth and under his swollen tongue. At one point he tried to cough and nearly choked himself again.

He tried to stand up. His body ignored him. It tried to convince him that he should just go back to sleep, just rest there and let everything sort itself out. When his brain ordered his muscles to function, they were unable to ignore him. He fought his way to standing and stood there like a wavering flag, symbolizing…he wasn't sure what. Maybe he just symbolized being too stupid to know when to quit.

He started walking again, but fell once more. This time he fell headfirst down to a dune. He knew he wasn't getting up again. He flopped at the bottom, spent as a dishrag, too tired even to think about standing.

Sinbad needed to roll out and take the measure of his surroundings the instant he hit the ground. The pain that was running through his body from teeth to toenails insisted otherwise. Pain won, and he lay where he had landed, groaning.

He sent out a silent prayer to any deity who might be listening to take him right now.

A dark figure rose from behind the dune. The sun blinded Sinbad and he squinted against it, morbidly amused that he had strength to maneuver his eyebrows.

It kept rising and that was when Sinbad realized it was a person. A face appeared above him, looking down at him. There was astonishment in its eyes, and then a concerned expression ran across it.

The first thing Sinbad noticed when he woke up was the throbbing headache. It felt like if every drop of blood that passed through the veins of his head carried a small explosive charge. For a while, the headache was his entire world. He couldn't remember pain like that ever in his life. He couldn't remember a life before the pain. He could only pray there would be life after.

A bit later it occurred to Sinbad to open his eyes. He started to do so, but the motion sent a lance of fire through his temples, so he stopped with the eyelid a quarter open, admitting a little bit of light but nothing else.

Still is better, he decided. *No movement at all. Movement is really, really bad. But thinking doesn't hurt much.*

He could think without moving. When that enlightenment hit him, though, the first thing he thought was obvious.

Where am I?

Doing his absolute best to ignore the screaming pain caused by the barest fluttering of his eyelid, Sinbad opened his left eye.

And he found someone had tended to his wounds.

With the gentlest of ease, he opened his other eye to discover his right arm was in a sling and his bare torso was wrapped in bandages. He probably had several cracked ribs, and he must have done something to his head.

He was reminded of what had happened to him on his Golden Voyage, where he found a golden tablet, which was dropped by a mysterious flying homunculus. Once he placed the tablet around his neck he was plagued by very strange dreams in which the evil magician Koura ruthlessly stalked him. And there was also a mysterious girl with an eye tattooed on her right palm. During his sleep a mysterious storm threw his ship off course, and the next day Sinbad and his men had found themselves near a coastal town in the country of Marabia.

But these recent surroundings were foreign to him. He didn't recognize the continent, or the architecture of this hut. The markings on the walls were nothing like he had ever seen before. The language was far more intricate than even his own native tongue. But the storm in which brought him to this strange land was far more violent than the one that took him to Marabia.

Before he passed out, Sinbad remembered speeding up into the sky on very violent winds all around him. He struggled to steer his ship, *The Chimera*, away from the terrifying storm, but the catastrophe was inevitable. The next thing he knew he was whisked away higher and higher into the maelstrom above the surface of planet Earth.

The eye of the storm was too intense and the atmosphere was very unstable. He fought against the gale force winds, trying to break the chaos. But he couldn't breathe because there was no oxygen for him to breathe and he could feel the painful freezing winds irritating his exposed flesh.

Then the ship shot up through the air, bursting through the maddening winds swirling around the airborne vessel

He was called to dinner by Azrak and met his caring family. His beautiful wife Zhara was a tall, slender Azurian woman. Her head was shaven as a fashion to the region's culture and her eyes performed a sparkle dance to the sunset. Right next to her was Matthias, the eldest son and then there was little Sobek the young man who spotted Sinbad out in the distance. Sinbad praised to Almighty Allah on guiding this boy to his hour of need.

They had very little to offer, but they managed to give the otherworldly visitor some of their portions. Sinbad ate and drank greedily. When he saw the unexpected blue people staring at his devouring, he quickly composed himself.

"My apologies, friends," he blushed. "I don't know how long I was lost in the desert. And it has been too long since I had anything to eat. Please excuse my unpleasant manners."

Azrak and his wife laughed. "There is no need to apologize, Sinbad. My wife is honored to have someone else enjoy her fine cooking."

Zhara's cheeks flushed with the sudden burst of red. Sinbad held up his glass and nodded to his hostess.

"Dinner is lovely, milady," he said to her. "Thank you."

Azrak's wife smiled, "You are very welcome, dear Sinbad."

"We have little to offer, Sinbad," said Azrak. "But we would be honored if you would stay with us until you have healed."

Sinbad finished off his soup with a very light slurp. He gave out a satisfying sigh and slowly stood up from his chair. Azrak and his wife were afraid he was going to fall over from his wounds, but the Earthman remained still. He gave the Azurian family a warming smile.

"One could not ask for a better host than you and your family, Azrak. I will stay."

The boys cheered and Sinbad gave out a hearty laugh. He looked at his bandaged body and then over to his gracious hosts.

"But don't expect me to lie around while I heal. I will help with the work around your home, until I am fit to leave."

"You don't have to, Sinbad," said Azrak.

"You and your boys saved my life, Azrak," Sinbad replied. "My life is indebted to you. I do not believe I could ever repay you, but consider this as only the down payment. It is the least I can do, my friend."

Azrak and his wife smiled and welcomed Sinbad to their family.

Through the next several weeks Sinbad was true to his word. He awoke every morning at dawn to help Azrak with his work, helped around the house much to Zhara's delight, and played with the children. During meals he would tell tales of his voyages through Earth's seven seas and entertained the children with childhood fairy tales from his hometown of Baghdad.

And when he ran out of stories about his adventures he began telling them about the epic fables of Greece. He went into full detail about the story of Perseus, the lost prince of Argos, and his journey to save a kingdom from the destruction of the gods.

Then came the chronicle of Jason and his mission to fetch the Golden Fleece, so he could defeat the evil tyrant Pelias, who killed and usurped King Aristo. The children were frightened when Sinbad brought up the horrific scene of when Jason found the blind soothsayer Phineas being tormented by two harpies, and then the infamous battle with the vicious skeleton warriors—an experience that both Jason and Sinbad vividly shared.

The children's faces lit up with joy and imagination on how beautiful and wondrous Earth must be. What Sinbad discussed the most was his love for the sea. To him the sea wasn't just water, fishes, or helming a ship. It was all about freedom. He would talk for hours on end about the subject and never get tired of it. Neither did the impressionable Azurian children.

This new experience could be easily related to Sinbad's first journey. Depending on the kindness of strangers, witnessing strange new things, and of course there was the adventure itself. He laid back and closed eyes, and recounted all the events that transpired in that old memory that felt like ages ago.

He had faced perils upon perils and endured such difficulties and discomforts when he was first starting out. Sinbad had made seven voyages, and an amazing story was attached to each. All of them happened through the decree of fate, from whose rulings where there was no escape.

Sinbad's father was one of the leading citizens and merchants of Baghdad. He was a man of morals and ample means. He died when Sinbad was a small boy, leaving him many possessions and estates. When he grew up and took all this over, he lived his life in complete excess. Eating the finest foods, drinking the sweetest wines, and went out with his friends to enjoy the city's nightlife. He was quite sure that these benefits would continue to be his, until he discovered that the money was all gone. His situation had chased and that all he had once owned was lost.

He found himself wondering what his father would have said had he lived to see the use to which he'd put his inheritance. He could still see his father shaking his head in discouragement and saying, "Sinbad, I've always warned you, if you don't learn how to handle funds, you're going to wind up with nothing to your name."

Sinbad was frightened and bewildered. Then he thought of something he had once heard from his father about King Solomon, the son of David.

"Three things are better than three other things. The day of ones' death is better than the day of one's birth. A live dog is better than a dead lion and the grave is better than poverty."

So Sinbad collected what he had in the way of furnishings and clothes, and sold them. Then he sold his property and everything else he owned. All of which got him was three thousand dirhams. It then occurred to him to travel to strange foreign lands.

He made up his mind to go to the sea and boarded a ship. The crew was reluctant to accept him, but he was able to win them over in time. The veterans only thought of him as some rich boy who wanted to play sailor. However, Sinbad carried his weight and did all the tasks the captain ordered. His smooth pampered hands soon grew into rough callouses, and he felt the satisfaction of a job well done.

The ship sailed downriver to Basra for Allah knew how many days and nights. Passing island after island and going from sea to sea and from one land to another. Whenever they passed land, they bought, sold and bartered, and sailed on like that until they reached an island that looked like one of the meadows of Paradise.

But the island wasn't an island.

It was actually a giant fish.

No—it was a whale!

It stayed motionless in the middle of the sea until it had become silted up with sand on which trees have grown over time so that it would look like an island. The heat of a blazing bonfire that one of the crewmembers suddenly ignited awakened it. Startled by the burning sensation, the creature began to move.

It was about to dive into the sea and the sailors were all going to drown. Some reached the ship before the "island" moved, plunging into the watery depths of the sea with everything that was on it. The sea with its boisterous waves closed over it.

Sinbad was one of those who had been left behind, and together with the others, he found himself underwater. But Almighty Allah saved him from drowning by providing him with a large wooden washing tub. He held on to it for dear life. He straddled it and used his legs like oars in order to paddle as the waves tossed him.

He followed the ship until it was out of sight. After that, Sinbad felt sure he was going to die. Night fell while he was still struggling in the water, and it lasted for a day and a night. Until, with the help of the wind and the waves he came to rest under the high shore of an island where trees were growing out of the water.

He had been on the point of drowning, but now he clutched at the branch of a lofty tree and clung on to it until he had managed to pull myself up on to the island itself.

His legs were numb and the soles of his feet showed traces of having been nibbled by fish. Something he hadn't noticed earlier because of his distress and exhaustion. He was, in fact, the nearest thing to a corpse when he was thrown up there. He had lost his sense and was plunged into dismay.

He stayed in this state until the sun roused him the next day. His feet were swollen and it was hard for him to walk. He made himself a crutch from the wood of the trees with which to support himself. It went on like this for a while, until one day, when he was walking along the shore he saw some kind of beast. He went to investigate to discover it was a fine mare that had been tethered to a tree.

When he got near, the horse scared him by giving a great scream and a man emerged from underground.

"Who are you?" the man asked. "Where have you come from and why are you here?"

Sinbad said, "You must know, sir, that I am a stranger. I was on a ship but I and several others found ourselves nestled into the sea, where Allah provided me with a wooden tub on which to ride. It floated off with me until the waves cast me upon this very island."

When the man heard Sinbad's incredible story, he took the sailor's hand.

"Come with me."

He led Sinbad to an underground chamber with a large hall, at the head of which he made the sailor sit. Then he brought Sinbad food and water.

"I would like you to tell me who you are, why you are sitting here in this underground room and why you have tethered that horse by the shore."

"There are a number of us scattered around here," the man explained. "We are the grooms of King Mihrjan, in charge of a number of his horses. On the new moon we bring thoroughbred mares that have never been covered and tether them on the island, after which we hide ourselves here underground so that no one can see us.

"Then a stallion, one of the sea horses, scents the mare and comes out of the sea. It looks around and when it sees nobody, it breeds with her and after it is done with her it would try to take her back to the sea with him. Because of the tether she cannot go, and he screams at her, butting her with his head and kicking her, and when we hear the noise we know that he has got down from her, and so we come out and yell at him.

"This alarms him and he goes back into the sea, leaving the mare pregnant. The colt or filly to which she gives birth is worth a huge sum of money, and has no match on the face of the earth. This is the time for the stallion to come out and after it dives, Allah willingly, I shall take you with me to King Mihrjan and show you our country.

"You must know that, had you no met us, you would have found nobody else here and you would have died a miserable death, with no one knowing anything about you. I have saved your life and I shall see that you will return from whence you came."

Sinbad thanked the man for being so exceedingly good to him, and while they were talking a stallion came out of the sea and jumped on the mare with a loud snort.

When it had finished its business it got off her, wanting to take her back to the sea with it. Once it failed, she kicked and screamed at him. At that, the groom drew his sword and raised his shield and went out of the door of the hidden room, shouting to his companions to help him and striking his sword against his shield.

A number of others arrived brandishing spears and shouting, at which the stallion took fright and made off into the sea like a water buffalo. It disappeared under the ocean surface without any trace or wake.

The man sat down briefly and was then joined by his friends. Each of them was leading a mare. When they saw Sinbad with the groom, they asked him why he was here, and the sailor patiently repeated his story to his new allies.

They had reached the city of King Mihrjan, and when Sinbad was placed before the ruler, he was given a courteous welcome and then was asked to retell his story. He told King Mihrjan of all that happened to him and all that he had seen from beginning to end.

The king was amazed by all of this.

"Sinbad," he said, "you have had a remarkable measure of good luck, and had fate not allotted you a long life, you would have never have escaped from these dangers, but, thanks be to Allah, you are safe."

King Mihrjan treated Sinbad with kindness and generosity, taking him as one of his own kinsmen and talking to him in the friendliest of terms. Sinbad was appointed as the king's port agent and was given the responsibility to keep a register on all ships that made port to the island. He stayed with the benevolent monarch as he carried out his business and received all manner of kindness and benefits from him. Sinbad was supplied with the most splendid of robes and took a principal role in presenting intercessions to him and settling the people's affairs.

Sinbad stayed with King Mihrjan for a long time. But whenever the sailor would find himself by the shore, he would ask the visiting merchants and sailors where the passage to Baghdad lay. He had hoped that someone would be able to tell him, so that he might leave with the crew and go back home. However, not one of them knew anything about Baghdad or about anyone who went there. So he remained helpless and tired out by his long exile.

After things had gone on like that for some time, Sinbad went one day into the presence of the king and found that he had a number of Indians with him. Their people were made up of a number of different castes, and among these were the Shakiris—the noblest of them all—who would never wrong or oppress anyone. Which left the so-called Brahmins, who drank no wine but lived happily, enjoying entertainment and pleasure and owning camels, horses and cattle. There were, in fact, seventy-two castes into which the Indians were divided, something that completely astonished Sinbad.

In Mihrjan's kingdom Sinbad noticed that there was an island named Kasil, from which there were to be heard the sounds of tambourines and drums being beaten all night long, although the other islanders and travellers who visited it told Sinbad that its inhabitants were serious-minded and cubits in length and another with a face like that of an owl. All in all, Sinbad saw so many strange wonders on that voyage that it would take too long to tell all of them to the king.

He continued to look around the island and noted what was there until he was standing by the shore, stiff as usual, in his hand, up sailed a large ship with many merchants on board. It pulled into the port and on the orders of its master, the sails were furled, the anchors dropped and the gangways ran out. The crew took a long time in unloading the cargo, while Sinbad stood there observing.

Then he asked the master whether there was anything left.

"Yes, sir," he said, "there are some goods in the hold, but these belong to one of our company who was drowned off one of the islands on our outward voyage. We have kept them as a deposit and we intend to sell them, keep a note of the price and then pass on what they fetch to his family in Baghdad, the City of Peace."

"Who is the owner?" Sinbad asked him.

The captain replied, "It was Sinbad the Sailor."

When Sinbad heard what he said, he looked at him closely and recognized him.

He gave a loud cry and quickly composed himself. "Captain, those goods are mine and *I am* Sinbad the Sailor. I joined the other merchants who disembarked on the giant whale that posed as an island. And when you shouted to us as the creature started to move, some got off while others, myself included, were submerged in the waves.

"Allah Almighty rescued me from drowning by providing me with a large tub. I got on to it and paddled with my feet until the winds and waves helped me reach this island, where I came ashore. Through Allah's help I met the grooms of King Mihrjan, who took me with them to this city and introduced me to him.

"When I told him my story he showed me favor and appointed me as clerk of this port, an office from which I have profited, and I have gained his approval. So these goods that you have are mine and they are my means of livelihood."

The captain quoted a passage: "There is no might and power except when Allah, the Exalted, the Omnipotent. No one has any integrity or conscience left.'"

"Why did you say that after you listened to my story?" Sinbad asked his former superior.

"You heard me say that I had with me goods whose owner had been drowned, and no you went to take them without having any right to them," answered the captain. "This is a crime on your past, and as for the owner, we saw him sink, and of the many others with him, not one escaped. So how can you claim that the goods are yours?"

"Captain, if you listen to my story and follow what I am telling you, you will see that what I say is true. For lying is a characteristic of hypocrites."

Then Sinbad went over for him everything that had happened from the time he left Baghdad with him until he got to the "island", where Sinbad was plunged into the sea. When he told the captain some details of what had passed between them both he and the other merchants realized on Sinbad's safety.

"By Allah, none of us believed that you could have escaped drowning. But Allah has given you a new life."

Then they handed over Sinbad's goods, marked with his name, from which nothing at all was missing. Sinbad opened the packages and took out something precious and expensive, which the crew helped Sinbad to carry as a gift to the king.

Sinbad explained to Mihrjan that this was the ship on which he had sailed and that every single one of his goods had been returned to him. It was from then, Sinbad added, that he had chosen the present.

The king was filled with amazement when he heard this, and he realized that everything Sinbad had told him was true. He showed the sailor great affection and treated him with even greater generosity, showering him with gifts in return for his. Then Sinbad disposed of all the goods he had with him at a good profit, after when Sinbad bought more goods of all kinds in the city.

When the other merchants wanted to depart to the sea, Sinbad loaded all that he had on to the ship. Then he went to the king to thank him for his kindness and then to ask him to allow Sinbad to return to his own country and his family.

The king said goodbye to him and presented Sinbad as he left with many goods from the city. When the sailor took his leave of him, and boarded the ship and with the permission of Almighty Allah they sailed off.

Good fortune attended them and fate helped them as they traveled night and day until they reached Basra in safety. Sinbad was delighted at his safe return and made his way to Baghdad with many vulnerable loads of all kinds of goods.

When he went to his house and was met by all his family and friends, Sinbad was more prosperous than ever, forgetting the time that he had spent abroad. Together with the toils and distress he had suffered and the terrors of the voyage. He occupied himself with pleasures and enjoyment, good food and expensive wine, and continued to do so.

Sinbad awakened from his reverie and then faced reality.

He wasn't stranded on an island.

There was no jolly king with power and influence to be his friend.

All of his friends and family don't know he was taken to Mars, or even know whether or not he was still alive.

And probably the most least is that there wasn't any gold, silver, or any kind of treasure to be sought on this floating red rock.

He started to weep and wail, blaming himself in his grief for the voyage he had embarked. Even the hardships he had inflicted on himself after he had been sitting at home in his own land at ease, taking pleasure in all of his luxuries. He was in no need of more money or goods. He regretted leaving Baghdad to go out to sea after what he had to endure in his first voyage, which had brought him close to death.

He prayed, "We belong to Allah and to Him do we return," and he was close to losing his sense of reasoning.

Then Sinbad finally realized he was now in the company of friends that kindly took him in. Not knowing if he were a man of honor or a villain.

For that, Sinbad was grateful.

One morning, Azrak and Sinbad set out into town riding on a pair of Azrak's stallions. Sinbad admired the surreal majesty of Mars. It was so much like his home world Earth, but there were some several dissimilarities.

"What a strange and beautiful planet you live on, Azrak."

"I'm sure I would say the same of your Earth," Azrak replied.

Before Azrak could continue the conversation, a loud explosion boomed through the valley. Both men turned around to see smoke coming out of Azrak's house.

"Oh, no," Azrak gasped. "My family is in danger!"

They rode their giant creatures back home. Azrak was so blinded by grief he didn't realize how fast he was going. He jumped off his stallion and threw open the door. His mind was obsessed of the safety of his family. Sinbad chased after him as they both ventured into the darkness, and then it was illuminated by peculiar blue fire.

Azrak went to the living room to see there was a struggle. Vases were knocked down and shattered all over the floor. The table was tossed upside down, and to Azrak's horror he found blood on it. He couldn't speak. His stomach was in a knot. His eyes were moistened into a pallet of mixed emotions. He glanced at the bodies of his slain wife and two sons where they lay etched in crimson and fell to his knees.

"No!" he screamed, shaking his fists in the air with rage.

Sinbad stopped dead in his tracks to see the horror. His heart sank and the color vanished from his cheeks. He had never seen anything this grim in all of his adventures.

"Allah, be merciful," he prayed softly.

Little did the two grief-stricken men know, the killers were still in the house. Two masked figures came hurriedly from a door, which a shadowy hand stealthily opened. They spoke not between swiftly into the gloom, cloaks wrapped closely about them, as silently as the ghosts of the ancients disappeared into the darkness.

Through the silence, which shrouded the corridor of Azrak's humble dwelling, the assassins' stealthy feet, cased in soft leather, made no sound either on thick carpet or bare marble tile.

The assassins ambushed them from the shadows. Their clothing was a mix of ethnic dress and modern combat garb. As they moved toward Sinbad and Azrak, they brandished bloodstained daggers and swords.

The hired killers subdued them quickly and put them in restraints. Then they fanned out, taking the lamps from the walls and pouring the oil onto anything burnable: rugs, pillows, furniture, and books. After they had set fire to the house, they took their prisoners to Zhar Akhdar's dungeons. Knowing they would provide excellent entertainment for their lord and master.

CHAPTER TEN
THERE IS NO GREATER MISFORTUNE THAN YOUR OWN

When Sinbad first began to awaken, he dared to hope that everything he had experienced up until now had been a dream. In his mind, he was rolling all the events when Azrak found him and took him into his home. It only took a few seconds, however, for the reality of his situation to come crashing down upon him. He was looking up and he was seeing not the ceiling of Azrak's hut, but instead the rocky surface of a holding cell. He was lying on the hard, flat surface of a cot.

In curious contrast to his environment, he heard a distant and oddly, discordant humming. He tried to lift his head and couldn't. So instead he turned it slightly and was able to make out a man standing a few feet away, humming went to Sinbad's ears. It sounded like a rather aimless tune. It was a bit patriotic but with a hymn feel to it.

"Azrak?" Sinbad weakly asked.

The strange Azurian man didn't acknowledge him with any reply.

Sinbad discovered a jug of water next to him. He tried to reach for it, but his hand wasn't coming anywhere close to it. He was parched, thirstier than he had ever been in his life.

He tried to say something else to the old Azurian man. He wanted to ask him for the water. But he couldn't speak. Instead, all he was able to produce were faint choking sounds.

"Water," he whispered hoarsely. "Water…"

The old man didn't hear him. Instead he continued to hum.

Sinbad tried to reach for the water, but there was a chain around his wrist that brought his hand up short. He yanked the chain from his arm and reached once more. But he came no closer. The restraints snapped taut, bringing him thudding back onto the bed. Sinbad inspected the shackles. Trying to find the weakest link.

"Don't waste your time."

The man had finally spoken. He looked straight at Sinbad. The sailor began to shake the chains. The Azurian looked as if he were about to offer a protest or advise against it. Instead he folded his arms across his chest.

Sinbad glanced around. The cramped room—if it could be called a room—wasn't looking any better once he was fully conscious.

"Where am I?"

Before the old man could respond, there was a *thunk* sound from off to the right. Sinbad repositioned himself on the cot and looked in the direction of the sound. For the first time he saw a door closely off the far end of the room. Inset into the door was a slat that had just been slid forcefully aside that been the source of the noise he'd just heard. A pair of bloodshot eyes was peering in.

The old man's reaction was instantaneous. He shot right up to his feet.

"Stand up! Now!" he ordered Sinbad.

Spurred by the fear that laced the old man's voice, Sinbad struggled to get to his feet. He was so weak that he literally could not harm a fly. If he tried to swat one, the insect would just shake it off and sneer mockingly at him.

The door opened and three green skinned men entered. Even though they had no hoods, Sinbad instantly recognized the two who were behind the round burly one as the murderers who infiltrated Azrak's hut and butchered his family.

Sinbad decided he preferred them with the hoods on. Each of them had similar features. Green, harsh, thick eyebrows, and the sorts of sneers that only bullies who had others in a weakened position could possess.

"Tarkhun," the old Azurian said in a voice so low that only Sinbad could hear, "is Emperor Akhdar's right hand. The two men with him are his top assassins."

Sinbad didn't nod or in any way indicate that he'd heard the old man. He wasn't even looking at him. His gaze had been drawn directly at the two thugs behind their fat superior. Flashes of the murders of Azrak's wife and children plagued his mind.

Sinbad had never wanted to kill anyone before. At the moment, what would have appeared to his captors to be rapt attention on Sinbad's part was actually Sinbad trying to figure out how he could gather the strength to cover the distance between himself and them, jump to the closest one and strangle him. He wanted to feel their lives fading between his fingers. These men, whom he had known for exactly five seconds, were men that Sinbad hated more than anyone he'd ever known.

Tarkhun was looking Sinbad up and down as it he was a prize horse that he just acquired.

"I have never seen anything like you before," he said to Sinbad. "No matter. The life you had is over. As of right now the rest of it belongs to me. You will follow my orders precisely or there will be dire consequences. Do you understand, outlander?"

Sinbad lifted his head and looked at Tarkhun squarely in the eye. "Where is the man that was with me?"

Tarkhun raised his eyebrow in curiosity. "You mean the Azurian?"

"He has a name. Azrak!" Sinbad snapped.

Tarkhun backhanded Sinbad, and sent him to the floor.

"I do not care for your tone, outlander. In time you will come to respect me."

Sinbad spat out some blood and then got back up. "What have you done with Azrak?"

"He is fine for the moment," Tarkhun replied. "My subordinates are taking very *special* care of him. But the poor fool has a habit of falling down."

"I swear if you harmed him, I'm going to—"

The old man held Sinbad back just when Tarkhun's two assassins drew their swords.

"Don't be a fool, outlander!" the old man viciously whispered. "You can't save your friend's life if you're dead. Right now you must abide to their rules. *Think*! Live to fight another day."

The old man was right. Clearly Sinbad was outnumbered and of course outmatched. Right now he had to bide his time, even though he didn't like it. Now Azrak's life hangs in the balance depending upon his behavior. He couldn't afford to have any more blood on his hands.

Sinbad stood down, watching Tarkhun squeeze out a smile on his rough face. He signaled his men to sheath their swords.

"That's more like, outlander," said Tarkhun, chuckling. "Perhaps you are not as stupid as you look."

CHAPTER ELEVEN
ASK THE EXPERIENCED RATHER THAN THE LEARNED

Sinbad had just been beaten senseless for the third time. His first week in Akhdar's dungeon had not been bad. The old Azurian man, who was in the same cell with Sinbad, unwilling agreed to watch the suspicious looking man's back, but he wouldn't let Sinbad sleep on the only available cot. Sinbad slept in the corner of the room, or whatever was left when everyone else had eaten, and worked harder than he had known possible in Akhdar's quarry. Lifting boulders, crushing them with crude pick axes, and cleaning the foul-smelling gunk in the hallways. At the end of each grueling day, he prayed to Allah with every muscle aching, but particularly the muscles in his back and calves. But despite the toil and discomfort, the first week was bearable because the other prisoners pretty much ignored him.

The second week was bad. He was not ignored; he was tormented. It began when a wiry Thulian man was beating up a youth of his own race in a blind area where the guards wouldn't see them.

Sinbad ran across the quarry, passing all the other inmates who were working. The taller man was delivering blow after blow, not showing the young one any mercy. He had tuned out all of the boy's cries and pleas. Only the sounds of bone against bone filled the attacker's ears.

"Stop what you're doing!" Shouted Sinbad, but the tall brute ignored him and kept pummeling the boy. "I said stop it!"

Sinbad dove through the air and tackled the assailant. Then with all his rage the man threw Sinbad off him and jumped onto his feet in a terrifying fighting stance.

"You have made a grave mistake, outlander," said the Thulian, as the young man fled out of the quarry. "Another time, boy!" he warned his prey.

"No, I believe *you* made the mistake. You think you can push people around because you are bigger and stronger than everyone else here. Well, *I'm* smaller than you. Let's see how you do against me!"

The Thulian smiled and muttered to himself, "And those were his famous last words."

He charged right at Sinbad, throwing the first punch. Sinbad blocked the punch and threw a left hook.

But the man caught it and kicked Sinbad in the groin.

The Thulian leaned forward to Sinbad's ear. "Would you like to know what's going to happen next?" he whispered maliciously.

Sinbad doubled over, falling to the ground, and without a word the Thulian kicked him on top of his head. Sinbad fell into a whirl of maelstrom color and awoke hurting.

Sinbad got up and looked around. The guards, who had not moved from their places along the wall, were grinning. Apparently they enjoyed a good fight. He could see one of them giving the other a small pouch of gems due to a lost wager. All prisons are the same in this universe. Apathy, corruption, and sadism existed in this region of the stars.

The following day, a member of the elite guards hit him with a shovel, and as Sinbad reeled against the stone wall, he tossed the shovel aside and punched Sinbad, twice in the chest and once in the face. When Sinbad opened his eyes his attacker was gone.

Sinbad went back to the cell he shared with the older Azurian male. He splashed cold, salty water on his bruises and tried to understand what was happening to him.

The only logical reason for all this abuse was because he was a stranger to this planet and the only human being in the prison. He'd accept this reality and took what he could from it. He didn't like being punched and the color of his own blood held no delight for him, but there were lessons to be learned here. And if Sinbad wanted to survive he had better learn them while he can still draw a breath.

"You have made a very powerful enemy today, outlander," said the Azurian.

"You mean that dog at the quarry? I've come up others like his ilk back home, and they had either met their end by my fist or the end of my sword."

"You would not find such a beast in your home world, Sinbad," replied the Azurian. "The man you just made a mortal enemy is Kasson Bay—the most notorious marauder who ever dared to venture through the dark mountains of Mars."

Sinbad scoffed, "So he has a reputation. That doesn't change that the next time him and I meet. *He* will be the one on the ground."

"Foolish Earthman!" scolded the Azurian. "We are talking about a man who takes pleasure on pillaging small villages and maiming innocents. Do not underestimate him."

Sinbad didn't heed the man's words. Now he had a name to go with the face, and he was busy visualizing his next battle with him. All he needed to do is to time his moves more quickly and he wouldn't be caught off guard.

Kasson Bay initiated the third attack. This time, Sinbad was ready and managed to land a blow before being knocked out. Sinbad awoke with water in his face. He looked up to see his ancient cellmate standing over him with an empty pail.

"If you want to live to see another sunrise," said the elder, "you listen to what I have to say. And I advise you to carefully pay attention because I will not repeat."

And Sinbad did—in odd, five-minute intervals between slave labor, the old man educated Sinbad in dirty fighting. Sinbad was aware that the weeks of brute labor in the quarry had physically changed him, coarsened his palms and thickened the muscles of his arms, chest, and thighs. The lessons included trust no one, hit first, preferably with something harder than a fist, and then hit or kick again, until the enemy can no longer resist. Then hit him once more, or kick him, or stomp him.

Sinbad had an idea of his own. Kasson, and a lot of his other prisoners, were bigger and more powerful than he—the hard work he'd been doing for weeks they've been doing for years. But none of them seemed exceptionally bright, including Kasson.

For the first several weeks, things focused on building Sinbad's strength and endurance. The old Azurian had him hauling water, shifting stones, and having him sprint. All the while increasing his weight by adding rock-filled pouches.

The combat drills Sinbad hungered for came at last, but not in the way he'd been expecting. The old man proceeded to teach the newcomer every aspect of infighting that he'd learned from a lifetime of adventuring and brawling—and Sinbad suspected that he made up a few on the spot. The elder, despite being three times Sinbad's age, tossed him around as if he were a ragdoll. Kicks, punches, head butts, and elbow strikes knocked Sinbad all over the cell.

The old man even bit him once!

Sinbad gave back as much as he could, and occasionally landed a fist or a kick on the unnamed Azurian. He never hurt him, though, but not because he pulled his punches. The elder still moved very quickly enough to slip most blows, and certainly knew enough to anticipate Sinbad's next moves. Still, as the weeks went on, Sinbad's hits became more consistent than misses, and his ability to block attacks improved greatly.

The old Azurian kicked him and Sinbad fell to the floor.

Fists on hips, the elder looked down at him.

Sinbad came up sputtering, "You're not fighting fair."

"Do you think anyone you will ever face in combat will fight fairly?"

"Men fight honorably."

"No. If you choose to believe that, you'll die in your next battle," the Azurian shook his blade slowly. "It's a miracle on how you are still alive. Men who *survive* tell other men they fought honorably. They lie. When you're in the company of your friends back on wherever it is you are from, have they ever told tales of an enemy who fought honorably?"

"No," Sinbad replied.

"And do you think anyone who survived fighting against them ever described them as honorable?"

"No."

"If you remember nothing else, Earthman, remember this: it's not the man who defeats the most who wins the battle, it's the man who *survives* who wins it."

Sinbad frowned, "And what if I vanquished them *all*?"

"Then you are the only man left standing," said the elder. "So, first I shall show you how to survive, then I shall train you in how to win. And if you can't win—*cheat!* You'll need that for the battles ahead. There is no shame in that, Sinbad."

Sinbad watched him warily, but did as he was told. The old man began by showing him how to keep his footing. The outlander's natural speed and agility made him adept at all of them, but his impatience to strike back diluted his focus. More than once, when Sinbad tried a clumsy retort, the teacher knocked his naïve pupil to the ground. The Earthman would bounce up again, fury blazing in those dark brown eyes. The old man knocked Sinbad down again and again, until the human could no longer rise—which took well into the night on some occasions.

Sinbad threw a punch at the ancient Azurian, who effortlessly evaded the blow, then flipped his head over heels onto the filthy floor of the spacious cell.

"Oomph!" Sinbad grunted, then swore profanely.

His self-appointed teacher was unfazed by his colorful invective.

"You must focus," he advised Sinbad.

"I *am* focused," he rose painfully to his feet.

"You're fighting like an angry wind. Your focus is fixated on a finishing move. It leaves you open for counterattack." His thin, but muscular arms were crossed atop his chest. His voice was calm, but stern. "Anger impairs your judgment and makes you do such foolhardy things."

Sinbad took out his hostility on the wooden door, making a dent with his fist. Blood covered his knuckles, and splinters stuck out of his hand.

"Akhdar's assassins should have learned that lesson."

The old man dismissed it with a shrug. "Someone else once said similar to that. And it destroyed him. If you let hate consume your heart, you will lose yourself. Remember that, Sinbad."

Having evidently decided he humiliated the Earthman enough for one afternoon, the old man wrapped up their training session. Sinbad took a moment to cool down and reflect what his teacher said to him. Then he was reminded of another saying, "A cold heart is a dead heart." He feared the prison had changed him. Not physically, but as a person. He came in here as a man, but he was slowly turning into an animal. He would further express this through prayer, hoping Allah would guide him through this difficult time.

He sat up on the floor with his knees bent and his palms placed on them. He closed his eyes and began his ritual.

"Greetings, prayers and
Goodness belong to Allah.
Peace be on you,
O Prophet
And the mercy of *Allah*
And His blessings.
Peace be on us and on the righteous servants of *Allah*
I bear witness that
There is no god but *Allah*,
And bear witness that
Muhammad is His servant
And Messenger."

The Azurian stood over him one night. "Do you know why I keep beating you?"

Sinbad spat blood from a split lip. "Because you will not teach me to attack."

"It takes no skills and no intelligence to inflict pain onto others. Anyone can do it. Even the animals," the old man sighed. "All the times we have trained, what have you learned?"

"You don't fight fair."

"Not that tired excuse. What have you learned?"

Sinbad sat up on the floor, his sullen eyes covered in shadows. "You move too quickly for me to close."

"And what does that tell you?"

"I have to be quicker. I have to be stronger."

"No, Sinbad," the old man shook his head. "It means you shouldn't be fighting me with your fists."

The Earthman blinked.

"Every man you face will have his strengths and weaknesses. Every group of men—every army—anything you will ever fight will have strengths and weaknesses. If you attack his strengths, you will lose. If you bring your strength to bear on his weakness, you will win."

Sinbad scowled. "You don't have a weakness."

The old man sat on his cot and rested his hands on his knees. "I do have a weakness, Sinbad. You don't see it as such, but I do. It's not one you'll ever be able to use against me, but it is there."

Sinbad looked up, "Then I will never be able to beat you."

"You will," the Azurian replied. "Tomorrow, in fact, I shall teach you how."

The Azurian spread his feet carefully, setting himself. "The weeks you've spent learning to attack, Sinbad. Do you really think you're ready to take me?"

The Earthman nodded, setting himself.

"Then come and face me."

Sinbad's eyes widened for a moment, then he darted forward, roaring a war cry. He attacked low, but the old man blocked low-left. The Azurian brought his right forearm up, deflecting the quick haymaker, and then he shoved.

Sinbad, off balanced, scrambled to keep his footing. He went down hard. The ground cracked beneath where he'd fallen, but the earthman bounced up again and drove at his teacher. Punches and jabs, knees and kicks, the outlander began combining things he'd been taught in ways the Azurian hadn't imagined he'd figure out so quickly. And the blows came fast, forcing the old man to dodge more than he ever had before.

Sinbad's effort made no difference. The Azurian never tried to attack, but concentrated on fending off the outlander's blows whenever Sinbad tried, whenever he hesitated, the ancient one would grab his fist and shove him back, again and again to the ground.

Gasping, Sinbad struggled to his feet and the old man punched him in the ribs. Sinbad staggered backward.

Snarling, Sinbad regained his footing. His eyes narrowed, his face tightened. He charged forward, he aimed to deal a hit that would split a man up from down.

The blue elder pivoted 340 degrees and aimed a kick at Sinbad's neck. But Sinbad raised his right forearm and blocked his teacher's foot. The Azurian man smiled.

Sinbad put his left leg forward and shifted his weight onto his left, and put his flattened, crossed hands at chest height: a fighting stance he had learned on the streets of Baghdad. He forced himself to remember everything else he had learned in his many voyages, and in all the dark alleys and filthy alehouses where he had fought, and won, and been defeated. The elder attacked and Sinbad responded with punches, kicks, blocks, and jabs. It was a smooth flurry of continual motion.

The elder said, "You are remarkably skilled. But this is not a dance. Slow down and keep your balance."

The blow's vigorously spun Sinbad around, and the old man knocked Sinbad off his feet. He landed hard, but come back up, balling his fists, rage on his face.

"Enough."

The Earthman came for him, not the least glimpse of reason in those brown eyes. The Azurian fended off two blows, then sent Sinbad flying back.

"*Enough*!"

Sinbad charged again.

When the Earthman threw a right cross, the old man caught Sinbad's face.

The blue man smashed the top of his head into Sinbad's face and immediately kneed him in the groin, driving his flat palm up into Sinbad's chin. Sinbad fell backward and tried to rise, but could not.

The Azurian shook his head, "You are not ready."

Sinbad shivered, "Does this mean you won't train me anymore?"

The ancient one sighed, "No, Sinbad, it means I have to train you even better."

One day the Azurian called a sudden halt to their fighting.

"Good. You've learned well."

Sinbad, doubled over, catching his breath, glared up at the old man.

"Is this how you were trained."

The old Azurian remained aloof. He was always the savagely forthright instructor, never the friendly mentor. But a bond grew between him and Sinbad regardless. Sinbad could not have given it a label, or even described it. In neither his personal experience nor any of his travels had he encountered anything like it. But he knew it was there, as he knew he had blood in his veins.

Sinbad began to question on whether or not it was possible to respect a man who did little more than brutalize another. He was on the verge of becoming emotionally attached to this wise powerful adversary. He had questions he could not possibly answer, at least not yet. He did not forget them, but he did not worry about them, either.

Sinbad never learned the names of his fellow inmates, and there had been hundreds of them. The old man had made it known that any unnecessary fraternization would lead to severe punishment, and no one ever crossed him. But Sinbad felt close to these anonymous men and women of varied races and walks of life. He felt closer to them that he had ever felt to anyone except for his old crew and his sweetheart Farah back on Earth. They may have been nameless, but they were pieces of something of which he, too, was a part and that gave him a commodity with them that often felt like affliction.

None of them stayed for long. New arrivals seem to be processed every few weeks or so. The men were either sent to the mines, or to fight and die in the arena. The women were enslaved to work in the palace kitchens and serve the royal court. The beautiful ones were fortunate to be handpicked by Akhdar to be part of his private harem. The children, however, weren't as lucky. When the slave traders brought in a family for processing, they would immediately separate the parents and the children. They were either sent to orphanage work camps or to be enrolled into various military academies where they would painfully get their spirits broken and brainwashed to join the ranks of Akhdar's ever growing merciless army.

Only Sinbad, the old man, and hopefully Azrak remained. He constantly asked himself if the emperor had something special planned for him.

Eventually, he would stop asking.

The next incident happened during the afternoon recreation break in the yard. The day was bleak. A cold drizzle was falling, turning the red dust on the ground to a dark burgundy mud. Sinbad was walking toward the cover of a tower when someone grabbed him from behind in a chokehold. Sinbad drove his elbow into his attacker's ribs, twice, and reached back, grabbed the man's hair, pulled him forward, and then got his shoulder under the attacker's chest and heaved.

The attacker, the young Thulian man, who Sinbad had saved in the quarry from Kasson Bay, was standing before him with a knife in his hand.

The green skinned man swung a roundhouse punch, almost gouging the outlander's eye with the blade.

Sinbad caught the fist, kicked the boy's knee. The pain caused the attacker to drop the knife and as he fell, Sinbad kicked him in the face.

Sinbad fought, using the knowledge he had learned from the old Azurian, until the boy conceded. He rested on his belly, struggling to breathe. Sinbad thought he may have broken several of the boy's ribs, but he couldn't restrain himself by kicking his assailant over to see his face.

Sinbad studied the young assassin and saw how the boy's skin was mottled and flaking when he fell into the mud. Sinbad came to the conclusion that the young Thulian was obviously a pledge to a prison gang. And the boy's initiation was to murder him.

Sinbad sighed, continuing his trek to the tower and hunkered down, scanning the yard; aware he was being stared at.

Emperor Akhdar Dadgar saw the whole fight through the window at the side of his lavish palace. He stroked his chin until he came up with a terrible thought. A delightful smile suddenly appeared on his face.

"Tarkhun," he called out.

The burly Thulian rushed to the emperor's side and knelt down before him. "What is your bidding, my master?"

"There is something I want you to do for me."

CHAPTER TWELVE
TRUST MAKES WAY FOR TREACHERY

The following days passed slowly for Sinbad. He was less than a prisoner but also less than a free man.

He had not heard from Azrak and presumed the worst for his friend. Sinbad had been observing the prison guards and had identified several he thought would be susceptible to bribes. But since his gold had been taken from him along with his other belongings, Sinbad had nothing to bribe them with.

Sinbad felt as if he'd just managed to drift back to sleep when he was rudely and abruptly jolted awake. Tarkhun shoved a hood over his head. For half a second Sinbad thought they were going to execute him. He was yanked to his feet. His strength had been returning, but very slowly, so he still felt off-balance as they hauled him out of the cell. He tried to figure out why they would put a head on him.

Then he realized they were taking him outside. By putting the hood over his head, he wouldn't be able to see the pathway out through what might well be a maze of tunnels. He was led there where he could make a break for it, but none readily presented itself.

Even with his face covered by the hood, he could still tell that he was moving from the relative gloom of the dungeon toward daylight. Moments later he felt fresh air wafting toward him, and then the hood was yanked from his head. He blinked like an owl in daytime, momentarily being blinded by the sun's rays. He raised one hand to his brow to try and ward off the sun even as he squinted, and then he saw something that stunned him. Considering all that happened to him since he was first brought into this cesspool of agony and despair. He would have thought there was nothing more that could happen to him that could have any sort of strong emotional impact. As it turned out, he was wrong.

Tarkhun stood right in front of him, giving a scowling smile. The sun was on his back that endowed him with a demonic aura. The huge Thulian man inhaled the fresh air with such enthusiasm and said, "I know, much better than the dungeon. But don't get used to it. This is going to be brief."

Sinbad surveyed his surroundings and noticed two guards roughly escorting a hooded captive.

"What is the meaning of this?" Sinbad asked Tarkhun. "Why have you brought me here?"

"Patience, outlander," scolded Tarkhun, "you will find out soon enough."

The guards brought the prisoner forward to Tarkhun, and threw him down on his knees. Sinbad recognized the two thugs as the men who slaughtered Azrak's family and destroyed his home. The assassins didn't show any facial reaction to Sinbad. It was as if they weren't capable of any emotion. Then Sinbad gazed upon the masked prisoner. He could immediately tell by the size, and bruises and cuts on the man's arms and legs he had been beaten repeatedly and he was also very malnourished. Then he noticed the man's chest heaving uncontrollably, as if the mask was suffocating him. But Sinbad knew that the size of the shroud wouldn't cause such a malady.

It was fear.

The man's hands were bound in chains behind his back. His wrists were almost thin enough for him to slip past the shackles. Tarkhun casually approached the prisoner, the sound of his footsteps crunched on the loose gravel that sent the captive fear piercing chills.

Tarkhun swiftly pulled the shroud off the man's head. Sinbad's jaw dropped as he discovered the poor man's true identity.

"Azrak!" he gasped, trying to fight back tears as he stared at his best friend's battered face.

Splotches of purple covered half of Azrak's face. His right eye had been swollen shut by the abuse of his tormentors.

His lower lip had been split and the dried blood glimmered in the sunlight.

With his one good eye, Azrak looked up to see Sinbad standing before him. He tried to force a smile, but the pain was too awful. The nerves on his teeth had taken their toll. He couldn't even eat without screaming in pain.

"Sinbad..." Azrak said in a weak, haunting rasp.

"You will speak when spoken to, Azurian scum!" yelled Tarkhun, as he kicked Azrak in the face.

Azrak fell backwards and landed on his side. He spat out several spurts of dark crimson blood along with some teeth as well.

Sinbad charged at Tarkhun with murder in his eyes. "Why the hell did you do that for, you walking deviant?!"

Before he could put his hands around Tarkhun's thick bulging neck, the two guards threw Azrak into position and held a blade against his throat.

Tarkhun didn't fear the outlander. He was running this show.

"Calm yourself, outlander," he warned, gesturing over to Azrak being held at knifepoint. "You wouldn't want to do something you may regret."

Sinbad stopped right in his tracks and abandoned his bloodlust. His angry twisted face quickly shifted into fear and worry.

"Please, don't!" pleaded Sinbad. "I'll do whatever you want. Just don't hurt him!"

Tarkhun gave Sinbad a very smug look. "Now that I have your undivided attention, I have a proposition on behalf of my lord and master, Emperor Akhdar—czar of the Dozhakian throne."

"What do you want?" asked Sinbad, not keeping his eyes off the dagger that was slowly slicing through the skin of Azrak's throat.

"Simple," Tarkhun began, "fight in the arena and your friend goes free. If you refuse he dies."

"Do not agree, Sinbad!" said Azrak. "I have lived my life. There is nothing more they can do to me. Tell him to go to hell!"

One of the guards backhanded him, and then the other pressed the sharp edge of the blade further against his neck, letting out a small trickle of blood.

Sinbad looked at Tarkhun, who stood there with his arms across his chest, waiting for a reply.

"If I agree, how would I know this promise will be kept?"

"You don't," Tarkhun said flatly. "What is it going to be, outlander? Fight for the amusement of my master, or sign your only friend's death warrant? The sands of the hourglass are dwindling to the very last grain."

Sinbad stared over to Azrak, exhausted by the tortures he had sustained all these months. He was ready to drop at any given moment. Then he noticed Azrak's lips moving, figuring his friend was reciting an inaudible prayer. Seeking absolution and telling his family he would soon be joining them. The guard with the dagger gave a slight chuckle, taking pleasure in his captive's pathetic cries for a god who had surely forsaken him.

Sinbad gritted his teeth. "I agree to fight," he said, bringing a smile to Tarkhun's face, "but under one condition."

"Which is?"

"I want you to kill those two guards," Sinbad pointed to Azrak's captors.

The two assassins looked at each other in confusion. They didn't know whether to laugh or to slit the Azurian traitor's throat right on the spot. Then they noticed the seriousness on their leader's face.

"Sir," said the guard with the knife, "you cannot be possibly considering—"

Something shimmered around Tarkhun's sleeve.

Something thin and metallic danced in the palm of his hand.

In one swift motion, Tarkhun slid the tip of the knife to his fingertips and threw it straight at his subordinate.

The knife met its destination between the assassin's eyes. The man doubled over, dropping the dagger onto the ground. The fallen guard's comrade couldn't believe his eyes, but there it was—his best friend and fellow hired murderer slain right in front of him on the request of this pink-skinned outlander.

"Daizha, help me!" the guard exclaimed in fear.

Then his eyes widened in horror to see Tarkhun coming for him now.

"Please, sir! Don't kill me!" he pleaded, reaching for his sword. "I don't want to fight you."

"I wouldn't fight me either," Tarkhun replied, delivering a right cross at the man's jaw.

The guard staggered to the side, trying to regain his senses and then finally unsheathed his sword.

He took a swipe at Tarkhun, but managed to dodge it. Then the guard slashed at Tarkhun's legs, but the burly Thulian man was able to jump over the stroke. Sinbad knew Tarkhun was only toying with the guard. It was just a matter of time before the bastard met his end.

The guard found a window of opportunity to strike his blade on Tarkhun's skull and took it. In one swooping arc, Tarkhun caught his wrist. His master's grip was strong enough to turn a piece of coal into a diamond. The force was strong enough for him to drop his sword, and it was hard for him to keep standing. When he heard the bones in his wrist snap he knew it was over.

With no effort Tarkhun pulled the guard's forearm forward, snapping it in twine. The beaten man howled in unholy pain, and nearly fainted to see a bone piercing through his skin. He tried to break free, but that only made things worse. With a flick of his wrist, Tarkhun broke the arm off and threw it aside. Then he brought in the guard closer, placing his hands on both sides of his head, and with a quick clockwise turn, he broke the guard's neck.

The guard's body lay limp in Tarkhun's arms, and then it was thrown to join the other corpse, like it was a sack of garbage. Tarkhun reached down to the pocket of his trousers and produced a handkerchief, and then proceeded to wipe the blood off his hands.

"You have made a wise decision, outlander," said Tarkhun. "Even though I ended up getting the raw end of the deal. But as they say, nothing ventured is nothing gained. Are you satisfied?"

"Very," Sinbad grimly replied.

Tarkhun gave a small laugh. "You may not be so weak after all. Your friend will be placed in your cell and no further harm will come to him—unless you decide to do anything stupid. Is that understood?"

"Yes."

"Good. Now collect your friend and bury these useless whelps."

Tarkhun left them to inform Akhdar that everything was going according to plan. Sinbad ran over to Azrak and helped him up.

"Azrak," Sinbad said, helping him to his feet, "are you all right?"

Azrak painstakingly lifted his head to look at Sinbad right in the eye. It wasn't a friendly look, but an angry one. "How could you agree to fight in the arena? It's suicide!"

"I had no choice," Sinbad replied. "They were going to kill you."

"You're only delaying the inevitable, Sinbad. You think these mongrels are going to keep their word? Their word is only worth *this*!" Azrak spat onto the bodies of his family's killers.

"I can handle my own," Sinbad assured him. "Back on Earth, I have fought and beaten the best."

"Stop it!" Azrak bellowed. "Just stop it. Those stories you told my children were fun and entertaining, but that's what they were—fairy tales!"

"Azrak, I swear on Almighty Allah that I spoke the truth when I told those tales."

"Especially when you said you slayed a giant sea serpent with your bare hands?"

Sinbad lowered his eyes and gave a small sigh. Azrak crossed his arms and scoffed.

"All right, so I had a knife. It's poetic license."

"'Poetic license?' Sinbad, you haven't seen the fights in the arena! The best warriors all over Mars fight to the death there! You won't stand a chance."

Sinbad gave Azrak a small smile, "Good thing I've got a great teacher."

CHAPTER THIRTEEN
IN THE SMALL LANES, THERE ARE NO BROTHERS OR FRIENDS

A horn sounded throughout the arena. On the main terrace, nobles had gathered to witness Akhdar Dadgar's latest source of entertainment. Festive banners fluttered from the high ceilings while attendants handed out golden goblets full of sweet drinks to the beautifully dressed guests. There was something lively in the air to the room as people chatted softly to each other and waited with eager anticipation for the fight to begin.

Sinbad stood in the shadows at the back of the arena. He watched the guards set up the primus. It was a huge place and poorly lit.

The arena's seats sloped down toward the ring; two hundred rows of rising seats separated the spectators from the combatants. The audience was still coming, only minutes before the main battle, and the arena was only half full. An audience of over twenty thousand, mostly men, filled the seats.

Sinbad watched the guards hose the blood from the previous fight out of the arena and began to purify the ring. He stood in the tunnel with the other three fighters, watching the blood get cleaned off the ground where he would shortly be standing and fighting on.

Beside him there the three other fighters were getting ready for the battle of their lives. There was a tall Azurian man who was covered in a series of tattoos. Sinbad didn't know whether to look at him or read him.

Behind the blue lanky figure was a hulking Thulian man, who looked he had spent the last several years at war. He was paunchy, but his upper body was very muscular. His face had been sliced to hell with dozens of knife scars.

"What are you looking at?" the scarred man growled at Sinbad. He looked like a rabid dog, showing his sharp teeth and drooling uncontrollably.

He was ready to pounce on Sinbad, but the guards pulled him back by the chains around his collar and harness. They weren't taking any chances with this psychopath. Once he is turned loose, there was no way they were able to restrain him again without the several guaranteed casualties.

Sinbad backed away and then noticed the last gladiator he was going to face for the evening. The man was a little short in stature and slimmer than all the others—including the tattooed Azurian. He wore some sort of golden armor that was all dinged up and lost its polish over past battles. The armor shimmered in the faint light, but it was nothing compared to the face. It was some sort of mask or helmet. Through the visual slit of the mask Sinbad could see a patch covered the man's left eye.

Sinbad could use this disability to his advantage. He wondered how long ago the man's eye had been gouged out. The masked fighter might've had some time to practice on improving his depth perception. But Sinbad remembered what the old Azurian taught him, and he shouldn't take anything lightly.

Then Sinbad noticed the mouth of the man's mask. It was permanently frozen into a demented grin with painted teeth running along the top and bottom. It was truly horrifying.

"Oh, no," gasped the old Azurian, looking through the bars that separated his cell and the arena. His eyes widened in terror when the gold plated fighter entered the ring. "Sinbad is going to fight Rajia."

"Who is Rajia?" asked Azrak, trying to get a glimpse of what was happening.

"Only the most deadly gladiator that even stomped the sands. He's more disturbing than Kar-Tyr the Kurwani. All Rajia thinks about is murder and he doesn't care who his opponent is—man, woman, child—he will not hesitate to kill."

Azrak stared at the old man with worry. "Does Sinbad have a fighting chance?"

The Azurian elder tried to avoid the question but Azrak kept on shaking him.

"He could easily dispatch the thin one," said the Azurian finally, "and it is going to take some time for him to take down that mountain of a man."

"But how would he fare against a warrior of Rajia's class?"

The elder lowered his head. "Speaking from experience, all three will gang up on him. They always go for the weakest one first. But if he remembers everything I taught him he wouldn't be harmed..."

Azrak gave a sigh of relief, and then cringed when the old man finished his sentence.

"...Much."

From where Sinbad and the rest of the gladiators stood, high above the arena, Emperor Akhdar Dadgar watched as the fighters came up, out of the tunnel and into the ring—four fighters—as he specifically ordered for a free-for-all. He waited patiently as the gladiators took their positions, as the full-throated roar of over twenty thousand people reverberated through the arena.

Three of the fighters were what Akhdar would have expected—murderous, bloodthirsty, and worst of all, sociopathic—for this type of combat had been the oblivious alternative to recruiting. The fourth one caught his attention. For a moment the man gazed at Akhdar; the fighter appeared to be staring straight up at him. Interestingly enough the impression was accurate. The outlander *was* staring at him. The Earthman stood up past the ceiling light, into the gloom, at the spot where Akhdar's terrace was located, as the other fighters limbered up in their stations.

The Earthman was what Akhdar had expected. He immediately forgot about the newly acquired moktar his hunters had captured for him the other day. He was gravely disappointed about the damage to one of its tusks. But he still had hopes his little pet would prove to be quite entertaining after his animal trainers were done modifying its behavior.

Akhdar raised his hands with his palms out. His voice echoed out across the arena and viewing audience.

"This is the final battle of the evening! I want a good murderous and treacherous fight, with as many punctured organs, shattered bones and ripped tissue as possible. These are the rules—there...are...*no*...rules!"

He paused, and the audience's cheers rose to a frenzied pitch as his voice boomed out. It was time to announce the combatants.

"From the wastelands we have Typhus!" He pointed to the scarred face Thulian, who let out a huge roar to the audience. "The master of murder and mayhem."

Then he pointed to the slim tattooed Azurian male.

"Cutthroat pirate and scourge of the Red Sands...Nukus!"

Akhdar then motioned over to the small masked figure that the audience really cheered the loudest. This fighter was truly his favorite.

"A true warrior who receives absolutely no introduction...Rajia!"

The crowd began to chant, "*Rajia, Rajia, Rajia....*"

Then it all came down to Sinbad. Akhdar stared at the Earthman with great interest. His sister Aella was more curious than him and the entire crowd combined about the origins of this otherworldly stranger. But by far as Akhdar was concerned, this provided the perfect gimmick for the arena fights.

"Lords and ladies, have I got a special treat for you all tonight!" he announced with great pride. "Our last competitor is from another world. Yes, you have heard me correctly. He hails from the giant blue planet known as

Earth, where he lived the life of a king. He was surrounded by unfathomable riches and living a life of total excess. But now he comes to you in chains and tonight he fights for his life. I give you, Sinbad, lord of the Sindth River, and outlander of Earth!"

The crowd marveled at the very sight of him. They haven't seen any form of beast nor man that was bizarre as him. Sinbad saw an assortment of many different races of the galaxy. There were so many different features, colors, and ways of life in the primus. To him they were more animals than men. Most of them had similarities to the gods of India.

Akhdar raised his arms in the air to silence the crowd. "Let us give the audience something gruesome to remember, shall we? The last one standing will be the victor!"

Akhdar watched the fighters, the outlander in particular, standing there alone and brave. Despite himself Akhdar found his pulse quickening as, with the rest of the crowd. He waited for the horn of battle to be blown that would signal the beginning of the fight.

The sound of the horn filled the arena. The three cutthroats moved in on the outlander.

From inside the dingy cell, the old Azurian sighed. "It begins."

Typhus was a very enormous man with dozens of knife scars on his face and he also had tribal brand on his right bicep, stared Sinbad down. The two other fighters stood behind him. Sadism and hatred danced in the light of their eyes.

The scarred man spoke in an accent Sinbad could not identify. "You have defied death for the last time, outlander."

He punched Sinbad in the face and the Earthman fell.

"Not only will I kill you, I will also devour your soul as well."

Sinbad got to his feet and smiled as he brushed dust off his chest. Then he noticed the sweat on his attacker's paunch glistening in the arena's lights.

"Has your mother ever told you not to snack between meals?"

Typhus took a powerful swing, but Sinbad caught the fist, kicked him in the groin, and as the Typhus fell, Sinbad punched him in the face.

The scarred man's two companions all charged at once—a mistake, because they got in each other's way. Sinbad fought, using everything he had learned from the old man. Seconds later, Sinbad threw rapid fire punches, blocks, and kicks. He was ignoring everything except the opponents in front of him.

They all got back up and surrounded Sinbad. They were closing in, but they weren't going to give the arena's champion Rajia any help.

Why would he need it, after all?

He was just going against a puny outlander.

They did however; made sure Sinbad wouldn't run away.

The masked gladiator swung a quick right, then a left. Either of them, had they connected, would have put Sinbad down for the count. If Rajia had been dealing with an ordinary weak adversary, of course. But Sinbad easily dodged them, making it effortless, as if he knew where they were going to be coming from and had already arranged to be elsewhere.

On some level, one of Rajia's cohorts realized that this wasn't going according to plan. Underneath the rusted golden helmet Rajia sported a befuddled look when his punches failed to connect, or perhaps it was the blindly speed with which Sinbad was moving. Either way the champion decided things would go more smoothly if the outlander were held immobile. So he lunged from behind with the intention of wrapping his arms around Sinbad's torso and keeping him still.

Sinbad, however, wasn't about to let that happen. Just as easily as he'd sensed Rajia's attack from behind, he perceived this one, as well. He ducked under the grab, leaving Nukus overextended and grasping the air. Sinbad then immediately straightened up, catching his assailant off balance, and sending them tumbling heels overhead to the floor.

Sinbad could tell by Rajia's single exposed eye that he clearly couldn't believe it. With a roar of outrage, the frustrated gladiator lunged at Sinbad, swinging an impressive combination of punches—right jab, left jab, right roundhouse, and a very mean left haymaker.

Not a single one connected.

Sinbad wasn't even backing away. He simply twisted this way, that way, pivoted, and then leaned back as if he were a contortionist.

Sinbad was clearly winning when Nukus suddenly managed to back him up against one of the walls. He pulled his sword arm back, ready to strike. As the slim Azurian warrior plunged forward, Sinbad swung up and over him. With one swift move, he knocked his humiliated opponent aside.

But Sinbad had the rest of Nukus' comrades to deal with. He knew these cutthroats needed to be stopped soon. The longer the battle continued, the worse the odds became. He was clearly outnumbered.

Then Sinbad heard a noise behind him and spun, bringing up his sword as he stepped inside a clumsy swing by at Typhus who had hoped to surprise him.

Swinging around with his sword in hand, Sinbad dodged Typhus' sneak attack but on doing so he met Nukus' blade. The terror of the Red Sands was ready to exact retribution. He was going to savor every bit of the sweet and glorious retribution.

Then Sinbad turned and held his weapon at the ready.

So far, the tide was on his side. But that could change any minute. The gladiators kept coming, and Sinbad had to fend for himself. It was going to be a difficult fight.

His scimitar didn't have either the reach or power of a cutlass, but he had confidence in his skill and speed, as well as the power of his right arm.

Sinbad swung his scimitar underhanded, up to Nukus' heart.

With surprising speed, the slender enemy swatted the blade up and away with his larger weapon.

But that was what Sinbad had been expecting.

His blade stabbed, not for a mortal blow, or even a disabling one. But for his opponent's vulnerable legs, slicing a cut across his upper thigh like someone carving a roast.

Nukus howled, staggering back with blood pouring down his left leg.

Sinbad might have been expected to follow up on the attack. Instead he stood back and assessed the situation around him.

He charged toward the other two fighters, with his sword held high, and came up on the nearest one's blind side. He roared a challenge as he swung at the Typhus' neck.

The big man turned, parried, easily deflecting the scimitar with his broadsword.

Sinbad used the energy of that deflection, riding it like a swimmer on a wave, leaping into the air and spinning past to land a step back.

Then Typhus' broadsword clanged against his opponent's steel, and Sinbad heard him grunt in surprise. He'd clearly underestimated his adversary.

A whistling of air from above caused Sinbad to raise his blade above his head. He caught the blow of the descending sword with his flexed elbows, his muscles shrieking with the force of the impact.

The huge blade stepped less than a handbreadth from his nose, and his arms shuddered with the strain of holding it there.

For an eternity, it hovered. Then Sinbad screamed with effort, throwing the broadsword backward, stepping under the giant. He stabbed across Nukus' exposed ribs. He roared and staggered back, but Sinbad's aching arms warned him not to press the attack. Instead he put his back against Rajia.

He felt the muscles in the gladiator's shoulders and back tense, and that was the entire signal he needed. They sprang away from each other, furiously attacking their opponents.

Sinbad charged at the wounded Nukus, ducking under his slicing sword, stepping into the pirate's right, stabbing his sword deep into his exposed flank. Just as quickly Sinbad yanked the sword out, sweeping past him, using his speed to keep ahead of the Nukus' turn.

Sinbad stabbed him in the back of his lower calf, missing the tendon, but still drawing blood, then spun and sliced his forehead with the smaller blade. Neither wound was critical, but he had reduced his opponent's abilities to move and see.

The illustrated man threw back his head and bellowed, swinging his blade wildly at the air, but already blood was beginning to flow down into his eyes.

Sinbad had planned to try for a critical strike between his ribs, but now he was going for the throat. He moved in, crouched low, seemingly leaving himself open.

Nukus swung his sword low, as though cutting grain, but Sinbad was ready. He sprang into the air, knees high, the blade passing harmlessly just under his feet, and as he did, he brought the pommel of his sword up, smashing it into the pirate's chin.

His head went back, and it struck bone at the back of the neck.

Nukus fell backward, making a gurgling, inhuman cry of distress, blood spurting from his neck in a warm fountain.

A few feet away, Typhus turned in response.

Then Rajia's sword flashed down, slicing his sword hand off at the wrist.

He screamed.

Rajia spun, his sword neatly slicing his throat. He gurgled and fell in a puddle of his own blood.

The blade flashed through the air, spinning once.

There was a wet, cracking noise, as though someone had split the egg of an enormous bird, and the point of the blade barred itself in the back of the Typhus' skull.

He staggered backward off-balance, mouth open, his own sword falling as he tried to grab Rajia's blade, now protruding from his head. His brain was pierced and fell and lay twitching on the ground just as the masked gladiator reached them.

Rajia put his foot against the fallen man's neck and yanked his sword free with some effort.

It was down between him and Sinbad.

The arena echoed with the clashing of swords and the shouts of battle.

Then he was taken off guard by a sucker punch executed by the merciless Rajia that sent Sinbad down to the ground. Then the masked fighter delivered a swift kick to Sinbad's ribs.

Sinbad rolled away instinctively, grunting in pain. Somehow he managed to spring back onto his feet even as the pirate circled him menacingly, keeping up his attack. A rapid-fire series of bone-jarring strikes and kicks drove Sinbad back across the arena. A driving force punch made his teeth rattle, but when the pirate threw a spinning side kick at his head, he caught the oncoming feet in an ankle-lock.

Sinbad was truly holding his own defense against the murderous thugs but he knew it wouldn't last. He was already tiring, and his attacker still had energy left to burn. Sooner or later one of them will fall. Probably sooner.

Between Rajia, he caught a glimpse of Akhdar's smiling face.

Sinbad growled. *It would not end like this!*

Sinbad felt his fear, his reason, his very humanly slipping off him like a snake shedding its skin. His sword flashed, again and again. He slogged forward into the attackers like a man wading into mud.

Swords clashed, mouths, faces contorted as the attackers shouted and screamed, but Sinbad heard only the pounding of his own heart in his ears. Time seemed to slow as one man fell, then two.

A sword sliced across his biceps, but he felt nothing but rage.

Sinbad saw Akhdar again, only this time his smile was gone.

Sinbad struggled to keep his breathing slow and even, that his body tensed, like a trap, waiting for the right move to put him in motion.

Time slowed.

He took one long step forward, then spun. He threw his shield up to interrupt the sword, which he heard slicing air long before he saw it.

He planted both feet, bracing for the impact. The sword clanged against Rajia's, and he was much slimmer than he was, and just about half his weight.

The sword slid off his shield to the left, and as it did, he shifted his left arm, pushing against the sword to throw Rajia off-balance.

He jabbed with his sword, but Rajia jumped back and the point of his sword only grazed the attacker's chest plate. He couldn't match his attacker's reach any more than he could his size or power, what he did have was speed and agility.

He prayed they would be enough.

Rajia replied, sword slicing through the air in front of him. The move was more defense than attack, and Sinbad sensed a momentary weakness. He lunged forward with the shield, taking the offensive. He feigned a high jab with the sword, pulling back just as his adversary moved to counter.

Sinbad used his shield to push Rajia's sword aside, making an opening. He swung the sword at his attacker's exposed right side. Once again, the man was too fast for him, stepping to one side, quickly recovering his stance. He made two quick slashes at Sinbad, back and forth, pushing the outlander back off to the center of the arena.

Sinbad stumbled in the loose gravel, lost his stance. Rajia pressed forward rapidly, his footwork sure and aggressive.

The sword swung down toward Sinbad's head, and he raised his sword defensively.

Blade clanged against blade, and pain seared down Sinbad's arm as though he had been struck by lightning, nearly causing him to lose the sword. His hand went numb from the impact, and he struggled for breath. Desperately, he swung the shield, striking Rajia's left arm edge on.

The blow landed solidly, but the man took advantage of the opening to grab the strap of the shield, using it to hold Sinbad defenseless. He stood eye to eye with the man for a fraction of a second, close enough to smell the sweat of his oily hair.

The man's sword jabbed, and Sinbad was barely able to direct the point past his body using his own sword.

Sinbad yanked his arm free of the shield, and it clattered to the ground. Rajia pressed his advantage.

He scooped it up in his left hand and turned to face his attacker just as the sword fell toward his head.

The Earthman bent his knees to absorb the impact, the swords crossed above his head. One sword met two, the twin blades slid across each other in response to the impact, until their guards locked together, stopping the blade with a loud report. Using both arms, he was better able to withstand the blow, and he straightened his legs suddenly, pushing the man back.

Sinbad followed him through the arena. Disengaging the lower sword, holding in his left hand he pushed Rajia's sword away with the blade in his right.

Unused to the left-handed attack, the man was slow and clumsy in his defense. The sword struck chest armor hard enough to knock the wind from the man's lungs.

Sinbad pressed again, slicing both swords back and forth in front of him. He changed his footing and attacked with the right arm again, using the left sword defensively. The sword struck the Rajia's left shoulder solidly, causing him to grasp in pain.

Sinbad shifted his feet again, feinting right, striking left, then left again, and then right.

The blades danced in front of him, and the outlander's confidence grew. His attacker was confused, off-balance. Sinbad struck with his left sword at his attacker's sword arm, forcing an awkward defense that left the man totally open to the right sword, the point of which struck out, viper quick to find the man's throat.

Sinbad charged at Rajia and hit his face with the hilt of his sword. Rajia grabbed hold of the weapon and yanked his opponent within arm's reach. He punched the side of the outlander's head, and Sinbad retaliated with a swift kick.

The two circled like tigers. Every time Sinbad made an offensive move, Rajia was able to counter it. Frustrated, Sinbad could not understand why he couldn't gain the upper hand.

Finally, he was able to land a powerful uppercut on the pirate's jaw.

Rajia countered by flying his foot upward and kicked him forcefully across the face. He staggered backward, tasting the coppery taste of his own blood, while he completed a gravity-defying backward flip, landing squarely on his feet less than two yards away.

This fierce duel was nothing like Sinbad's fights in the mines. In contrast, this battle was in deadly earnest, with at least Rajia determined to make it into a fight to the death. He threw a right palm punch at Sinbad's stomach, which the outlander blocked with a downward swing of a left punch.

He kicked out defensively, trying to drive Rajia out of striking range. But the mysterious fighter took advantage of the sudden distance between them to draw back his right leg and executed a side kick to the head.

Rajia leapt toward Sinbad, following with a left cross. He ducked beneath his opponent's headlong charge and grabbed him in an elbow lock.

Sinbad swiftly wrapped his arm under Rajia's throat. But he countered with a savage jab of his elbow into his ribs. Sinbad doubled over, gasping for breath, and the pirate pulled away from his grappling embrace.

Rajia suddenly punched him in the face. Sinbad fell to the ground, reeling in shock and pain. Blood was spilling from his mouth.

He saw the people's champion standing over him. Underneath Rajia's helmet, a twisted grin ran across his face.

Then he kicked Sinbad in the face, and the outlander groaned and collapsed.

Sinbad tried to roll over, but Rajia had a foot pressed against his back, pinning him to the floor. He felt his head nearly explode as he struggled back to his feet. The back of his skull was throbbing, and he could barely see what was directly in front of him.

Then Rajia smashed his foot into Sinbad's back. He laughed again as Sinbad recoiled in pain.

Rajia hunkered down and looked Sinbad in the eyes.

Rajia stood up again and smashed his heel into Sinbad's side. He thought he heard a bone break, and he laughed out loud.

Sinbad groaned again as a foot smashed into the side of his head.

Rajia's elbow crashed down on his side. Sinbad heard several ribs cracked.

A foot smashed into his face. He felt blood spill from his broken nose.

Rajia kicked him again, but this time Sinbad didn't feel it.

Then Rajia kicked him again, reveling in his anger, living for the violence, crude and barbaric.

Sinbad could feel blood smearing his face and hands.

Sinbad forced his eyes to look up, his expression turning from agony to realization. Rajia laughed at his dumbfounded look.

Sinbad tried to speak, but blood was filling his mouth. Rajia glared at him again as he kicked him once more in his side. This time Sinbad yelped in pain. Blood splattered across the grounds of the arenas.

Rajia watched Sinbad squirming on the ground like a worm in a freshly dug hole. His body sported red welts and blood was seeping out of open wounds. A couple of more swift kicks, Rajia thought, and the alien fool would be no more. And it was not a second too soon.

He slammed his foot into Sinbad's side again and laughed as his victim groaned in pain.

Rajia leaned over him again, their faces nearly touching. Everything he had ever wanted to tell Sinbad was spilling out faster than he realized.

Then he slammed his fist into Sinbad's stomach for effect.

Rajia stood up again and kicked Sinbad as hard as he could. This was the kick that was going to break the last of Sinbad's ribs. It was going to be the final swift and deadly kick that would crush Sinbad's heart.

"Come on, Sinbad!" shouted Azrak. "You have to get up!"

"He put up a great fight, Azrak," consoled the old man. "I could not ask any more from him."

"What are you talking about?" Azrak snapped with much anger in his voice. "A man is dying out there and you don't even seem to care!"

"He knew what he was getting himself into. Don't blame me for his decisions."

"Damn you," Azrak cursed him. "I heard all about you. What you did that got you thrown in here. Whatever happened to that man?"

"He died a long time ago."

"I suppose he did." Azrak heaved, and then he watched hopelessly as his best friend was being to a bloody pulp.

Aella couldn't bear to watch anymore. Yet she couldn't look away. Her brother found this ghastly display quite relishing. He got what he wanted. Even though he was surprised that the Earthman lived longer than he expected.

"Smile, Aella," said Akhdar. "People may think you're not having a good time."

He was about ready to present judgment, but he couldn't find it in his heart to deprive Rajia of his fun.

In a last desperate effort, Sinbad grabbed a handful of sand and threw it through the eye-slit of Rajia's helmet. The masked man let out a terrible scream that his one good eye was blinded.

Using this to his advantage, Sinbad reclaimed his sword and engaged his enemy. He was quickly on the defensive, as Rajia posed to be a powerful, if not swift, foe. As he fended off blow after pounding blow, he allowed himself to be maneuvered in with his right arm close to the wall of the arena, a position that should have put him at a disadvantage.

Sinbad made a momentary show of looking weak, then tossed his sword from his right hand to his left and went on the offensive.

Rajia was taken by surprise, off-balance and uncertain how to respond, he stepped back. Sinbad followed, pressing in close so his sword worked to his benefit. The heavy metal pommel smashed into the pirate's sword hard. He heard bones crack, and the cutlass went flying and so did the champion's helmet.

Silence had fallen over the arena. They have never seen someone beaten Rajia, or in this case tumbled him.

"He did it!" cheered Azrak. "He's beaten, Rajia!"

The old man threw Azrak aside and peered through between the bars. "Inconceivable!" He spat, while he just witnessed the impossible. "This is truly miraculous."

"It's no miracle, my friend. Sinbad just showed you that nothing is hopeless and anything is possible." Then Azrak paused and pat the elder on the back. "And he has a great teacher."

Sinbad had humbled the old man. He had made the sailor into a warrior, and Sinbad made himself a hero. For the first time in years the old man smiled.

Sinbad tread carefully across the sands and towered over Rajia. He laid face down on the ground, and Sinbad took him by his long shaggy hair, turning his head around to look into his opponent's eyes.

"The battle is over and you have lost," he told Rajia, holding the scimitar against his throat. "Yield, impudent dog."

Then to his horrific discovery, Rajia wasn't a man—he was a *woman*!

She was actually a young Thulian female with dark ravenous hair that had been freshly cut so her attackers wouldn't use it to their advantage. She wore a patch over her left eye, and behind it were very deep scratches that were made by some wild animal.

Sinbad couldn't believe what he was seeing. All this time he had been fighting a woman. And the worst part of all was he was going to kill her.

Then he heard the crowd rising to their feet and began chanting, "kill, kill, kill," and the cheering grew even louder when Akhdar approached the edge of the royal terrace. Sinbad raised his head to stare at the emperor who was ready to make an announcement.

"Lords and ladies," Akhdar said, applauding the spectacular fight, "this has indeed been an outstanding evening for all of us. I am pleased to announce that our new champion of the arena is Sinbad, outlander of Earth!"

The arena was filled with a laundry list of cheers and jeers. The women screamed the loudest, which attracted the hidden jealously Aella harbored. She was fairly impressed by the outlander's courageousness. She could easily arrange to be alone with him and make him forget about all those lonely Earth women. But she knew her brother Akhdar wouldn't allow such a dalliance. He must be persuaded, or in this case manipulated to invite the outlander into the palace. Whatever it maybe, it had to be soon. She couldn't slake her lust for him any longer.

Akhdar smiled down at Sinbad, and frowned at his fallen champion. He held out his fist and stuck out his thumb. He waved the thumb upward, and then sent it down, following an uproarious approval from the crowd.

"The people have spoken," Akhdar said to Sinbad. "The time for change is now. Strike her down and become my new champion. You will be granted all the luxuries and pleasures only royalty have the privilege to enjoy. All this can be yours if you drive your blade through her heart."

Sinbad looked down at Rajia, who spat at his face and showed no fear of death. The chanting grew louder and louder. He couldn't even hear himself think. It was starting to overwhelm him. All he could hear was, "kill, kill, kill." Then he even heard himself saying that.

He threw his sword across the arena and listened to the sudden silence of the crowd. Akhdar's smile and admiration for him had faded very quickly. He frowned upon this newfound sense of rebellion.

"Her life is not mine to take!" Sinbad shouted over to the royal terrace. "It also doesn't belong to you or them!" He gestured to the audience. "I can never kill an unarmed opponent. Even if the opponent is a woman. You can do what you want with me, but I beseech you, Emperor Akhdar, please spare her life!"

Akhdar couldn't believe what he was hearing. This pathetic excuse for a life form refused being showered with riches and women, only in return if he would preserve his enemy's life. Even when said enemy was going to kill him a moment earlier. Akhdar didn't understand the true meaning of compassion. He thinks of such feelings as a weakness.

"Long live Sinbad the Merciful!" yelled a man in the audience.

Akhdar swiftly turned his head to see a middle-aged Thulian man standing out of his seat with his arms in the air.

"Yay, Sinbad!" said another right next to him.

Then a woman cheered, then several others joined, and one person started to chant Sinbad's name, which led the whole arena to join in.

"*Sinbad, Sinbad, Sinbad, Sinbad, Sinbad…*"

"They think he's a hero," Akhdar softly said.

Then he heard his sister chanting for the outlander under her breath. Akhdar turned to face her and shot her a dirty look. Aella blushed and looked sheepishly away, laughing at look of her brother's face. For a moment he looked like their uncle. He was a man who took no nonsense on absolutely everything.

During all the commotion, Rajia reached down to the back of her tunic. Under there was a concealed dagger. She gripped the handle very tightly and then proceeded slowly towards Sinbad. He was distracted by the loud cheers and waited for Akhdar's response.

Akhdar watched the disgraced Rajia slither her way to the unsuspecting outlander. A small grin appeared on his face. That would certainly put an end to this minor problem.

Then he began to have second thoughts. Letting Rajia kill Sinbad would grant this insignificant little nobody martyrdom.

Akhdar would never hear the end of it.

Azrak couldn't breathe.

He saw the glimmer of Rajia's blade and she was ready to avenge her honor.

With a primal yell, Rajia made her move.

"Sinbad, look out!"

Sinbad turned around and saw her sending the dagger toward his chest. But out of the corner of his eye, he could see something speeding by and then noticed his attacker doubling over and fell straight on her back.

Sinbad went closer to investigate to find an arrow embedded into her covered left eye socket. His assassin had died instantly, and whoever shot her was very deadly accurate. The angle of the shot had originated from right on top of him.

The only place he could think of was the royal terrace.

He looked upward to discover his protector.

Akhdar looked at his sister with disgust.

There she stood at the edge of the balcony with a bow in her hand, feeling satisfied. Behind her was a bewildered guard whom she stole the bow from. She took pleasure in the rush she received on taking a life. It was better than anything she had ever experienced before. She took several steady breaths to compose herself, and she finally let out a smile.

"Why did you do that, sister?" asked Akhdar. "Couldn't you see things were starting to get interesting?"

"Brother, dear," Aella answered, lowering the bow, "you wouldn't want to disappoint all these people by letting your new champion die in such a cowardly and pedestrian fashion. Like it or not, I've just did you a favor."

"You have a lot of nerve to undermine me, Aella. But this is *my* arena and I'll determine who lives and who dies."

All around them the crowd kept chanting Sinbad's name. The cheers were even louder than before, and several of them praised Aella for saving their new champion.

"Do you hear that, Akhdar?" Aella playfully asked him. "You do not in control the arena, *they* do," she motioned over to the audience. "If I were you, I should take the people's needs into careful consideration."

"Fine," Akhdar growled. "The outlander lives...for now."

Aella smiled and watched as Sinbad was being escorted back into the dungeon by the arena's guards.

"Tarkhun!" Summoned Akhdar, feeling very agitated.

His main bodyguard hurried over to his side and kneeled before him. "What is your command, my lord?"

"Tend to the outlander's wounds and escort him back to his cell. And make sure you dispose of the *garbage* in the arena."

"As you wish, my lord," answered Tarkhun, still waiting for further instructions.

"What is the delay, Tarkhun?"

"Forgive me, sire; but what of the outlander's friend—the Azurian?"

"What about him?"

"You said if the Earthman would fight in the arena you would free his friend."

Akhdar gave Tarkhun a very stern look. "I did promise him that, Tarkhun. But he intrigues me. He will fight in the arena until I say otherwise. I believe it is high time that this Sinbad of Earth should be educated on the way we do things here. Make sure he doesn't hesitate on carrying out his gladiator duty when he decides to disobey me the next time."

"Do you wish for me to kill the Azurian, sire?" asked Tarkhun.

"No," answered Akhdar, "well, at least not yet. So far that blue devil is our only bargaining chip to keep the outlander in his place. As of right now, he is off-limits. But please do give Sinbad a daily remainder on what would happen if he dares to make me look like a fool again."

Tarkhun raised his eyes to his master, displaying his trademark sadistic smile. "Yes, sire."

CHAPTER FOURTEEN
EVERY HEAD HAS ITS OWN KIND OF HEADACHE

Sinbad shivered as consciousness tossed him with his return. The world moved around him, but resolved itself into a steady, rhythmic motion. Combined with the sound of dust being scattered in the wind and the humid climate, he concluded he was near the desert. He tried to move an arm and wasn't certain he'd been able to do so. Still, he felt no band around his wrist, nor heard the clank of chains, so he assumed he was not in the hands of his enemies.

As more of his senses returned, with them come on awareness of aches and pains, and general stiffness. The wound on his right shoulder burned still, but not poison.

A gentle hand laid a cool compress on his forehead. Another cloth dubbed at the wound on his shoulder, soft words in distant whispers reached his ears, and his mind reconstructed his world. A woman was attending to his wounds. Her hand so gentle and her voice sounded very warm.

When he opened his eyes, even the sunlight burned them. He began to tear up, but not quickly enough. He could not recognize the woman perched on the edge of the bed. A tremor shook him, then all strength fled his limbs.

Qani pressed a hand to his chest. "Don't speak, Sinbad. Don't try to move. The poison gave you a fever. It's only just broken."

Sinbad finally awoke drenched in his own sweat. Crazed by the violent fragments of his past. He shot right up scaring Qani who was right beside him. Sinbad saw her and began to back away to the wall.

"Who—who are you?" he said in fright.

The green woman stayed where she was and she was cautious on not making any sudden movements.

"I'm Qani. I'm—"

"One of Akhdar's concubines sent to seduce me?" said Sinbad, sweating profusely and frantically checked his surroundings.

Qani gave the dazed and confused sailor a grim look. “Your tongue is quick, Earthman.” She drew a dagger from behind her back and pounced on the human. “Let’s see if your reflexes are as fast!” She raised the blade over Sinbad’s head with her face consumed with passion. “Savior or not. No man speaks to me that way!”

Sinbad grabbed the dagger and threw his elbow at Qani’s face, which sent the furious green woman on her back.

“I am no savior,” said Sinbad, holding her at knifepoint. “And I assure you my reflexes are quick enough, woman.” He looked at her carefully and then around the chamber. It was quite unfamiliar to him. “This is not Akhdar’s palace,” he said, lowering the dagger, “and you are no concubine. A narrow mind has a broad tongue. Please forgive my ignorance.”

His words were deliberate, spoken slowly as if trying to twist them into something calmer, less patient, then he felt, but his anger still shook him.

Qani gave him a sneer. “Your ignorance almost had you killed, outlander. Still you showed mercy and bested me.” She detached a veil from her attire and presented to Sinbad. “This is yours.”

Sinbad accepted the article of clothing and exchanged it with the dagger. “And this is yours. Would you care to enlighten me as to why I’m here?”

“You were wounded,” answered Qani, casing her dagger. “I healed you.”

They stood quiet, neither having anything left to say. He watched her for several minutes, knowing she did save his life. And he was silently grateful to her.

He couldn’t give up hope if something could still be salvaged. He stepped up in front of Qani. They looked at each other for a moment. Then Qani slapped him hard in the face with the back of her hand.

The anger and rage in Qani’s eyes as she looked at Sinbad was real, and it stung him deeply.

Sinbad's body and mind froze. It was as though he had been turned into a statue. Qani's words frozen at the entrance to his mind, what he refused to let them in.

CHAPTER FIFTEEN
ALL STRANGERS ARE RELATIONS TO EACH OTHER

A shadow was cast against the wall. The figure moved with grace, each movement a sign of practice, exuding strength. The arms slashed through the air, extending a sword against an imaginary foe. Each parry and thrust resounded with a faint echo in the bedchamber, fighting with the persistent sound of dust and small pebbles scattering through the humid desert wind.

A sole woman trained in the center of the room. Her only witnesses were the images on the walls, which owed her fealty. Her breathing was heavy but controlled, her training session well into its second hour. Sweat ran down her brow, each drop hitting the floor next to her feet.

An occasional grunt accompanied thrusts and as she would during her practice. She now swiped at the air, swinging its sharp end up until it nearly scraped the ceiling. She swung it in a complete circle around her body one way, then another. After several more minutes, she ended its session with a vicious thrust that would have torn an opponent in two.

But there were no opponents.

She was alone in the center of the room.

Qani decided it was time to conclude weapons training, and practice on unarmed combat. She stood in front of the window in her chambers, letting the dawning sun's rays bathe her with their warmth. It had been the habit to do since she was a little girl. The ritual's regularity instilled a sense of order. The sun's presence reminded her that forces were more titanic than she ruled the world. And yet, at the same time, she felt she was a critical part of it, made whole by it as she, in turn, helped make it wider.

As the sun cleared the horizon, she bowed to it, and then began her morning exercises. Her years of training made her an expert in a variety of the combat arts. Primarily unarmed, but she was not unacquainted with a bow or a knife. While she recognized them as useful tools, and diligently studied until she had mastered their uses. She preferred unarmed forms. Knives and arrows, after all, could do serious harm even without the intention to do so. As the saying went, "A falling knife has no handle." Arms and legs, however, feet and fists, could be used to help even more eagerly then they could be used to hurt.

So, in the early morning, Qani's slender body moved from one form to another. Her flowing robes easily accommodated her movements. Her long hair had been gathered back and tied with a band. It delicately brushed her shoulders as her exercises continued. As she did each morning, she battled a succession of shadow warriors, turning their attacks back on themselves, using their force and hatred to destroy them.

The simple flowing motion rooted her in the world. Life itself was energy. She recognized it, moved with it. Just as she would use another's energy against them, so she used the world's energy to help her. This was, after all, her role. By doing what she did, she established order in what would otherwise be a chaotic world, fostering peace where there would be alternatively been an ocean of misery.

Qani leapt and spun between her imaginary attackers, striking at them ferociously. She expertly threw her punches while constantly battering the nearest victim with a brutal roundhouse kick. Without missing a breath, she segued from the completed kick into a flawless front kick and then followed with a side kick to complete the combination. The next move was hard enough to fracture a skull.

Her wrists ached from all the sparring, and her back and shoulders protested to the vigorous workout as well. Then she finished the session with a spinning back kick.

She ran through an entire range of advanced forms of unarmed combat. She pushed herself to the brink of exhaustion. She was an image of slick perspiration in painful fatigue. She was tired enough to drop instantly into unconsciousness as soon as her depleted body dropped into her waiting bed. But she couldn't afford such luxury. There were plans for the day. The kind of plans that could she never dared to reschedule. They were important for her and the future of her people.

Ankhara paused at the edge of the door, then dropped to his knees. He bowed his head, not looking up, unmoving, while Qani's exercises continued. Qani had noticed him immediately, more because he had disrupted her routine than because of any inherent interest the man may have possessed. He hesitated to complete her exercises—an action that left him slightly unsettled.

"How can I be of assistance to you, Ankhara?"

Ankhara kept his eyes downward. "Qani, we await your command."

Several other rebels sat at each side of a large granite table. Sunlight streamed into the room from an opened doorway. At one end sat Qani's lieutenant Barbatus who was drawing slowly on a pipe. He slowly exhaled a fragment of smoke, and then it drifted upward like a curtain that further hid his face.

Qani entered the room with Ankhara following a few steps behind her.

"Officer on deck!" said one rebel.

All the rebels stood in attention. Qani walked causally to the chair that was opposite of Barbatus. She could felt his gaze upon her.

"Be seated," she said, beginning the meeting.

She looked up to her lieutenant's face. He had always been old in her sight, but aside from the lines around his eyes and the corners of his mouth, he had not changed much. True, time had altered his appearance ever so slightly, but his eyes retained their kindness.

"This man, Qani. This outlander; he is the answer to our prayers."

"How can you be so certain Barbatus? The prophecy foretold that the chosen one would be a great warrior. When we found him he almost managed to get himself killed."

"By saving the life of another," Barbatus interrupted. "Looks can be deceiving, child. This Sinbad has come a long way like the prophecy foretold. He is indeed a warrior and a great destiny is upon him."

"Are we going to abandon our search for Prince Muqari?" she asked.

"Daizha, no, child," said Barbatus, taking another puff from his pipe. "We are putting the search for him on hold until we can figure out what to do with this outlander."

"Why are we even continuing the search for the prince?" asked Ankhara.

Qani, Barbatus, and the rest of the rebels turned their heads to his direction. This was the first time Ankhara had ever spoken out of turn in the group meetings. He didn't feel a bit intimidated by their analytical gawking.

"For all we know he may be dead like his uncle before him. We should focus on another attack where we could get to Akhdar. Or perhaps use his sister against him."

"An unwise plan, Ankhara," said Barbatus. "We already risked a lot on helping Sinbad escape from the arena. Akhdar must have raised his defenses and gotten more guards. He will be impossible to get near to now."

"We had Akhdar right where we wanted him." The vein on Ankhara's forehead was growing larger with each thought. "We had the element of surprise with the explosion. If we didn't concentrate solely on the outlander Dozhak would be free as we speak."

Barbatus gave the silver-haired Thulian a weary look. "I understand your frustration, Ankhara. But even though they were blindsided we were still outnumbered. We wouldn't have stood a chance. Brute force is not the answer, son."

"What are a few sacrifices to save the many?" blurted Ankhara, escalating the tone of the conversation. "Maybe you're too afraid to follow through on this, but I am not. We might have been outnumbered but all we needed is one good shot and Akhdar will be gone forever."

"Ankhara," said Qani, "stand down."

He looked at her in confusion. "You know I'm right, Qani. You lead the rebellion, but still you listen to this foolish old man who hasn't done anything for our cause."

"I said *stand down*!" she bellowed, hearing her own echo through the conference room.

Ankhara couldn't believe what he was listening. He has been Qani's most trusted lieutenant since the rebellion began and one of her closest childhood friends on top of that as well. She of all people should understand what he was proposing to do with the Akhdar situation. But now she was looking at him with very mean eyes. The kind where an overbearing mother finds her child doing something he isn't supposed to regardless on how many times she has told him no.

He scowled at her. "Fine! You are all damned fools."

Ankhara seethed through his teeth and stormed out of the conference room. He slammed the door very loudly, causing Qani to flinch.

After a few minutes of awkward silence Barbatus spoke. "Now back to the outlander."

Qani took a moment to gather her thoughts. "I don't believe in him," Qani replied. "I'm going to take him to Farkhunda the Sage so we could some answers."

Barbatus set the pipe down and rushed a hand over his forehead. "Then I bid you a safe journey, and I'll pray to Daizha that you will find what you are looking for, Qani."

"Thank you, Barbatus."

The rebels rose out of their seats and noiselessly exited the dimly lit chamber to prepare for their quest to seek the great sage Farkhunda.

Sinbad sat on the ledge on top of the Thulian rebel base. He was deep in thought. His mind was going back to the prison escape. He was indeed grateful for getting out of that accursed pit. But Sinbad had a feeling it was all too easy. He heard the rhythmic scuttling of Kar Tyr's gorilla-like toes across the sands as he emerged from the entrance. The centaur turned around and found Sinbad on top of the rock hanging like an idle gull on a beach.

"It makes no sense," Sinbad told his fellow fugitive. "Akhdar had us outnumbered. Why would he allow our escape?"

Kar-Tyr looked at the human wondering if the poison hadn't gotten out of his system yet.

"You are free, Sinbad. Is that not enough?"

"Enough to make me wary," Sinbad replied.

"Wary of what?"

"On my world, it is said that better a hundred enemies outside the house than one within."

Kar-Tyr raised his eyebrow in curiosity. "You talk in riddles. Speak your mind, friend."

"I am a stranger here," Sinbad confessed, holding his hands together. "I trust no one. Least of all one who was granted reprieve from genocide."

Kar-Tyr stomped his oversized feet with anger, and clenched his fist in front of Sinbad.

"You dare question my allegiance?" said the sole survivor of the Kurwani race. "No one—*no one*, wants to see Akhdar breathe his last more than I."

Kar-Tyr's face was written with angst. He lowered his fist and stared Sinbad in the eye.

"You saved my life, Earthman. That is the only reason you will survive that remark."

Qani, wrapped in her long purple cloak, mysteriously appeared right beside Sinbad. She was fed up with this quarrel and took command of this situation.

Belted around her narrow waist, her flowing robe of iridescent silk covered her from ankle to shoulders, baring only her arms, neck, and a tantalizing triangle of a chest. A matching purple head cloth wrapped her hair, held in a place by a think braids around her forehead.

"Enough!" she hollered. Her lower face was covered with a long scarf that flowed through the light breeze. And her long auburn hair was neatly coifed in a ponytail that was tucked inside back of her colorful cape.

Sinbad didn't bother to get up from his current position. He merely looked up to see his rescuer taking a dominant pose. He pondered why she should be giving orders. Not only was she a woman, but a child simply playing soldier.

The Earthman saw a distinguishing mean look in Qani's eyes that she had not forgotten that bawdy comment he inadvertently made when he woke up from his venom induced nightmare. That affront would hang over his head indefinitely throughout the rest of this journey. Qani shifted her attention to Kar-Tyr and the rest of her loyal followers in her faction, who were awaiting her orders.

"It is time to go," she said, pointing to the cavern.

Inside the caverns were as dark as the night and as wet as a fallen rain. The party consisted of Sinbad, Kar-Tyr, and four of the resistance's strongest warriors with Qani leading the way. The torch Qani yielded in vigilance illuminated the damp hollow. She was intimate in this region. She knew every path and grotto the cavern had concealed. The echoes on the other hand were very dangerous. If a novice had ventured into these caves they would surely be lost and won't find their way out in weeks. If they were lucky survive that long.

Qani hoped her friend Tanoo was guarding the exit. She would hate to go all this far without someone to open the barricade at the other side. This was very essential to her plan.

Qani's warriors were dressed in similar cloaks as the one she wore. The train to these ridiculously long capes was very long. Sinbad noticed this right away. He thought of the concept as ridiculous. An enemy could easily overpower them by simply pulling down on their hoods over their eyes, or snaring the end of their capes.

He then began to query on what kind of campaign was this Qani woman was running here. In all of his adventures he had never met such a creature who could walk like a woman and talk like a man. The interception at Akhdar's palace was sloppy and badly calculated. They barely escaped with their lives. Then he recognized Qani saved his life of course. He owed her every bit of gratitude as he did with Azrak many months ago when he crash-landed on this world.

The expedition into the caves was a quiet one. Especially between Sinbad and Kar-Tyr, who wouldn't dare to look at each other without shrinking their own egos. They both knew one of them should speak, but it was part of the game on who would be man enough to swallow his own pride.

"I may have spoken hastily, Kar-Tyr," Sinbad finally spoke, easing the tension between them. "Forgive my imprudence."

"Let's hope your sword is as sharp as your tongue when the time comes, then," huffed Kar-Tyr.

Qani sharply turned and glared at the both of them. "Enough bickering, you two."

She came to an abrupt halt. Sinbad and Kar-Tyr looked at each other. The Kurwani warrior shrugged his broad shoulders and then turned his attention over to Qani's direction. The female trooper raised her torch for the light to reveal a dead end.

"We're here," she proclaimed.

Sinbad looked around the cavern. He knew this couldn't be right. Qani must have made some sort of a mistake.

"Are you daft, woman?" he rudely asked her. "There's no way out of here. You've led us down a wrong path."

Qani's soldiers became silent, and started to mutter among themselves.

"Did he just question Qani's methods?" said one of them with agitation in her voice.

"The Earthman has a lot of gall, I tell you," said a male rebel.

"No one has ever defied Qani," retorted a soldier at the rear.

"Insolent fool!" Qani snapped at Sinbad. The rebels held their tongues. They did not wish to invoke the wrath from their mistress.

There was a very awkward silence in the cave.

Qani reined back, stopping, and fixated him with a harsh stare.

The sailor crossed his arms akimbo. Whatever she was doing, she was wasting time. Qani stepped toward Sinbad, holding the blazing torch between him and her. She pulled down her scarf that hid her beautiful face. This time she didn't give him a friendly smile or the spiteful grimace she delivered in her private chambers. This as the expression she reserved for those who had the audacity to challenge her patience. She was ready to leave this chauvinistic barbarian to fend for himself in the caves.

Qani looked at Sinbad like she wanted to fight him. However, the outlander didn't believe in striking a woman. Only a coward would do such a savage act. He stood there motionless, waiting for her to calm down. Sinbad had learned many lessons in his life, and one of the most important ones was Hell hath no fury for a woman scorned. The next move was up to her.

Qani pulled back her loathingly gaze and waved her torch over to the stone wall. "Watch and you will learn," she said to Sinbad, as she walked up to the partition and started knocking on it. The sound was complex in a multitude of rhythm and sudden stops. Sinbad realized what she was doing. She was dispensing a code to the outside.

Then there came a soft rumbling in the cavern. It was so unexpected it spooked Kar-Tyr so bad he bucked with his front lower feet in the air. The vibrations were only coming from their end of the cave, and to Sinbad's surprise the wall in front of them began moving to the right. Just like the Forty Thieves' den from the tale of *Ali Baba*, a secret door was magically opened.

"The walls!" said Sinbad, startled. "They're moving!"

The stone door only moved far enough for the three travelers to pass through. Sunlight beamed into the gloomy cavern. Qani doused her torch and motioned to Sinbad.

"Watch your first step, Earthman," she cautioned him.

"What do you mean, Qani?" Sinbad asked, taking a giant step. "It looks very—"

Sinbad's foot slipped and began to fall down a steep chasm. Before he slipped off the cliff, Qani pulled him back on the ledge.

"That's why, Earthman," she berated him.

Sinbad looked down to see it was a long drop to the ground. He looked over to the skyline to see the clouds have met the plateau. He had no idea where the earth ended and the sky began. Then he saw a city at the neighboring mountain surrounded by the ocean. It would take at least a week's trek to reach there.

"If you're done admiring the view, Sinbad," said Qani, "that's *two* you owe me."

"You could have warned me," he replied.

"I did. I told you to watch your step."

"Did it ever occur to you to also mention we are on top of a mountain?"

"As much as I would to enjoy arguing with you, Sinbad; but we must move on."

"Agreed," he concurred, observing the area. "Is there a bridge or a path we can talk down to the bottom?"

Qani pushed him out of the way as one of her soldiers charged off the cliff. The cloaked rebel plummeted down the sky and slid his hands into the activating pockets of his cape and immediately the cloak became a rigid wing, smashing into the wind, halting his downward plunge. The contours of his cloak spread out and stiffened to take a batwing shaped formation. His fall became a glide, controlled by his arms.

He tilted his body and swirled in midair. The mountain winds granted the freedom fighter the ability to glide towards the magnificent city.

Sinbad watched while another member of Qani's faction took flight.

"Are you all mad?" Sinbad addressed the group. "Not even an eagle would dare!"

Qani grabbed Sinbad from behind. "Fortunate for you, I don't know what an eagle is."

"What are you doing?" Sinbad gasped, when Qani held on to him while they jumped the cliff. Sinbad let out a frightful scream.

"I assure you it's perfectly safe," Qani calmly said to him.

Qani launched herself into the empty air between the cliff and the city. Her cloak burst open and re-formed itself into wide, stiff glider wings. Her descent slowed, and Sinbad held on tightly. He screamed as he and Qani soared through the clear sky.

The story of Icarus ran through his mind. He was afraid they were going to fly too close to the sun and plummet to their deaths.

Sinbad could feel the wind blowing against his face. "I'll believe that when we are on the ground."

Cradled in Qani's slender arms, they flew toward the city. The beautiful mountains loomed ahead, while remote plains and valleys stretched out far below them. The cool breeze did little to dampen their spirits.

Two of the rebels had to hold onto Kar-Tyr because he was the heaviest. The Kurwani didn't want to go, but he was taken by force. If there were a contest on who could scream the loudest, Kar-Tyr would be the grand champion.

They were all heading to the city. Qani was able to steer clear through the clouds and over the water.

"The clouds should break right about…now," she said to her unwillingly passenger. The clouds parted to reveal the majestic hidden city. "Welcome to my home, Sinbad."

Qani soon indicated that they had flown far enough and the party descended onto the western slope of a towering mountain. Sinbad's feet sunk into the sand as Qani gently put him down at the base of a steep incline.

CHAPTER SIXTEEN
DILIGENCE IS A GREAT TEACHER

Once the group had settled on land, they prepared to go to the docks. Qani had a vessel berthed in the marina, which was ready to go with charts and previsions. Sinbad finally found something he was accustomed to—the sea. He couldn't wait to get behind the helm and set sail. He was as excited as a child on his way to the circus. Along the way Sinbad took in the village. It was dry and dusty with houses made of sunbaked bricks that squatted alongside simple structures of mud and stone. But nothing captured Sinbad's attention more than Qani's vessel at the harbor.

Sinbad stood in the village square, and looked across the great waterfront. From here he could see the vast sweep of low buildings, most walled with mud and brick, many roofed only with awnings of hide, woven straw, or for those who could afford it, colorful silks.

It was a dizzying cacophony of sights and sounds. Sinbad marveled at the kiosks and shops, as they sold a meager supply of goods but an array the likes of which he'd never seen before. Most vendors and shoppers seemed hunched over, shuffling from place to place, lastly going through the motions.

The streets were crowded with people as well as many animals. Everywhere there were feline-like creatures, perched on windowsills, walking the tops of walls, prowling the garbage-strewn alleys among the feasting swine. They protected the city's granaries from vermin.

In one place, a broad boulevard down the hill, he could see the crowds part and the animals turn aside, moving verily around a spot as though parted by some hidden force.

Beyond all this lay the dark, towering skyline of the inner city, surrounded by a huge wall of ancient stone turned black as coal by some unknown growth. Ornate spikes and carvings covered the parapets, and great guard towers, topped with statuary of long forgotten gods, stood to warn away attackers.

The towers within great palaces and temples that rose up to meet the cloudless sky dwarfed the walls. They were tall only for the sake of intimidation and pride, some decorated with gold and carved marble, others hung with silks printed in religious signs, and still others black as ink even in the fall light of day.

Outside of there, nestled at the base of the walls of the inner city, he could see the much lower, white-marble walls. Within these walls, merchants, diplomats, and other welcomed foreigners of status lived. Within the enclave Sinbad could see the houses, small palaces, and roaming houses where short-term visitors of wealth stayed.

His pace was carefully chosen, not so fast to appear to be in a hurry, not so slow so as to appear to be dawdling. He kept his eyes ahead, not making eye contact with people he met, not looking around like a gawky sightseer. His goal was to appear to have legitimate business passing through wherever he went, but nothing so urgent or immediate as to draw attention.

It left him with little to do but think, and lately, that had been something he could do without.

He had confidence in his own abilities, yet he was placing himself at great risk. He didn't fear death, or so he held himself, but he didn't look forward to it either. If he were captured, he would most likely be taken back to Akhdar's palace for immediate execution.

He noticed that the sun was now out of sight and the sky had turned red as blood. There were few pedestrians now, most of them in a hurry to get out of there.

"I don't trust the Earthman, Qani," said Ankhara, looking at Sinbad with much disdain. "Why are we risking our necks for this pathetic creature? He's going to get us killed."

"Why, Ankhara; if I didn't know any better I could have sworn you sound scared."

"I am *not* scared," he glowered. "We have the planet's most wanted rogue in our company and here he is in broad daylight with nary a disguise at all. He's going to be the end of us. We should leave him and keep the Kurwani. His strength might be of use to us."

"Listen, Ankhara," Qani scowled at him, "you and I have been friends since we were very small children. We have been through a lot together, and when I was elected leader of the resistance you have never questioned me—not even once—until now. Why is that, friend?"

"I agree with you that he's not what the prophecy foretold of. Just look at him!"

Qani turned her head to see Sinbad marveling at the sights of the village. Seeing and listening to everyone and everything he came in contact with, like he was experiencing the world for the first time.

"He's like a child!" Ankhara retorted. "Do you want to jeopardize all of our plans on an idiotic man-child?"

"But Barbatus said—"

"Barbatus is an old fool!" Ankhara snapped, viciously. Qani was taken aback by this surprised outburst. "He spent his entire life reading that blasted story over and over again, and prays to Daizha, whom turned a deaf ear to all of us a long time ago. I suggested that you come to your senses and see what is really going on here."

Qani looked at Ankhara with her mouth open. She didn't know what to do. She had never heard her friend talk to her like that before in a tone she hardly ever thought possible to come through his lips.

She sneered at him and shoved him alongside of the wall on a passing building. Bystanders either stood there and watched, or proceeded to their own affairs. Qani's group stopped and wondered what was going on. Sinbad came forward to Qani's aid, but the other rebels held him back.

"Barbatus," she began, slowly composing herself, "is the closest thing I have ever had as a father. He has done more than you have ever known. As of right now, I do not care who you are. If you ever talk that way to me or about Barbatus like that ever again, not only will I expel you from the group I will personally cut off your tongue. Is that understood?"

Ankhara could only nod in response. He was too terrified to answer. Qani let him go, and then motioned to her fellow rebels to keep moving. Right now they were wasting daylight.

As Sinbad and his companions made their way to the docks, they were like fish swimming upstream—the flow of traffic against them—burdened with supplies to see them through all the long night to come. There was a festive yet nervous energy in the air, smiles and laughter all around. There was also a stink of fear, noticeable even under the usual smells of the street of cooking food, strange spices, wood smoke, and the ever-present stench of livestock.

When Qani led the party to her vessel, Sinbad was in awe. It was a grand ship. The main sails were outstanding and the structure was well balanced. Suddenly, Sinbad was at home. No more drifting through the desert, rotting in a dungeon, or flying through the clouds. He was where he belonged.

"She looks like a good ship," she said to Qani with admiration. "I should have no problem captaining her."

Qani pulled him back with a boorish jerk. "It's *my* ship, and I'm her captain," she said, sounding like a greedy child who refused to share her toys. "If anyone has a problem with that, they can stay here. Understood?"

Sinbad nodded grudgingly, as Qani strolled aboard the seaworthy vessel. He had felt the harsh sting of emasculation being reduced to a mere deckhand. He considered that the female population of this planet was the domineering gender. He placed his hand on the side of the ship and briefly fantasied on how he would to steer her through the raging waters.

"I'm sorry," said Sinbad, "about what happened back at the base."

She scowled at him. "I don't care what the prophecy says, outlander. But if you ever talk to me like that again, I will beat you until but a spark of life remains in your body. Is that understood?"

Sinbad gave her a soulful glance. "Yes."

"Yes, what?"

Sinbad hid his annoyed snarl. "Yes, *Captain*."

Qani gave out a satisfying smile. "Good. Now man your station."

Sinbad turned his back, rolling his eyes. *The nerve of that conceited woman.*

He was trying to make peace, but all she did was spat on his face. Maybe he deserved it, but this was totally uncalled for.

Qani stood above deck waving to her crew. "Set sail!" she bellowed, as the Thulian rebels took their rightful positions. Sinbad tended the main sail, but everything was foreign to him. He couldn't comprehend on how it works.

"There's no rigging, hardly any sail," he said to Qani. "What am I to do…*Captain*." He used the term loosely.

"Just sit there and be quiet," she abrasively rebuked him. Qani sauntered over to the helm and settled into her captain's chair, and took hold of two levers. "I've got everything under control."

Under his breath, Sinbad muttered, "That's what I'm afraid of."

With every position filled and his lack of knowledge of this unfamiliar craft, Sinbad went over the front of the ship where Kar-Tyr rested. After their high-flying adventure to the city, the last of the Kurwani became silent and didn't interact with the small squad. Sinbad took space on the opposite side of the deck. They were right back to the silent treatment. This one was much more uncomfortable than their previous row in the caves. In retrospect, Sinbad believed their morose attempt at friendship might have gone a little better.

Sinbad looked over Kar-Tyr's direction. The proud centaur was still as a statue and became part of the ship. His long hair swayed gently to the breeze. He had a serious expression on his face. It was as if it was craved in marble. It appeared Kar-Tyr had left this world and sought solace in his own.

Sinbad tried as he might to find the right thing to say without appealing any insult to this half horse hybrid. On what seemed to be well over a millennium, Sinbad finally spoke.

"Tell me of your people, Kar-Tyr."

"So you can once again accuse me of..." the Kurwani nastily replied, and then quickly changed his tone peremptorily. "Forgive me. I get nervous on the open seas. There are no more of my people, Sinbad. That is all you need to know."

The Earthman obliged to Kar-Tyr's request. The last son of the Kurwani tribe had been through so much trauma; just speaking of the unimaginable massacre of his people was much more painful than swords. Not only Kar-Tyr's upper body displayed many scars, he also had some in both his heart and soul. Sinbad knew Kar-Tyr would open up to him when he is ready and able. Right now he was asking too much.

"I have done a great disservice, Sinbad," said Kar-Tyr. "I have taken part in a horrid act that I thought would do more good than harm."

Sinbad looked at him with great concern. All he could think of was all the fights Kar-Tyr endured in the arena. All those inmates and monsters he killed. All of who were murderers and terrorists. He had no choice to fight back.

"Do not put yourself at blame, Kar," Sinbad said to him. "You were only following orders."

"It is no excuse," Kar-Tyr replied. "If I could do it all over again, I would have just let Akhdar kill me."

"You shouldn't say such a thing."

"I take no pleasure on taking one's life."

"Nor do I."

"But what's done is done, and I have to live with it. I have a lot to answer for when I leave to the next world. And I expect that the gods should not take mercy on me. I deserve whatever penance they will give me."

Sinbad sighed in despair and studied Kar-Tyr's tattoos on his massive right arm. It was a closer look when he first saw them in the arena. The Kurwani man noticed the Earthman staring at them.

"They're not names," he said.

"What?"

"They're not names of the people I've killed. I was only saying that to intimidate you."

"Then what are they?" asked Sinbad.

"They are religious symbols of my culture, Sinbad," Kar-Tyr confessed. "Each design represents each sin I must atone for. So I have quite a few," he laughed.

"You will get a chance to make up for what you did, Kar."

"I expect no leniency from it."

Then Sinbad shifted his attention over to the horizon, and spotted an upcoming chasm.

"There," Qani pointed to the abyss, "can you see the straits, Sinbad?"

"Aye," he replied, squinting his eyes so he could further make out the shape of the structure. "It looks a little narrow. Think you can handle it?"

"I've done this a thousand times," Qani assured him, manning the controls. Then she gave an almost inaudible mumble, "In theory." Hoping Sinbad wouldn't hear her.

But to her dismay, he apparently did and started coaching her through the tight fit of the channel.

"Easy now," he told her, trying to keep his cool. "*Don't* pull too hard. Feel how the water is guiding the ship."

Qani took Sinbad's advice into consideration. She followed all of his instructions seamlessly. Sinbad's stomach began to unknot. He was no longer tense and managed to squeeze out a smile.

"That's it. Well done, Qani."

Once they had entered the chasm, Sinbad's thankful smile slowly vanished as he checked out their current location. Darkness fell upon the ship and her crew. Kar-Tyr felt a chill shooting down his spine. It was enough for the centaur titan to get off the deck floor. He trotted over to the center of the ship and joined in on the surveillance. Something was amiss in this daunting outlet. He made it his personal mission to watch all directions in case the group would fell victim to a trap set by a band of murderous marauders.

The trees were all twisted and dead. The branches looked like giant boney fingers that resembled sharp claws. Kar-Tyr felt the talons would swoop in and collect the rebels one by one at any given moment.

"Not a very friendly looking place, is it?" he asked his friends.

Nearly halfway through the channel, the group heard very violent sounds coming on land. Then a voice shot out.

"Go away!" it called from the shoreline.

At first Sinbad thought it was a siren, using its song to lure them to crash their ship to the rocks. He had lost several good men to those creatures when he had to sail *The Chimera* through the Dragon's Teeth valley back on Earth. The sirens sand their heavenly serenades and mesmerized the crewmembers. They lured the men to the side of the ship and pulled them into the darkened abyss one by one to drown.

But the cries weren't attracting Qani's crew at all, but only sending them away. Then he realized the feminine voice wasn't speaking to them, but to someone else. Sinbad peered through the light at the end of the tunnel and made a shocking discovery.

"It came from over there," he pointed to a woman being beaten by a pair of bandits, and her children where cowering beside her.

One of the thieves was going through her things, looking for anything valuable. She kicked him in the shin, and elbow-jabbed the mugger next to him. She tried to squeeze past them, hoping to break loose and run for it, but then her luck ran out.

They converged on her, snarling, and shoved her into the ground and one of them kicked her in the stomach. The assailant was armed with only a mace, and his partner was only equipped with a small blade. Her three children, two girls and a boy, gave very loud hurtful sobs.

The tall one brought his small blade toward her chin, while his partner held her immobile. There was no way she was going to give these punks the satisfaction of hearing her scream. It was unlikely she would be able to maintain the resolution.

Sinbad glowered at the two brutes and grabbed his sword. "Impudent dogs," he growled, as he jumped ship and ran towards the robbers.

"Sinbad! Wait!" yelled Qani, who was too late to stop him.

Sinbad charged at the two marauders, who quickly forgot about the woman and engaged in an unfair fight of two against one. The one with the dagger threw his blade at Sinbad, only for the sailor to deflect it with his sword. He plunged his scimitar forward, feeling the meaty crunch as it rushed deep into the thief's belly. The man's eyes went wide with shock, then wider as Sinbad jerked the blade upward to finish the kill.

Sinbad kicked the man backward off his sword before it could be entangled in the cadaver's fall.

Sinbad was fighting like a wild beast himself, in silence except for his gasps of effort. The remaining mugger swung his mace to Sinbad's head, but the Earthman ducked and capitalized on his attacker's side, which he left open.

Sinbad took a swipe at the man's side. The thief hobbled and held the bloody wound in tremendous pain. With a furious roar he swung the mace on a forehand swerve. Sinbad struck the weapon's handle that diminished its drive for the severed top to go flying in the opposite direction. Steel glittered in Sinbad's hand and with a heave of his great shoulders he drove the sword into the marauder's body. The assailant's high thin squeal broke in a struggled gurgle and his whole, lanky body fell face down in a slowly widening pool of dark crimson in the Martian sands.

Qani and Kar-Tyr came running after Sinbad, only to find the battle was over and their friend had emerged victoriously. Sinbad knelt down to the ground and wiped his bloodstained blade on the ground and then enclosed it.

Qani, fearing by that sudden movement meant Sinbad had taken a dire hit rushed over to him. "Are you all right?" she asked, catching her breath.

"I'm fine," he replied, wiping blood from his face.

Sinbad staggered dizzily up, shaking the sweat and blood out of his eyes. Blood dripped from his sword and fingers, and trickled in rivulets down his thighs, arms, and chest. Qani caught at him to support him, but the outlander shook her off impatiently.

"You're injured," Qani shuddered, looking him over.

Sinbad took a step back. "It's not my blood," he told her. He gestured over to the children who were helping their battered mother. "Check on the pilgrims."

Sinbad directed his team. He raked back his sweat-plastered hair with a shaky hand as he leaned against the wall, weak from the reaction of relief.

Kar-Tyr made haste on going over to the young ones. The woman was covered with bruises and she was inflicted with several cuts. No superficial damaged had been done. But the trauma had left an immense impact on her. She wasn't willingly to accept Kar-Tyr's at first. But with a sympatric face and a kind heart, he softly persuaded her to trust him.

The children were taken aback from Kar-Tyr's appearance. He was different from the people they usually intermingled. They should have been afraid, but that fear was lifted when they witnessed him helping their wounded mother. The children quickly embraced their mother. The woman gave a soft moan, knowing she would be sore for the next several days, but managed to take it in stride that she was alive and able to hold her babies.

Qani looked at them with a heavy heart. "What are a mother and her children doing out this far?" she asked Sinbad.

"They are unharmed," Kar-Tyr said with a compassionate look. "Frightened, but unharmed. Shall they accompany us?"

Qani was about to give the Kurwani her answer, but Sinbad had already made the choice. "Yes, Kar-Tyr," he said with benevolence.

Qani should have felt angry regarding Sinbad not knowing his place. But she was impressed by his humanity. He was an alien to this world and he was willingly to sacrifice his life to save a family of strangers he had certainly had no personal ties. She greatly misjudged the Earthman. Maybe there was hope for him yet.

The woman smiled at Sinbad and embraced him. "Thank you, sir. I knew Daizha had heard my prayers."

"It is all right, milady. You were in trouble and I could not just sail by without ignoring your pleas. My name is Sinbad."

"I am Shondi," said the pilgrim, and then she motioned over to her three children. "These are my children Aratus, Navi, and Nonni."

"Thank you for saving my mommy, mister," said Aratus, the little boy.

"You are most welcome, young master," smiled Sinbad, and then he looked over to Kar-Tyr. "Kar, see that they are provided with food and water. If we do not have enough, they are welcome to my share." Qani was awestruck. Sinbad turned to her and said, "Which way now, Captain?"

The look Qani gave him was surprisingly tender. She stared at him with such admiration and grinned, "You may call me Qani."

Before the group could continue on their journey through the wide-open tundra, Qani ordered her band of rebels to stay in the ship. She appointed Ankhara in charge and assured everyone they will be back in the morning to plot their next move.

It was a barren desert. The monotony was unbroken by even the slightest trace of vegetation, stretched for miles before them. Qani's flowing purple cloak and matching head cloth protected her from the merciless sun. But it offered little relief from the suffocating heat and lack of moisture. Not a single cloud could be seen in the sky. Even though she had been here less than an hour, her mouth already felt dry and parched.

It was growing dark out. When the sun went down in the desert, it went down fast. Then the children were getting tired. To their delight, Kar-Tyr offered them to ride on his back. Excitedly they mounted the centaur and cheered joyously.

"Faster!" said Nonni, hugging Kar-Tyr's neck.

"Giddy-up!" laughed Navi, while the boy held onto Kar-Tyr's waist.

The ride was a bit bumpy, but he was having fun. For the first time in ages, Kar-Tyr smiled. It was good to hear the laughter of children again. Something he hadn't inured since he was captured. He forgot how soothing it was. He hoped this trek would last as long as possible.

Kar-Tyr rode ahead, while Sinbad and Qani went over the disposition. Shondi kept a watchful eye on her children. She was beginning to get worried if they were too heavy for the Kurwani's back. Her qualms waived, when she noticed his muscles. She averted her eyes and felt a small pinch of shame.

Qani looked at the tundra. "This place is so desolate."

"Reminds me of the desert," said Sinbad. "How far is it, Qani?"

Over the hill sat single house. Isolated from civilization and enveloped in solitude. Qani pointed to the lonely dwelling.

"There it is," she said to her company. "Farkhunda's hut. I haven't seen him in ages. I hope he remembers me."

Sinbad stared amorously at her. She was pleasing to the eye, but so had been the women in Akhdar's private harem. He saw something different about her.

"I can't imagine anyone not remembering you," he said absentmindedly.

"What do you mean by that?" Qani asked.

Sinbad couldn't find his tongue. He couldn't believe he let that slipped out. He hesitated to answer. Or did he even have an answer?

"Let's race them there!" said Aratus on Kar-Tyr's back, pointing to the hut.

"You're on, lad!" said Sinbad, quickly changing the subject. He challenged Kar-Tyr to a footrace where the centaur won. The children laughed and cheered.

The hut was small and humble, and at the right side sat a giant goat-like creature. Its fur was green and its snout was pink. It had a pair of long curved horns on its head. It looked at Sinbad and his friends, and gave a low baa. Then it returned to graze its small portion of grass.

The creature wasn't as bizarre as the giant, two-headed roc that nested on the island of Colossa—a place where a giant Cyclops dwelled. But the green goat that stood before him now wasn't the least bit hostile. It continued to munch on the grass and allowed the strangers to come forward to the hut.

Sinbad waited for Farkhunda to emerge from his home to greet them. But something was terribly wrong. Even though how troubling Sinbad had to admit it.

"Surely he's heard us by now," he said to his party.

Shondi sheepishly replied, "Sorry. The children are a bit excited."

Sinbad and Qani approached cautiously the modest residence. The Earthman slowly opened the door, prepared for anything. He insisted Qani to stay behind him in cause of any danger. She lightly brushed Sinbad aside and peered through the opening.

"Farkhunda?" she hailed to her old friend.

Inside of the house was pitch black. She didn't hear him answer, or hear any sounds of movement.

"It's me, little Qani. We've come for your help."

Sinbad opened the door all the way, letting more light into the room. The light formed an outline on the floor where it encased figure of a man. Qani gazed down on the floor, as her breath was taken away. She gasped with horror and put her hands in front of her mouth. There laid the bloody corpse of Farkhunda with his eyes still open. His own blood that originated from his throat blemished his blue Azurian skin.

He was brutally murdered in the sanctity of his own home. A pool of his red blood flowed deeply in the crevices of his tiled floor and seeped into his rug. Qani couldn't control her emotions. At the terror of this scene, Qani screamed uncontrollably and threw herself bodily upon Sinbad in the abandon of her anguish. Sinbad embraced her tightly as she continued to howl like the damned. She could feel her whole world crashing down and her heart was shattering like glass.

She shrank against him, and cried out. She had seen the corpse at her feet. Farkhunda lay twisted and contorted, his hands and feet were exposed to view, and at the sight Qani went livid and hid her face against Sinbad's powerful shoulder.

Sinbad shared her pain. He was immediately reminded when he and Azrak ran back to his home to appallingly learn his family was murdered in the same fashion. Qani wept hysterically inside Sinbad's nurturing arms. Her eyes were burning with rage and sadness. Sinbad turned her head away from the grisly sight and slowly closed the door.

CHAPTER SEVENTEEN
HE WHO SPEAKS ABOUT THE FUTURE LIES, WHEN HE TELLS THE TRUTH

Kar-Tyr watched his two friends somberly walked back to the group. He looked at Qani, who was in tears. She threw her hand up in a gusty gesture of wrath and despair as the horrific sight she had just witnessed shattered her psyche.

"What is wrong?" he asked them.

Sinbad was in repentance. "The sage is dead," he informed the group. "His throat was slit. Akhdar knew we were coming."

Before Sinbad could continue, a buzzing noise filled the air. It was getting louder and stronger each second.

The collective attention was diverted by a high-pitched whining sound. Looking for the source of the sound, the group looked over to the horizon.

Kar-Tyr pricked up his ears. "What's that noise?" he said, following the racket from behind him.

It seemed to be coming from overhead. There were only a handful of clouds in the sky, but whatever it was, the sound originated from there. Sinbad craned his neck, shielding his eyes against the glare of the midday sun. There seemed to be something speeding their way.

"Sinbad! Look at this," the centaur pointed up to the sky to reveal something flying their way. "Is it a bird?"

"I don't think so, Kar-Tyr. It's very big," said Sinbad.

The whining of the object was getting louder, as if it was powering up somehow.

"What is that?" Aratus, Shondi's only son, demanded impatiently.

With a rush of air and what sounded like a jet turbine, the object that was so high up suddenly got much closer, much faster. It dropped like a rock, but it wasn't in free fall. Instead it was many with confidence and assurance.

Quickly it was almost at earth level, zigzagging through the sands.

The flying thing curled backed up into the sky, banked and hovered, pausing to make a dramatic entrance, apparently. Then it moved right toward the hut, and Sinbad couldn't believe what he was seeing.

"It appears to be some sort of flying ship," said Kar-Tyr.

"A flying ship?" Sinbad asked in bewilderment.

Lights were glowing on the front of it, with an array of armature underneath. Turbines were powering it from behind. But even the outlandishness of the device floating in front of them was as nothing compared to the riders.

The image of the flying craft was getting closer, something caught Sinbad's eye on the front of the ship. "Is that a cannon?"

Then he saw someone on board taking aim at him and everyone else. Sinbad's jaw dropped and quickly motioned his group to scatter.

"Everybody run!" he exclaimed at the top of his lungs.

The flying assault craft zoomed over the rebels and shot at them with their mounted laser turrets. The ship was filled with Akhdar's elite guards, and they were accompanied with a familiar face only Qani could recognize.

"It's Ankhara!" she identified the traitor in heartbreaking disbelief. "He must be working for Akhdar!"

Ankhara was the field commander of this operation. He climbed on top of the ship, watching the rebels flee like little rats.

"Die Azurian sympathizers!" he cursed at them.

Fighting to maintain his balance, Sinbad reached out to help steady the pilgrim family and escorted them to safety. Shondi was holding her youngest daughter Nonni, while Aratus was covering his ears from the terrifying blast, as the group scrambled out.

"Mommy, make it stop!" Aratus shrilled, while his face turned red and his eyes were burning from his tears.

Sinbad turned to Shondi and he saw her face quickly changed from surprised to fear. She held her children in panic and shouted to them, "Keep moving!"

Sinbad looked at Ankhara with hatred in his eyes. He knew there was a spy in Qani's faction. He just didn't thought it would be the white-haired Thulian who he caught making eyes at his female superior on several occasions.

The ground shook wildly. Everyone was shouting. Qani was barking orders, and suddenly Kar-Tyr's jaw dropped at what he saw flying through the sky.

"Traitorous scum!" Sinbad shouted at the green Judas, just barely dodging a plasma discharge.

More explosions. Smoke was billowy everywhere.

Sinbad started to run. He had no destination in mind. All he knew was that he had to put some distance between himself and the infernal flying machine. Smoke was everywhere. He covered his mouth with the palm of his hand, trying not to breathe in the smoke, fearing his lungs could collapse. Laser fire was all around. Ionic pulse beams flew past him. The ground erupted directly in front of him. If it had struck even a second later, he would have been right in the middle of it and would be incinerated on the spot.

Kar-Tyr and Qani had been running, diving, and dodging for so long now that he could not be sure of anything. Another explosion sent earth and gravel vomiting skyward behind them as they were forced to take cover behind Farkhunda's hut.

They were dealing with fire and destruction that was out of proportion to anything they had encountered before. It was leaving a trail of carnage with licking flames and billowing smoke. At times it seemed as if the ground itself had vanished, to be replaced by gouts of flame and geysers of earth and pulverized stone. Ankhara's flying gunship was a stone's throw away, but the barrage beneath which they were presently trapped. It would be suicide to engage a full frontal attack.

Sinbad shielded his eyes, trying to see Kar-Tyr or anybody. He caught fleeting glimpses of running forms.

He heard an explosion behind him and to the left. Naturally he moved forward and to the right.

Kar-Tyr ran clear out of the gunner's sight and unleashed his kunai. He reeled in back and lashed the rope around the muzzle of the cannon. The soldiers on the ship looked in amazement and then became frightened, because they all knew how this was going to end.

"Let's see how well this bird fights on land," said the mighty Kurwani warrior.

With a hefty tug, he sent the whole ship smashing to the ground. The impact left a giant crater on the earth and the guards bounced out onto the cruel red dirt.

The crash caused the ground to shake, making everyone fall. Sinbad was on his knees and he had a hard time getting up. He heard an energetic hum from one of the guards' sword-gun. The guard stood behind Sinbad and aimed at his back.

"Now you die, Earthman!" he said with his finger on the trigger.

Before the masked assailant could take Sinbad's life, he was struck down by an incoming blast. The assassin fell to his death, as Sinbad investigated the origin of the shot.

"In Allah's name?" he whispered, looking at Shondi holding the smoking laser rifle. She shielded her children behind her, and she shed a tear of regret.

"Daizha, forgive me," she pleaded to her god.

Sinbad shifted his attention to the fallen guard's weapon and made a mad dash for it.

"Shooting swords!" he exclaimed. "Magnificent!"

Qani somersaulted through the air. She landed in the ground right in front of the Dozhakian honor guards. They came in first, the three of them converging as one. All they managed to do was slam into each other, because Qani—having barely touched the ground—immediately bounced up as if she were on strings. Before they realized it, she was behind them. She grabbed the respective heads of two of them and slammed them together with a resounding crack.

The third and burliest attacker swung his sword at her. Qani ducked under each seep. On the fifth swing, she caught the arm effortlessly. Her enemy was stunned, unable to believe that he was being immobilized with so little effort, and the nimble young woman punched him on the nose.

And with that, she tossed the Thulian man on top of the heap of his already fallen associates. He started to get up, but a quick, casual spin kick from Qani knocked him out.

Qani delivered a swift high kick to an assassin's jaw, making him throw her sword-gun in the air. The female warrior then grabbed him by the shoulders and performed an overhead somersault to retrieve the weapon in midair. While soaring through the pink sky, she shot a guard who was sneaking up Kar-Tyr while the Kurwani man was too busy grappling an enemy. Powerful fingers crushed the startled Thulian man's windpipe as easily as though it were a paper cup.

Qani landed softly to the ground and held a defensive stance. Kar-Tyr held his opponent by the throat and kept squeezing until the Thulian had lost consciousness.

"You act as if you've used one of those before," Kar-Tyr said to her, throwing the hired killer across the tundra.

The Kurwani warrior spun toward to another attacker before he could lay a hand on Kar-Tyr. He savagely brained Akhdar's agent with his fist, shattering his skull in a single blow. The second Thulian man joined his companion on the ground, and that was that. Two men were out cold in a matter of seconds.

Qani quickly replied, "I'm a quick learner."

Sinbad collected the sword-gun and aimed it at Ankhara who was trying escape from the wreckage.

"Surrender, Thulian dog or taste the sting of this light-sword!" commanded Sinbad.

Ankhara declined the Earthman's orders and started to make his escape. Sinbad took aim and fired, but heard a strange click instead of pulsing blast.

"It doesn't work," Sinbad complained, trying to find the malfunction of this inexplicable device.

Ankhara chuckled at Sinbad. "You're out of juice, outlander," he mocked, giving him a shrewd smile.

"Juice?" puzzled Sinbad, while he examined the gun.

What an absurd planet I am on, he thought. *Women hold titles of authority over men here. I was on the deck of a ship that for the life of me I couldn't rig. And now I am dealing with a weapon that only can be fueled with **fruit juice**. Allah, help me.*

He gripped the handle of the gun and pitched it at Ankhara's head. "If it doesn't work, I'll return it."

The weapon was nothing, but the man who wielded it was everything. Sinbad's impression of guns was crude and impersonal whereas a blade is not. With a sword, the one who would hold it could do more than learn combat. It developed character.

The blow broke Ankhara's nose and blood sprayed in a splattering arc. The traitor fell to the ground, as Kar-Tyr placed him in restraints. Qani watched as Sinbad collected all the unconscious bodies of the Akhdar's enforcers, and then advanced into the smoke and murk. She studiously stared at them with a puzzling look on her face.

"How did they know we were here?" she asked, still not believing what happened. "How did they find us?"

"Akhdar had eyes and ears everywhere, Qani," replied Shondi.

Sinbad looked at her with a sudden coldness in her eyes. "And how are we to know you're not another spy?"

"You cannot," the pilgrim honestly answered. "Only know that I came to help, Sinbad.

"Help?" Qani said in repulse. "Farkhunda is dead and with him the knowledge of the location of the prince. How can you possibly help?"

Shondi frowned and took a breath. "I can help because *I* know his location."

Qani was taken back from this news. It was inconceivable. She was going to say something, but refrained and allowed this inexplicable individual to explain herself.

"Years ago, Zhar Dadgar outlawed certain technologies in Dozhak, hoping to make it more peaceful. Some Akhdar included, did not agree with this policy and took what they wanted.

"Akhdar led them to an underground chamber, and from there, began his plot to take over as ruler of Dozhak. I was a slave there," she confessed. The tone of her voice was somber as a floodgate of terrible memories came gushing through. "Kept for breeding purposes. I along with three of my children, escaped when we heard rumor of the prophecy."

Sinbad solemnly replied, "I'm sorry to disappoint you. But there is no prophecy. Akhdar as much admitted so."

"That is not quite true, Sinbad," boomed an ominous voice coming from Sinbad's left.

He quickly turned his head and was startled by the sight of the giant green goat spoke to him.

"By Allah!" Sinbad exclaimed, as all of his friends stared wide-mouthed at the barnyard behemoth.

He thought his heart would stop when a voice hissed in a low baritone voice. He stared appalled to see the creature in such a state of nerves, and he pulled himself together with an effort.

"Do not be afraid, children. I mean you no harm," said the creature with age and wisdom. The strange inhuman voice rose in a sort of low chant. "My name is Ostath. I have walked the Martian soil since before the dawn of either Azurian or Thulian. I have seen great civilizations born and ruined," perceived Ostath, as he spoke with both pride and humility. "I have learned many things in my time, Earthman, and one of them is that even the most outlandish of rumors starts with a truth."

Sinbad's interest was piqued. He gazed upon Ostath with wonder and inquisition. The sailor had seen just about every demon, deity, and magic in his whole life. But for once, Sinbad couldn't believe his eyes. He was afraid to speak, not knowing what this magnificent animal was capable of. Sinbad realized that this strange creature must be centuries ahead of his generation. But he put it down to witchcraft, and troubled his head no more about it. He just stood there with his mouth gapped open and listened what the wise old beast had to say.

"Your coming has been foretold for millennia, Sinbad," Ostath informed the baffled Earthman.

It was surreal. Sinbad felt as if he were watching a puppet show, or a disembodied ghost possessing the giant green goat.

"Akhdar merely used the whispers of it for his own gain." The amazing creature turned to face the setting sun. It etched the pink and hazy purple of the sky in brief gold. When Ostath began to take his leave, he looked back at Sinbad. "Is it not said on your world that a man's capacity is the same as the breadth of his vision? Open your heart, Sinbad, and you will find the truth."

"Forgive me, Ostath," Sinbad said carefully, "if I am the savior the prophecy foretold of, then how am I going to unite the two races together? As you can see I am foreign to this planet. Everyone sees me as an outlander. I am worthless to their eyes, and the compassion in their hearts. I am only a sailor, not a holy liberator for justice."

"Oh man, listen," said the strange being, "I am foul and monstrous to you, am I not? Nay do not answer; I know. But you would seem as strange to me. There are many worlds besides Mars, and life takes many shapes. I am neither god nor demon, but flesh and blood like yourself, though the sublime differ in part, and the form be cast in different mold. But with courage you can make them see the light."

Sinbad paused and then tenderly replied, "If I even manage to rally a resistance against Akhdar's forces, how will I succeed? I'm more concerned on the lives of others than my own. What if I make a mistake and send them to death's door?"

Ostath narrowed his stately eyes on the Earthman. "You know better than anyone else here, Sinbad. I've been watching you, Earthman. No matter how the odds are against your favor you always managed to turn the tide and vanquish those who dare to spread their evil across the realm. Not because you wield a sword or command an army, but respecting life for your fellow man. Believe what you want, Sinbad. However, I am never wrong when I see greatness."

Sinbad, touched by Ostath's words, watched the sacred beast begin his journey through the Martian tundra; he felt the weight of the world on his shoulders. Then he looked at his friends. All of them stared at the Earthman in a newfound light. Qani was shamefaced on how she treated him earlier.

Sinbad had saved countless lives, slayed many monsters and occasionally saved a kingdom every now and then. But this was beyond anything he had ever endured. Now he had been tasked to save an entire world where he certainly had no stake in from sheer destruction.

Then he recited several lines from his favorite poem.

"It is through toil that eminence is won;
Whoever seeks the heights must pass nights without sleep.
The pearl fisher must brave the depth of ocean,
If he is to win power and wealth.
Whoever hopes to rise without effort,
Will waster his life in search of the impossible."

Sinbad's shoulders had just gotten heavier.

CHAPTER EIGHTEEN
ALL SUNSHINE MAKES A DESERT

The next day was quite challenging. Sinbad, Qani, and Shondi salvaged whatever was left of the Thulian airship. For where they're going they would need that ship up and running. Qani and Shondi surveyed the vehicle, while Kar-Tyr kept watch of the children who were playing nearby. The pilgrim studied the gears and the mechanics with such scrutiny.

"You are sure you can repair this ship?" Sinbad asked her. He wished he could help, but all he knew was how to repair common sea vessels. Not star cruisers.

"My job, other than bearing the next generation of the Thulian population, was to fix the engines of the cruisers," Shondi replied, and shot the Earthman a quick smile. "I am sure."

Hours of hard work, deconstruction, and rebuilding took all morning and early afternoon. Whatever Shondi needed, either tool or component Sinbad was gladly to lend a helping hand. It was better to be an errand boy than to do nothing at all. After Shondi closed the engine compartment she looked at Sinbad who was above deck behind the helm.

"Try it, Sinbad," she said, as the sailor turned on the ignition.

They could hear the engine sputter but it wouldn't turn over. Sinbad tried again but it was no use.

"Nothing," he told her, wiping his brow.

The pilgrim woman gave him a determined look. "I think I have it," she said with more confidence. "It should start now."

Sinbad took a deep breath and rebooted the controls. The steady whirl of the engines hummed miraculously as the craft began to hover off the ground. Movement was stable, while the red Martian sand was spraying off from both sides because of the revolving turbines.

"It works!" Sinbad said in triumph. His face resembled a young boy with all the excitement and glee one could ever imagine.

Shondi smiled at him and dusted her hands off. "I would expect no less."

Sinbad jumped off the ship that was hovering eight feet above the ground, and raced to his friends who were standing idly by Farkhunda's hut.

"Kar! Qani!" he called out. "We are ready to go! We must leave while the sun is still up."

Qani and Kar-Tyr looked at Sinbad. They were perplexed on what they were going to ask him. Only Qani had the courage to approach the Earthman.

"What are we to do with them?" she asked, pointing to Ankhara and the rest of Akhdar's hunters who were tied around a large wooden post.

Sinbad checked Ankhara's bonds. The traitor's hands were secured behind him; his feet were bound to a stake that was driven into the ground. Sinbad double-checked the knots, fairly certain the Thulian man could not free himself, but completely confident that Ankhara wouldn't do anything in his power to escape.

Sinbad glanced at them and drew his sword. Qani ran to Kar-Tyr and held onto him. The Kurwani held her tight, and felt her pressing her face against his chest. She stood in stunned silence, tears freely falling over her cheeks. She refused to watch the forthcoming grisly scene. She kept her eyes closed, prayed to Daizha and waited for the bloodshed to be over.

Sinbad knelt down to the bound prisoners and looked at the traitor Ankhara. His nose was swollen and the blood around his mouth had dried. Ankhara scoffed at Sinbad and saw the glimmer of the outlander's blade in the hot sun.

"You have come to dispose of us, outlander?" he asked Sinbad, holding his head high. His broken nose distorted his voice. "Even if you are not either Azurian or Thulian, but you and I are just the same."

"I do not believe that," he replied to his enemy.

Ankhara chuckled. "You have no choice, Sinbad. You have to do it, or we will be considered as loose ends. And you of all people should know that loose ends should be tied up. I am not afraid to die. I will go into the next world as a warrior to the great Dozhakian Empire."

"Were you the only spy in the group or were there others?"

"I acted alone."

"What have you done with the rest of the rebels in our group?"

Ankhara looked away, and then Sinbad grabbed his face and forced him to look him in the eye.

"I will repeat the question: what have you done with our friends?"

"Have you tried looking in the bottom of the river?" Ankhara answered him with malice. "They have to be floating by now, if the fish didn't get to them yet."

Sinbad punched him in the face, further damaging the traitor's broken nose.

"You bastard! How could you? They were your brothers and sisters!"

"They were traitors to the crown and they died like the dogs they were!" Ankhara shouted back. "If you're going to kill me, you better do it now. But I must warn you, outlander; when you throw a rock at Akhdar Dadgar, he'll throw a knife back at you. If you throw a knife, he will send a whole battalion and kill your whole family while you sleep. Are you ready to handle those consequences?"

Qani slowly turned to see Sinbad conversing with the prisoners. She wondered why he hadn't executed them yet. And then she saw him holding the hilt of his sword.

"What is he waiting for?" she asked Kar-Tyr.

Then she felt something in his satchel. With natural curiosity she pulled it out.

It was a smoking pipe.

Similar to the one Barbatus always inhaled from.

"Kar-Tyr, where did you get this?" she asked.

"I found it when the ship crashed," he answered. "I don't smoke, but it's in real fine condition. I thought I would use it to barter with a trader in the next village for food and supplies."

A sharp pain struck Qani. "Oh, no." She began to weep. Her best friend betrayed her that led to the slaughter of her fellow comrades, and he also murdered the only father figure she ever known.

Now she was alone to her cause.

"Death is a black camel that lies down at every door," said Sinbad, holding his blade against Ankhara's throat. "Sooner or later you must ride that camel, my friend."

He lowered his blade down to Ankhara's shoulder and cut through the ropes that bound the traitor and his comrades.

"But not today."

Ankhara and the rest of the guards got up and proceeded to leave the camp. Ankhara looked at Sinbad contemptuously, and felt he had been denied a warrior's death.

"You have dealt me a great insult, Earthman," said Ankhara, clenching his fists. "You have never experienced such pain once you have been through Emperor Akhdar's chief torturers. And I hope they keep you alive long enough for you to realize the foolish error you have made."

Ankhara turned his back on Sinbad and began to curse incoherently beneath his breath, while his cohorts followed his fellow Akhdar supporters through the desert, where they would hope to find some assistance or to steal a transport back to their master's palace. Qani kept an eye on them until they were out of sight. Then she shifted her gaze on Sinbad.

"Why did you let them go?" she asked, with anger in her voice.

"Akhdar already knows our next move," Sinbad replied, thrusting his blade back in its sheath. "Their deaths would have served no purpose. And I am not a cold blooded killer." Then he turned around to see the pilgrim's children playing on the airship. "Besides, mercy is a virtue that should be impressed upon everyone."

"You should have killed them, Sinbad," argued Kar-Tyr. "This place is now compromised."

"It was compromised the moment we arrived here, Kar-Tyr," Sinbad replied. "Their wandering through the desert just bought us at least several hours. Karma will get back at them. But in the meantime, gather your things. We're leaving as soon as possible."

On the way to the airship, Qani and Kar-Tyr noticed two of Shondi's children playing at the other side of Farkhunda's hut. Navi and Aratus were playing with sticks and wielded them as swords. They were reenacting the battle from the night before. The game caught Sinbad's attention and he laughed softly with delight.

Navi argued with Aratus. "No! I get to be Sinbad."

"You can't be Sinbad. You're a girl!" Her brother contested. "You have to be Qani!"

"Nuh-uh!" Navi protested.

"Uh-huh!"

"Nuh-uh!"

Then Aratus gave his older sister a smirk and threw down his stick. "Okay, I'll be Kar-Tyr," he said flexing his arms. "He's the strongest anyway."

Qani laughed, while Kar-Tyr found this form of hero worship very flattering. Not once in his life he would be perceived as a positive role model.

"Kar-Tyr," said Qani, "are you blushing?"

"What?" the Kurwani said, snapping into attention. "What are you talking about?"

"Your cheeks are turning red."

"No—no they're not!" he protested, but his cheeks were turning even more shades of red by the second.

"You *are* blushing!"

"It's sunburn," Kar-Tyr lied.

Qani smiled, "Yeah, right."

"It is time we were on our way," Sinbad said to them, as he didn't try to conceal his laughing smile. "Come on, children. It's time to go."

"Aw, do we have to, Sinbad?" whined Aratus.

"Yes, Aratus, we have to."

Aratus frowned, and then Navi placed her hand on his little shoulder. "Don't pout, Aratus. We get to go ride on the flying ship."

Then Aratus' face lit up with excitement. "Why didn't you say so? Let's go!"

He raced across the sands, passing Qani and Kar-Tyr and stopped at the airship that was hovering over eight feet into the air. Aratus tried to jump into the ship but he was too small. Sinbad lifted the pilgrim child up to the craft as Shondi carried him onto the deck.

"Me too, me too!" said Navi, holding her arms out for Sinbad to lift her on board.

"All right, then," the sailor smiled and gladly handed Navi off to her mother, while she extracted the ramp for the rest of her friends to enter the ship.

Kar-Tyr moved to the head of the ship with the children while the rest of his comrades were at the helm. Sinbad stood across the craft as Shondi was by the controls.

Sinbad sighed, "Again, I am at the mercy of a woman guiding the ship."

"Would you care to fly?" she generously asked Sinbad.

The Earthman was awestruck. "Is she hard to handle?"

Shondi showed Sinbad the control panel and went by the instruments step by step.

"The lever controls your height," she began, as Sinbad paid closely attention.

Back on Earth all he had to do was turn the wheel and let his men tune the sails. But this was entirely another animal.

"This stick steers. Everything else you can pick up along the way."

Sinbad pumped his fist in the air and gave a mighty yell. “Everyone secure themselves!” Then he let out a devilish grin that reached from ear to ear. “It’s time to sail.”

Then he pulled on the throttle and the ship was suddenly granted maximum thrust in mere seconds. The front of the ship bucked upward with Shondi’s children holding on to Kar-Tyr as they let out squeals of enjoyment and shock. Kar-Tyr shot straight up and lost his breath.

“I don’t think I like flying,” the Kurwani warrior said, trying to steady himself.

The thrill of being in the command of a new ship had spread Sinbad’s smile so far his cheeks began to hurt. How he loved to hear the engines and turbines hum when rev up the throttle and how the air would whisk through the air when he took it up to high speed.

“Whoo-hoo!” Sinbad yelled with gratification.

Qani and Shondi looked at each other and smiled. They finally let the Earthman have his fun.

After everyone had fallen asleep, Sinbad kept on driving the airship. He never left the controls since Shondi allowed him access. He was a quick learner in this new technology and how he savored every minute of it. Then he understood that he couldn’t settle on just mastering the sea, but also the sky too.

Sinbad suddenly felt someone’s hand on his shoulder and heard Qani’s soft voice.

“Sinbad? What you did back there? With Ankhara and the others…thanks.” Sinbad turned his head to the side to see Qani, who was trying to find the right words. “They were once my closest friends, and—and…”

“Truly, it was nothing,” Sinbad tenderly interjected.

Qani coyly turned away, and then met him in his eyes. A sultry breeze rustled through her hair.

“Still…” she said, as they both close in on each other’s lips, but quickly pulled away by the piercing loud shrieks and the loud flapping of several large wings in the wind.

There was movement in the air about them. Such as a swirl was being made in water as some of the creatures rose to the surface to investigate the disturbance. A nameless, freezing wind blew on Sinbad briefly, as if from an opened door. He felt a presence at his back, but he did not look about.

Flap! Flap! Flap! A clamorous fluttering of wings overwhelmed Sinbad's ears. He kept his eyes fixated at the dark sky, on which several questionable shadows hovered.

Out from the blackened gray skies came four winged creatures. They flew closer and closer to the airship. Sinbad strained his eyes in the darkness and saw a hint of motion. Qani's eyes widened in horror and violently gripped the helm. Sinbad stared at her hands digging into the panel. Then he shifted his focus onto the incoming creatures.

"Qani, what are they?" he asked, as the creatures came to the light.

The four monsters were humanoid but had brown bat qualities. Their claws were long and sharp, and their wings had the span of twenty feet. Their tails acted as rudders in their steering among the clouds.

For a moment Qani lost the ability to speak. She quickly snapped out of it and answered Sinbad's question.

"Marseilogos," she gasped, holding Sinbad's hand. "But I thought they were never extinct!"

The air was filled with the sound of laser blasts illuminating the dark galley. Sinbad and Qani saw the shot came from Shondi, who was shielding her children from the onslaught.

Squared jawed, with no trace of fear in her eyes, her light green skin shone from perspiration. She was firing a plasma rifle she had taken from one of the Dozhakian hunters. It was impossible for the children, who cowered behind her, to determine whether she was shooting at something in specific or just laying down suppressing fire or maybe simply shooting wherever he she can and hoping to Daizha she managed to hit one of those monsters.

"Get away you foul beasts!" she cried, as she kept firing at the night sky.

Sinbad wondered how she could see what she was shooting at. Maybe she was not. Maybe she was firing blind.

Kar-Tyr untangled his kunai and lashed it at the marseilogos, hoping it would scare them away. But these monsters were much more cunning than the creatures that he and Sinbad fought in Akhdar's arena.

Sinbad was in the center of the ship now, going stooped forward, head thrust out warily, sword advanced, when again death struck at him soundlessly. A flying shadow that swept across the gleaming floor was his only warning, and his instinctive sidelong leap all that saved his life. He had a flashing glimpse of a hairy black horror that swung past him with a clashing of frothing fangs, and something splashed on his bare shoulder that burned little drops of liquid hellfire. The cuts were deep and the smell of blood attracted the monster's brethren. Springing back, sword high, he saw the horror strike the floor, wheel and zoom toward him with appalling speed—a gigantic black bat, such as men see only in nightmares.

It was much bigger than an ordinary man, its evilly gleaming eyes shone with a horrible intelligence, and its fangs dripped venom.

Sinbad leaped high, and it passed beneath, turned and charged back. This time he evaded its rush with a sidewise leap, and struck back with a vengeance. His sword severed one of its long arms, and again he barely saved himself as the monstrosity swerved at him, fangs clicking fiendishly. But the creature did not press the pursuit. Turning, it flew over the heads of all the crewmembers, where it hovered for an instant, glaring down at them with its sinister red eyes. Then without warning it launched itself through space.

Sinbad stepped back to avoid the swooping body, then ducked frantically, just in time to escape being decapitated by its razor sharp claws. Then began a desperate game, the wits and quickness of the man matched against the wicked craft and speed of the giant bat.

One of the marseilogos dove in and grabbed Qani and brought her to the air.

"Sinbad!" she exclaimed, trying to break free from the monster's grasp.

"Kar!" he called out to his centaur friend. "It's got Qani!"

"Not if I can help it!" Kar-Tyr said, as he whipped his kunai around Qani's waist.

"Easy!" Sinbad shuddered.

"Calm yourself, Sinbad," Kar-Tyr assured him. "I know what I am doing."

"Have you ever tried anything like this before?"

"Yes, back when were on the run from Akhdar's men through the canal."

"How did that go?"

"Great."

Sinbad gave a sigh of relief.

"But only this is a little bit different," Kar-Tyr confessed. Then Sinbad's confidence in his Kurwani friend had rapidly been lowered.

Kar-Tyr pulled Qani from the marseilogo's clutches and filled through the air. She could feel the rope breaking apart, and she let out a bloodcurdling scream. Sinbad ran to the starboard of the craft and caught her.

"I've got you!" he said, bringing her back on board.

Shondi kept on firing her laser rifle until the monsters flew away out of sight. She tended to the controls while Qani looked after Sinbad. She inspected him for any injuries he might have sustained in his recent encounter with more of Mars' vicious beasts. She didn't like the look of the long slash marks that were dug into his shoulder.

"This should help," she said, applying some ointment to Sinbad's cuts. "It may be a little stiff."

"A stiff shoulder I can handle," Sinbad replied, acting virile. "If I were a little slower, it would have been my head."

"Are you well enough to fly, Sinbad, or should I remain at the controls?" asked Shondi.

Sinbad used the railing of the ship to raise himself to his feet. "A scratch will not keep me from sailing, my friend," he told her. "I shall fly."

"We won't reach our destination until morning," said Shondi, as Sinbad relieved her of her post. "Wake me if you need to rest."

But everyone in the ship knew Sinbad would never rest until Akhdar has been dealt with. And he is more stubborn than all of his crew combined. Sinbad kept sailing and didn't even stop—not even for a moment. He kept his focus over to the horizon and he never left the helm.

"Are we there yet?" Qani jokingly asked him.

Sinbad gave her a smile. "How are you, Qani?" he asked. "That was very close."

"Truthfully, Sinbad, I was frightened," she admitted, trying to hide her embarrassment. "For once in my life I felt so helpless. I never wanted to feel that way ever again."

"It all happens to the best of us, Qani," Sinbad replied. "There's a saying back in my world."

"What's that?"

"We're all human."

Qani looked at him as if he were speaking another language. "*You* may be human, but for me it's very different."

"What I meant was, don't blame yourself. It's okay to show a little fear and weakness."

"On this planet, Sinbad that could get you killed," Qani pointed out.

"So you're saying might is always right?"

"If you are among the followers of Akhdar, it is."

"Have you ever heard of, 'live by the sword and die by the sword?'"

"Yes, we have that here."

Sinbad smiled again. "Are all the women on this world like you?"

"What do you mean?" she asked, feeling intrigued.

"Strong, brave…and beautiful."

Qani blushed and shyly turned away from his chestnut brown eyes. Then she glanced down at her besmirched attire. Qani couldn't care less. Her slippers were in tatters, her robes and silken undergarments torn to shreds that scarcely held together decently.

"You probably say that to all the females in your species."

Sinbad took her hand and felt her smooth skin. "Only the ones I care for deeply."

She paused and looked into his eyes. "You saved my life, Sinbad."

"You saved my life *twice*," he said, showing her two fingers. Then he slowly reached out and touched her cheek. Then his fingers gently traced her jawline, down to her chin. "It was the least I can do."

"Who is Farah?" she asked.

Sinbad didn't blink. "How do you know of Farah?"

"When we got you out of the arena, you were delirious from the poison the guards shot you with," Qani explained, looking at the healing entry wound from the arrow on Sinbad's arm. "At one point you mentioned the name 'Farah.' Is she your wife?"

Sinbad remembered the fever dream vividly. Farah appeared to him heartbroken and very scornful. Most of all was the diamond ring around her finger and how she cruelly rejected him. He knew all of that wasn't true, but he could not be sure. Does he really expect her to wait for him forever?

"Farah is my betrothed," Sinbad confessed, the sound of sorrow and loneliness was weaved into his voice. "I was supposed to marry her back home, but I decided to go on one last adventure before I took my vows. I heard of a rare and beautiful gem that was supposed to be hidden on an island in the Far East. I thought it would make a great wedding present for Farah. So I took my ship and crew to the direction of where the island was supposed to be, but we got caught in this terrible storm. The typhoon pulled us into the sky, and when I woke up I was here on Mars—alone—until a friendly farmer and his sons found me."

Qani was stunned at this realization. Then he saw the shame in Sinbad's eyes as he took his hand off hers.

"How long since you've last seen her?"

Sinbad sighed and shook his head in quail. "It has been so long I'm afraid I do not know. She probably thinks I have abandoned her, or worse."

Qani held his hand. "We will find you a way back to Earth, Sinbad," she assured him, sharing his loneliness.

"What if I do find a way back, would she still want me?"

"It's better to know than wonder what would have been."

She placed her arms around Sinbad's neck. She felt his muscles tense and tremble.

"What are you doing?" he asked.

"I'm repaying you for your heroic services."

She leaned in and kissed Sinbad on the cheek. Then he pulled her in towards him and held her tight.

Her skin was warm and soft to his touch, and he gratefully explored every subtle nuance of her exotic splendor.

"This Farah must be most fortunate to have you," cooed Qani, closing her eyes and felt the warmth of his skin.

Sinbad held her close and smelled her hair. He thought the fragrance of Princess Aella's hair was heavenly, but this was more real. He never wanted this moment to end. For a precious heartbeat, the rest of the world slipped away. But still he felt something was wrong.

"Qani, I have a feeling you are not telling me something."

She opened her eyes and looked up at him.

"Why are we traveling to this destination? Are we going to meet more of your friends?"

She stared at him despondency. "All my friends were killed by Ankhara's betrayal. There is no one else to turn to."

"But we are still on a voyage."

Qani sighed and decided it was time to tell Sinbad the truth. "You do know that Akhdar came into power after his uncle died?"

Sinbad nodded in response.

"What you don't know that the previous zhar had a son, and he was next in line to the Dozhakian throne."

"Yes, I remember Akhdar mentioning that to me," Sinbad replied. "He said his cousin disappeared. Is that what happened to him?"

"Nobody knows," she said sadly. "Hearsay on the cobblestones says that Prince Muqari fled into exile, or like his benevolent father…murdered."

Sinbad's eyes widened. "You think Akhdar killed his own kinsman in cold blood?"

"No," Qani replied, "I pray to Daizha that it isn't so. I know Akhdar is evil but he wouldn't kill a little boy."

"Then you suspect he sent him away somewhere?"

"All I heard are rumors of someone fitting Prince Muqari's description was seen around the region we are heading, but I don't know where. If we can find him, Akhdar would be stripped of his power."

Then she looked at Sinbad. Watching him take in everything she revealed to him.

"I know this isn't you fight, Sinbad. When you find a way back home you can go."

"No," he answered, "this became my fight since that day Akhdar destroyed the lives of the only people who ever helped a stranger like me on this world. I will not leave until he has paid for all the crimes he has done to you and your people."

Sinbad pulled Qani close and held her.

"I swear to Almighty Allah."

The next morning the group reached their destination point. Shondi directed Sinbad to the landing site.

"You can land there, Sinbad," she directed, pointing to the most level area on the tundra.

Sinbad gently landed on the ground as the sand and dust settled. The hum of the engines had ceased.

As Kar-Tyr played with the children, Shondi gathered Sinbad and Qani with very important news.

"I have something for you, my friend," she said to Sinbad, as she reached into her robes and pulled out a sealed scroll. "This is a map to the caverns. It will lead you to the lair where Prince Muqari is kept."

She handed Sinbad the scroll and looked at him with tears in her eyes and a quivering smile.

"I cannot thank you enough, my friends. You saved the lives of my children and have helped us to start a new life together. I will never forget you."

She rushed into Sinbad's arms and held him for what seemed like an eternity. She finally let go and called her children.

"Children! It's time to go!"

"Aw, Mom!" groaned Navi.

"We were just about to get him!" said Aratus, who was wrestling with Kar-Tyr.

Kar-Tyr lifted Aratus up and twirled him in the air. "Next time, little Aratus," he smiled. "Next time."

After they said their good-byes, Sinbad unraveled the scroll and studied the map. By the looks of it, this quest was going to a treacherous one. Already their journey had been long, but Sinbad felt like it was only the beginning. There was absolutely no doubt this trek will be dangerous. But now they have guidance, they're focused, and Allah willing, their mission will be completed. And the rule of the usurper Akhdar will be nothing more than a wretched memory.

CHAPTER NINETEEN
THINK OF GOING OUT BEFORE YOU ENTER

Over shadowy spires and gleaming towers lay the ghostly darkness and silence that runs before dawn. Into a dim alley, one of an authentic labyrinth of mysterious winding ways, Sinbad, accompanied by Kar-Tyr and Qani entered the gloomy cavern.

A shiver ran down Sinbad's spine as he explored the dark ominous cave. The gloom reminded him of a tale he heard from the Greek islands about a young adventurer named Perseus. His mind was set at the part of the story where the lost prince of Argos led a small number of men to the lair of the all-knowing Stygian witches, who held the knowledge on how to slay the monstrous kraken so Perseus could save the beautiful princess Andromeda from the wrath of the vengeful goddess Thetis.

Now Sinbad was cautious on every step he took. He couldn't take the chance to be taken off guard. The caverns of Mars were foreign to him. Unlike what he was used to back on Earth. Luckily for him, he had two locals to guide him through such dark territory.

Kar-Tyr also took no joy in this. His gorilla-like bottom feet gripped the stony earth anxiously. He felt suffocated as Qani walked too closely to him. He couldn't dare share his troublesome feelings with a fellow warrior—and in this case a woman.

Her face was filled with confidence. She wasn't threatened by the lack of light, or the cold breeze that breathed through from where they had entered the cave. She had been exploring caves as early as she could walk. Qani knew it would be essential to her life as a rebel and an enemy of the state if she could familiarize herself with such dismal surroundings when she would go into hiding.

Despite Sinbad's own capabilities, she found it at best if he should let her hold the map and lead the expedition. But after hearing Ostath's words, Sinbad felt he was destined to take charge. Qani felt it was the least he could do. She even let him fly the airship for Daizha's sakes. No matter how many times she tried to give Sinbad a hint, the Earthman wouldn't share the map.

The great book says Beware! Verily there is a piece of flesh in the body of man, which when good, the whole body is good; and when bad, the whole body is bad, and that is the heart.

This passage was running through Sinbad's mind when he, Kar-Tyr, and Qani entered the caverns. Kar-Tyr brought up the rear and checked if they were being followed or being spied on. Sinbad led the party down the dark and damp cave, checking the map the Shondi had given him. Qani looked over his shoulder to see if he was reading it right. Sinbad caught her a few times and quickly blocked her view. They came to the end of their route and were face with three tunnels, leading into different directions. However, fallen rocks have sealed off the last one on the right. It was clear they wouldn't be able to take that way.

Sinbad checked the map. "I have not seen such a labyrinth since the winds blew me through the lair of the Iblis."

Qani looked confused. She clearly had no idea what he was talking about. She briefly scanned the map, but couldn't see over Sinbad's shadow. She put her hands on her hips, and waited for Sinbad to pick a tunnel. The Earthman hesitated and began to track back through the path.

"Which way, Sinbad?" she asked impatiently. "It's not that hard. It's either the first or second tunnel."

"It does not say, Qani," Sinbad replied. "The map shows only one tunnel, but I cannot tell which one."

Along its labyrinth ways he went with the certainly of familiarity. It was indeed a maze of dark alleys and enclosed courts and devious ways; of secretive sounds, and stenches.

There was no paving on the streets; mud and filth mingled in an unsavory mess.

Qani rolled her eyes and stuck her thumb out to the second cave. Sinbad rolled up the map and signaled for Kar-Tyr to follow.

"Choices are the hinges of destiny," Sinbad nodded in agreement, and his companions began groping their way at random down the dark passageway.

They were following no marked trail, but dipping down to ravines so deep the sun never struck bottom, laboring up steep slopes where loose shale threatened to slide from beneath their feet, and following knife edge with blue-hazed echoing depths on either hand.

The further they walked; the walls became narrow and constricting. Qani had difficulty getting through the taut rocks. Kar-Tyr did not like this at all. He added extremely tight spaces to his list of the many things he despised. This even topped his fear of flying.

"What is said about the road not taken?" he asked Sinbad, holding his breath while squeezing in through a compact spot.

"Or the shortest distance squeezed between two points?" Sinbad replied to Kar-Tyr.

Qani turned around and raised a finger to her lips, and shushed her two complaining comrades. "I didn't realize I was travelling with old women," she said, finally making it out of the tight walkway and found a light at the end of huge corridor.

"Ye of little faith," Sinbad remarked, helping Kar-Tyr out of the tunnel.

Sinbad followed Qani to the light while Kar-Tyr, emerging from the narrow hallway, stood up and stretched his heavy arms, enormous in the despair of the cavern. The cracking of his bones and ligaments echoed throughout the cavern. When they reached the other side, Sinbad immediately frowned. They were on a ledge on top of a very high cliff. He looked down to see a river with dock on that connected to a several stairways from the other tunnel. There were two longboats tied to the dock, he also saw several flying gargoyles soaring around the cavern.

"Congratulations, Qani," Sinbad growled, "you led us to a *dead end*."

"How is this my fault?" she rapidly defended herself. "Don't blame me that you don't know how to read a map. However did you become a sailor in the first place?"

"Even a blind camel could see this coming," Sinbad's voice reverberated through the great shadowy cavern. "And I navigate by the stars."

"I didn't see you taking the lead of a sailor through the labyrinth of Iblis."

Sinbad's blood was up, and since he had come so far, and overcame so much peril, he was determined to go through to the grim finish of the adventure, where and whatever that might be.

Kar-Tyr's feet clacked on the red stone ledge, and broke up the fight between his friends. "Does this blind camel fly?" he asked them.

They needed to improvise on how to get down to the docks. There was no way Kar-Tyr was going through that tight passageway ever again.

Sinbad was not a man who throws his fate to the wind. He created his own destiny. But there were times when the totems hewn from ancient wisdom made destiny easier to achieve. Be they a gift bestowed by the king of Java or a simple turban of Kolhapuri cloth.

"Wait," Sinbad said, looking down at the docks, "I have an idea."

He took off his turban and collected the golden medallion he put there for safekeeping. He put the chain around his neck and began to untie the knots in his turban. Kar-Tyr and Qani looked at each other in bafflement. Not knowing what the Earthman had up his sleeve. Sinbad straightened the cloth until it was in its full length.

"Kar, would you mind if I borrow your weapon?" Sinbad asked the centaur.

Kar-Tyr was uncertain at first, but he was pushed into it by Qani's constant nudging her elbow to his ribs. Kar-Tyr reached for his kunai on his belt and gave it to Sinbad.

The outlander smiled and took it from Kar-Tyr's bulky grey hand. "Thank you, my friend."

Sinbad tied a knot around the handle of Kar-Tyr's kunai with the long cloth. Then he wrapped the rope around a rock, and checked the distance from the ledge to all the way to the dock.

"Here we are!" Sinbad said, revealing a way out.

Kar-Tyr cringed at the sight of it. "I don't think it would bear my weight, Sinbad," he said, showing his size. "The rope will break."

"You're not going first, Kar," Sinbad said, pointing to Qani. "*She* is."

"What?" Qani yelped. "I am not going down that thing."

"You have to, Qani," Sinbad replied. "Out of all of us you're the lightest."

"This is insane, Sinbad. Why don't we just go back the way we came and go through the other tunnel?"

Kar-Tyr stepped back and waved his hands. "Unacceptable!" He yelled.

After much coercing, Sinbad was able to persuade Qani to wrap the long fabric around her slender waist. She was the edge of the cliff and Sinbad gave her an assuring smile.

"You have no reason to worry," said Sinbad, trying to comfort her.

"Easy for you to say," Qani grumbled. "You're not dangling like a worm on a hook."

Sinbad ignored that last remark. "If you reach any trouble, Kar and I will pull you back up."

Kar-Tyr positioned himself behind Sinbad and took hold of the rope. He gave Qani a promising look and a thumbs up.

"Are you ready, Qani?" asked Sinbad.

"No," Qani replied soundlessly.

"Here we go," signaled Sinbad, as Qani began to carefully climb down the overhang.

Qani gripped the rope and crooking a knee about it, began the descent. The unpremeditated rope swayed and turned on itself, but the Thulian woman was not hindered.

Down and down she went, silently, the images of her comrades grew further and further away. She put one foot under the other and held on to the cloth with all her might. She reached the point where there wasn't more footing and she hung in the air.

"Is it long enough?" She heard Kar-Tyr ask Sinbad.

"Enough to reach the end of its length," Sinbad answered, making Qani feel uneasy. "Beyond that and the river, only Allah knows."

She tried to pull on the rope, but as she did, she felt her foot slip again. It was ripping the skin on her knuckles. Then her feet slipped completely out of the crack. Her fist held for a moment, then ripped free as well.

She held on to the cloth-made rope, still slack in her other hand, and struggled to squelch the cry of alarm trying to claw its way out of her throat.

The rope went tight, almost ripping itself from her hand. She flailed with her now-free right hand, and grabbed the rope with it as well. She slammed into the wall, hung there, spinning in the darkness.

It was a strain to hold on, but after a minute or so she caught her breath and was able to slip her toes through the loop as well.

The fabric stretched as far as it could. Qani got caught up on watching the thick sheet expand she lost her grip and fell right into the water. Sinbad and Kar-Tyr raced to the edge to see if Qani was all right.

"Qani!" Sinbad exclaimed. "Qani! Can you hear me?"

Sinbad saw something emerging from the water. Qani quickly reached the surface and gave out a loud gasp for air. The cavern was filled with her laughter.

"That was fun!" she shouted back up at them. Kar-Tyr gave out a sigh of relief, and Sinbad smiled down at her. "You should try it. The water's great!"

Sinbad followed suit and joined Qani in the water. Kar-Tyr nervously shimmied down the rope and undone the grapple to his kunai and fell in the water. As the three friends reunited they swam to the docks, and took one of the longboats. Sinbad felt good to be back on the water. Sea salt ran through his veins and there he can best master the ebb and flow of what the sea would provide.

They took the gondola through the mysterious stream, like Charon the ferryman escorting souls through the river Styx. Sinbad's eyes probed the murky waters, looking for any surprises along the way. But he only saw the rushing current. Qani steered the small boat with the very long oar. It churned the water slowly.

Sinbad had his nose stuck on the map, while Qani wringed her hair dry. The gondola wobbled awkwardly. She gripped the shaking oar with both hands. Out of the corner of her eye, she could have sworn something was swimming their way. She briefly shrugged it off, but the very sight of it took her back. Along to the rapid vibrations of Kar-Tyr's startled jumping. He would be glad when they were back on dry land again.

"Oh, no," Qani said in fright.

Kar-Tyr looked at the abyss that it had a growing shadow. His jaw dropped and he shouted, "Hold on!"

Sinbad felt he was left out on a private joke. But the looks on his friends' faces made it clear there was nothing funny about what was going to come.

"Hold on for what?" Sinbad asked, when a sudden spray of water struck behind the back of his neck as an unseen force surged out of the water behind him.

A huge sea serpent jumped out of the water and knocked the boat over. The three adventurers flew off and landed in the water. The monster was ferocious and it looked like it could swallow the boat whole in one big monstrous chomp.

Sinbad didn't even have enough time to fill his lungs before he suddenly found himself in the deepest part of the river. Air bubbled from his lips and nostrils as he fought to hold on to whatever air he had left.

Sinbad knew too often the sea was a cruel and fickle mistress. He was reminded of an old story told to him by an old Bedouin about a man who ended up in the belly of a leviathan. He did not choose the path. Sinbad unsheathed his sword and swam down to the depths of the river and faced the monster head on.

The creature was in its domain now, where its strength was supreme. The gargantuan monster's malevolent countenance leered at Sinbad triumphantly. Long pieces of seaweed were stuck between its piranha-like teeth.

Watching him.

It could strike at any moment, crush him in its great jaws, and swallow him whole.

It did not.

It just watched him.

The water was cold as he pushed himself upright. He reached into the water and grabbed his sword.

He kicked his legs through the water, as if he were churning butter.

His muscles were getting tired.

He was in dire need of oxygen to soothe them.

The beast snarled at him as Sinbad swam quickly and slashed the serpent at the side of its mouth. As with most creatures of the sea, this monster must have a blind spot. Then it was a simple matter of striking quick and decisively. Blood swarmed through the water, while the serpent turned around and charged at Sinbad.

Sinbad's cheeks bulged. His lungs screamed for air. His vision dimmed as he felt his life ebbing away. He reached down deep inside for the strength to fight back.

The sailor readied himself for the next assault, but the water was filled with a warm, white blinding light.

The laser blast went through the monster's head and the beast sunk down to the blackened depths to its doom. Sinbad looked to his right to see Qani swimming above him with her laser rifle in her hand. Now Sinbad owed her another life debt. This world and its people never ceased to amaze him.

CHAPTER TWENTY
THE HOUSE OF DANGER IS BUILT UPON THE BORDERS OF SAFETY

The raft was kindling from the battle with the sea monster. The only option Sinbad and his crew were to continue their journey over land. They reached the shore and exited the broken gondola.

Sinbad looked over to the hills to discover very thick smoke rising up to the heavens.

"Look over there!" he said to his comrades. "If there's smoke, there must be people."

Kar-Tyr crossed his arms. "And we don't know whether or not if they're friendly."

Qani flashed a quick smile. "Only one way to find out, boys," she said, as she led the way.

Kar-Tyr didn't move a single step. It seemed if something agitated him. Sinbad and Qani stopped where they were and noticed their friend's worrisome expression.

"Kar, what's wrong?" asked Sinbad.

"The Mons of M'Aragk," he replied, with a very soft tremble in his voice. "I've heard stories."

"Just stories, Kar-Tyr," Qani giggled. "Told by Azurian mothers to keep children from misbehaving."

"Well, that's what they said about the serpent you killed a while ago."

Sinbad cleared his throat. "If you truly feel about this, Kar-Tyr, maybe you should stay here and keep guard. Qani and I can complete the mission without you."

Kar-Tyr hesitated, looking to find the right words to convince his friends he wasn't afraid. He briefly looked at Qani who was trying to hold back from laughing. But the lowering of her eyes was a dead giveaway, and Sinbad waited patiently for the Kurwani's reply.

Before Kar-Tyr could answer, he heard the rapid fluttering of a bird from behind him. He let out a small yelp that humiliated him when he turned around to see his friends laughing at him.

"Maybe it is better if you come with us, Kar," said Qani, covering her mouth in order to hide her giddy smile.

"I will take that under consideration, Qani," Kar-Tyr retorted. "In case if you and Sinbad get into trouble."

"Yeah, I bet," she taunted him.

Sinbad smiled in amusement. "Now, if you two are through we should get going," he unsheathed his sword and began to walk through the path. "I will take point. Qani, you're behind me. Kar-Tyr, you bring up the rear and watch our backs."

As they went into the trenches, they discovered many cobwebs that filled the cavern. It looked like nobody has ever visited this part of the cave in years. Qani was impressed by the grandeur of the webs. It was as if someone had taken a lot of time to put this together. It reminded her of a ceremonial reception she attended when she was a little girl. The gossamer webs were indeed quite beautiful, but it was all gloomy and gothic. She could feel her skin crawl as she kept moving further and further into the ghostly dominion.

Sinbad led on, using his scimitar to slice his way through. He felt like he was on safari through the jungle. Ever since he arrived on Mars, he didn't see one single tree or any green fields whatsoever. Nothing but red dry land.

"How can you be so calm, Sinbad?" asked Kar-Tyr. "It feels like the ceiling is getting lower on each step we take."

"This is nothing compared when I was on a quest for the Fountain of Destiny," answered Sinbad, keeping the sword in front of him and kept a sturdy vigil of his surroundings.

"What is this fountain?" asked Qani.

Sinbad took a deep breath. "The legend stated that whoever should find the fountain would receive youth, a shield of darkness, and a crown of untold riches."

"I wish that fountain was nearby," said Kar-Tyr, wiping his brow. "Especially, the part about the shield of darkness."

Several quick images of the final battle with Koura the magician flashed through Sinbad's mind. Koura drank from the fountain's waters and he was rejuvenated and he was awarded the cloak of darkness—the power to become invisible at will. Sinbad's duel with him was a very strenuous one. He had to rely on his wits to finally vanquish the dark magician.

"Everything is not always what they seem, Kar-Tyr," said Sinbad.

He paused for a moment, and could have sworn he had heard something scuttling about around his party.

"What is it, Sinbad?" asked Qani, picking silk webs out of her hair.

"Did you just hear something?" he asked, giving the cavern a once over.

"No, I didn't," she replied. "What about you, Kar-Tyr?"

The Kurwani man looked behind him and listened closely. "Nothing at my side. You must have imagined it, Sinbad. These old caves and the total lack of light can play tricks on your eyes."

"That may be so, but I'm not taking any chances," replied Sinbad. "Be careful, my friends. Something tells me we are not alone."

Kar-Tyr pulled down the webs from his face and continually to look over his shoulder. Sweat protruded from his huge brow, and he started to have heavy doubts about this expedition

"This was a mistake," he confessed, taking a very loud gulp. Then several webs tangled him and it was very frustrating on getting them off. "This muck costs us any tactical advantage."

Sinbad cut through a few more webs and faced Kar-Tyr. "There is no reward without risk, Kar-Tyr."

"Then how about the higher the risk, the bigger the payoff? We are risking too much, Sinbad."

Out of the corner of Qani's eye, she saw several yellow flickering lights all around them.

"Sinbad," she said, looking around the cavern, "looks like someone lit these candles. We must be getting close."

Sinbad studied the glow carefully. The flames of the supposed candles didn't sway into the air and he couldn't smell anything burning.

"Those aren't candles."

Then he felt something snare his left arm with this quick wet sound that whisked through the air. Then several more whipped through wrapping some strange rope around Kar-Tyr and Qani's arms.

The yellow lights grew larger and larger, as the sound of many feet scurrying around them. Then several hisses and screeches filled the cavern. Qani's face lit up with horror, and Sinbad held his sword ready with his one free hand.

A horde of giant spiders descended down and surrounded them with their numerous yellow eyes glaring at them with hunger. The tips of their legs were pointy and resembled small daggers. They rounded up their intruders with their very strong silk web lariats from their spinnerets. They tagged on their preys' limbs very tightly, but the captives put up quite a struggle.

Waiting for the unwary, waiting for their prey, waiting for the chance to trap and cocoon the intruders and drain them dry. Unfortunately nothing seemed to be cooperating. No flies or insects of any kind were presenting themselves as a bountiful meal, and the creatures were going mad with hunger.

Kar-Tyr gave Qani a dirty look. "Do *these* look like your mother's tales, Qani?"

"Shut up, Kar-Tyr," she grumbled, reaching for her plasma gun in the holster on her right thigh.

"Where ye are, death will find you," said Sinbad, "even if ye are in towers, built up strong and tall."

Qani gave the Earthman a puzzled look. "What?"

"Take them down, *now*!"

Sinbad pulled himself free from the web, while his comrades followed suit.

Kar-Tyr bashed one spider's head into its body with his massive fist. Then he lashed out his kunai spear and wrapped it around an incoming spider's neck, pulling it down with a tremendous tug and sent it crashing into the ground. The creature tried to get up, but Kar-Tyr pulled the lariat taut and snapped the damned thing's neck.

"I got two down! How about you?"

"Working on it!" said Qani, delivering a spin kick across an arachnid's head, and then stomped its brains in.

This is where all the training finally paid off. All the morning rituals, weapons practice, and total concentration. She wasn't fighting against shadows or imaginary enemies anymore. This was real and she couldn't afford to make a mistake. If she lost focus—even for a moment—she could die. Not only had she had to protect herself, but also her friends as well. Not that they needed it. Kar-Tyr was doing fine by himself. He felt right at home whipping his signature weapon around. Sometimes he just felt he was back in the arena, going up against one of Akhdar's vicious beasts.

Sinbad was hacking one spider after another. Never flinching or showing any signs of squeamishness from all the blood and gore. He swung his sword over his head and split the spider in front of him in two. Green blood dripped from his blade, and spun around to cut the one behind him in half. However, after each of them had killed one spider two more would take its place.

The bright white blast from Qani's plasma gun distracted Sinbad while a spider pounced in front of him. It was the largest of them all. It tended to stay away from the others, daunted by the disparity in size. While the others moved in leisurely groups, clumps of mandibles and black furred abdomens.

The creature pinned him to the ground and thrust its head forward, with its mandibles clicking rapidly in Sinbad's face.

The Earthman tried to push the eight-legged beast away from him, but it was so heavy. The more Sinbad resisted, the closer the spider would get to gnawing his face off.

Sinbad gritted his teeth and started to feel the strength in his arms go. "Allah, give me strength!" He pleaded; digging his fingers into the spider's sides, hoping it would hurt the beast and would grant him a window of opportunity to throw it off his chest. But it was to no avail.

He was drawn heavily to those horrible yellow eyes. It was as if the creature was hypnotizing him. Bending him to the monster's will. Telling him that resistance was futile. That he pulled up a great fight, but now it was time to claim his final reward.

The spider had lost its mind.

It wasn't as if it had a large mind to begin with, but hunger had overridden its desire for caution. Feasting was all it could think of, and continued on its hunt.

The huge spider approached its trapped prey. Its fangs were dripping in anticipation of a long-overdue meal, but still cautious. It was impossible to know if it was thinking about its pack mates that this interloper in their caves, this soft, two legged thing with a sword had already killed, or if it even possessed the capacity to remember them. But same instinct told it that this helpless-looking creature, which was staring right back at the spider, might still be a danger.

Kar-Tyr saw the horrific sight, while he was grappling with a spider of his own. Sinbad reached his fingers to his captor's head, and with his thumbs he gouged the eyes at the side. The spider let out a terrible shriek. It bucked up, leaving Sinbad little room to crawl out from underneath the monster.

"Sinbad!" cried Kar-Tyr from the other side of the cavern. "Heads up!"

With a mighty swing, Kar-Tyr hurled his web spinning opponent at Sinbad's foe. The two spiders crashed into each other and slammed against the wall. Sinbad quickly got back to his feet and reclaimed his sword to finish each of them off with single killing stroke.

Kar-Tyr picked up a dazed spider and ripped off its limbs one by one. "I should have mentioned that I hate bugs!" he said, as he threw the maimed creature down, took the two severed legs, and used them to impale the spider into two of its many large eyes.

Qani was blasting away, trying to scare the creatures away. However, the rapid gunfire only angered them. Sinbad saw a spider creeping up behind her using its spinnerets to lower itself gracefully down, closer to its prey. It began its last ditch effort to fill its belly, and lunged at Qani.

With lightning speed, Sinbad slew the accursed thing through its bulbous abdomen. Qani quickly glanced at what was going on and saw Sinbad smiled.

"There you go," he said, retracting his blade from the spider's body. "*Now* we're even."

"You *still* owe me, Sinbad," she replied.

"What are you talking about? There was the poison and the cliff."

"You forgot about the sea serpent."

Sinbad looked at her aghast. "You didn't save me. I was ready to slay it."

"With that little butter knife of yours?" she mocked. "I don't think so. I just did you a favor, Sinbad."

"We can argue later," snapped Sinbad. "Now shoot something!"

She gave him only half a smile and then returned shooting the monsters away. "These creatures are only protecting their home. *We* are the intruders."

"Then Allah will note their sacrifice and provide for them in the afterlife," Sinbad replied, after decapitating another spider's head.

There was only one spider left, and Kar-Tyr had it by the neck over a cliff. His powerful fingers were once again around an adversary's neck. This time he wasn't going to try to knock it unconscious. He was going to crush the monster's windpipe. He wondered if he held its neck too tightly the head would pop off like a daisy. Kar-Tyr could see the light of the spider's many eyes fade away.

Qani watched in terror. The battle was over and they already won. There was no further bloodshed necessary. But this encounter was too close a call. They were almost killed in this cave of unspeakable horrors. But what Kar-Tyr was doing was far too much she and Sinbad could possibly bear.

"Kar-Tyr—enough!" ordered Sinbad.

The Kurwani warrior began to loosen his grip around the arachnid's neck, and noticed the shallow breathing the creature was giving off. He let go of the surviving spider and it fell into a sudden drop onto the ground. The creature covetously breathed for air. Its stomach was moving in and out, in and out to indicate it was still alive, and it wasn't going to fight any time soon.

The hideous, black, hairy-legged monster, whose body shone like black onyx, limply scuttled into a crevice of the rocks and disappeared.

Kar-Tyr looked over to Sinbad, and a thought ran through his mind. "Of course, leave one alive to tell their kin."

"Hopefully, we would be long gone before they come here with bigger numbers," said Qani.

Sinbad removed his sash and cleansed his blade from all the green blood that soiled it. Then he wrapped the cloth around his waist and sheathed his sword. He let out a weary sigh.

"What is our plan now?" Qani asked him.

"Plan?" he replied in confusion. "Try not to be killed. That's a good plan."

CHAPTER TWENTY ONE
DO NOT STAND IN A DANGEROUS PLACE TRUSTING IN MIRACLES

In all of his travels Sinbad had seen many wondrous and horrible things. He had been to the end of the Earth and back. Lived by his wits and imposed his will by the sword. But this strange land…he was beginning to understand it wasn't so much unlike his home.

Sinbad led his friends down a winding path. All he could see was a bright light at end of the tunnel. The floor was green as the jade statue in Akhdar's throne room. Halfway through the tunnel, he turned to his friends and signaled for them to stop.

"Stay here," he said to them. Qani and Kar-Tyr nodded silently in response, as the fearless Earthman slowly proceeded alone to the other side of the tunnel.

He passed through the hall quickly enough, traversed the pointed ridges and approached the next chamber that let upon the gallery with uncertainty.

He could barely see now, but he noticed the distinct markings were carved in the stones at the corner of the building. His soft sandals allowed him to move along the bricks and cobbles in near silence. He paused periodically, straining his ears into the darkness, taller than his eyes.

The path followed a fold of rock, winding intermingling down from tier to tier, and Sinbad caught a glimpse of the ruin that had fallen.

The valley floor was still far below him when he reached a long and lofty ridge that led out from the slope like a natural causeway. He could trace ahead of him the trail he had to follow.

He found himself in the middle of this crude rocky balcony that overlooked to what seemed to be a hidden temple. Then he heard a few muffled footsteps. He stepped back into a doorway, looked into the gloom to his left, waiting for some sound or sight of their inevitable passage.

When the sound came, it was to his right, not one set of footsteps, but many.

Then the light of the torches.

Sinbad stepped as far back into the shadows of the doorway as he could, sliding down into a tight crouch to hide even his shape.

He saw the torches, the dark, rippling shapes of their robes, right in front of him, at least a dozen large men. They passed so close in front of Sinbad's hiding place that he could smell the rich incense on their clothing, the perfumed ceremonial oils in their hair. If one so much as turned a head in his direction, he was doomed.

But none did. He listened as their footsteps became more distant.

Sinbad poked his head over the rocks to discover thousands of people dressed in white ceremonial robes, and they were on their knees paying tribute to a giant jade statue of Kali.

The statue was the focus of the temple. It was the first thing anyone would see upon entering the subterranean place of worship. Its outlines and size slowly becoming visible in the reflected light from the many torches that brought illumination to the cavern. It was a godlike statue, beautiful jade, and it was on its knees. It appeared to be at least thirty or forty feet tall. The statue held two giant stalagmites in each of its hands. Sinbad discovered it had six arms.

That's the same statue from Akhdar's throne room, Sinbad thought. *Are they in league with him?*

Sinbad silently asked himself what is with that particular idol. Could it be their god Daizha, or some other holy deity? Something about that statue scared Sinbad. It was so lifelike and it was very well proportioned. Whoever sculpted this masterpiece must have taken a lifetime to complete.

The Kali rested on its knees with its first pair of arms rested on the floor. The other three pairs held onto the stalagmite arches, as if it was ready to break them off and use them in combat. In front of the statue was a stage and on it was a man wearing hood that concealed his identity. But the people on the floor knew him well, and got onto their knees and were ready to receive his gospel.

The temple was monochromatic, bleak, and forbidding. The dark ambiance Sinbad picked up from the place was not a good one as the hairs on the back of his neck rose to attention. It was quiet, like a very large mausoleum, and the air was stale, in need of freshening from the outside world. Too long, he imagined, this place had sealed itself off from the world above.

Sinbad silently motioned for his friends to come over to him. Kar-Tyr made sure his many feet didn't make a sound on the stone floor, and Qani was hugging the wall to hide herself from any spies.

Sinbad furtively eyed the holy ceremony. He, Kar-Tyr, and Qani were all crowded behind the stone rail of the mezzanine overlooking the grand floor of the temple. Looking away from the acolytes, Sinbad turned his attention back to the priest presiding over the ritual.

The crowd actually served Sinbad's needs. He wanted to scout around the temple discreetly, and having all eyes on the idol of the great Martian god was quite convenient.

Sinbad lowered his voice to nearly a whisper. "There are thousands—*thousands* of them. They pray to some idol." He looked over to the right side of the temple and pointed to what seemed to be monument. "If we can get to that monolith, maybe we can—"

"It's not a monolith," Qani interjected. "It's a ship—a *Thulian* ship. It is forbidden science." She closed her eyes for a brief second and quickly opened them with a sudden spark dancing around in her irises. "Listen, I've got a plan."

The hooded man raised his eyes from the leather-bound tome laid open on the pulpit before him. Sputtering torches and candles illuminated a cavernous temple deep beneath the avid desert sands. Shadows capered upon forbidding stone walls, into which were carved into graphic depictions of forgotten lore and theology. A black silk ribbon marked his place in the book.

He threw back the hood of the ebony cloak, revealing to be a member of the Thulian race with green skin and red eyes. His ceremonial robes appealed to instincts more intimidating than spiritual.

"Through the age of ignorance and the arrogance of the kingdom itself, the people cease to be the masters of their own fate: they have become the puppets of these alien forces!" said the priest, delivering his sermon to many of his followers. No such innovations came from the dozen or so acolytes standing on the stone steps between the priest and his cult.

"Praise Daizha!" his flock, a congregation of Thulian followers, answered him in unison. They bowed their heads, their assorted fingers folded together before them in prayer.

The people would have kept their distance from the statue, giving it wide berth and moving away as quickly as possible. Here, the Kali drew a crowd, all of whom were the worshippers of Daizha, some commoners, and some nobles.

They gathered quite close to the jade monolith, often less than thirty feet away. They all knelt and begged favors of Daizha, some for health, love, and safety. But more often for power, wealth, or harm to an enemy, requests Daizha was said to be most favorable to.

Before the priest could lead his people in prayer, something had caught his eye. A lone young Thulian woman was approaching the pulpit. The priest arched his eyebrow in curiosity. He had never seen this woman before in his life, and he doubted anyone else in this cult had either. It was clearly she wasn't one of them. She didn't wear the sacred trappings of the holy order. He found it quite offensive that she had entered this hallowed ground dressed as a harlot. Somehow he felt she was here so she could repent her sins and start her life anew. She wouldn't be the first, and he always welcomed outsiders if they should seek clemency.

The woman reached the front row of worshippers and stopped in front of the pulpit. She seemed a little embarrassed on interrupting their prayer. Her throat swelled with anxiety and cleared her throat.

"Excuse me," she began, still feeling unsure about this plan, "I don't mean to interrupt your little friendship circle, but I bring a message from the prophet!"

The priest's eyes widened in amazement. *How could this foolish girl know anything about the prophet?*

His ears were filled with the echoing murmur of his congregation. They all knew this day was going to arrive, but they didn't think it would be so soon. The faithful argued with the skeptics, while the priest helped the woman to get on the stage.

With an encouraging smile from the priest, Qani continued. "The umm, great and mighty Sinbad bids you, umm…"

She felt all this sounded much better in her head, but she didn't have enough time to prepare. She closed her eyes and pictured the flock as her group of rebels. Suddenly she felt she was back in her comfort zone and was ready to follow through with her plan.

With a burst of confidence she found reason to continue. "He calls upon you to pave the way for his coming! He shall return the empire to its glorious past and boundless future!"

The congregation cheered and raised their arms in salvation. Smiles stretched their smooth green faces, and tears of joy dripped down their cheeks. All they have been hoping and praying for has led up to this.

"He knows the sacrifices you've made!" Qani persisted with more poise in her voice. "He shall set free the forbidden knowledge that will bring us back to glory. You must go home and prepare because he will be here sooner than you think."

Many of the worshippers have taken heed to Qani's words. They all rose up and began walking back to their homes to prepare for the coming of their savior. The one that would lead them into freedom and a better life.

Qani just hoped that it gave Sinbad and Kar-Tyr enough time to make their move. Because she had no idea how long she was going to keep up this charade.

Back from the green-stoned mezzanine, Sinbad and Kar-Tyr watched as all the members of the cult left the area. Nothing was going to be in their way to the ship.

"Whatever she said, it certainly cleared the way," said Kar-Tyr.

Sinbad looked at him with caution. "Don't expect it to be that easy."

"It's always isn't."

They both began their silent descent down to the temple floor. Sinbad kept ever so vigilant on whether or not all the worshippers had left the region. Kar-Tyr's three-toed feet barely managed to get to the ground. He was holding to the side of the wall very tightly until he was able to gain his balance.

When they were about to make their move to the ship, Kar-Tyr noticed Sinbad's turban was giving off some kind of heavenly glow. A golden aura shone through the very fabric, and Sinbad could feel its tantalizing heat.

Kar-Tyr pointed the unnatural sight to Sinbad with fear. "Your headdress—it glows!"

Sinbad's eyes widened with enchantment. "It is a harbinger of destiny," he explained, removing the turban to see the golden medallion he had kept secret to everyone else.

The mystic charm was glowing like the sun itself. Kar-Tyr took a step back, dreading the talisman would burst into flames. Sinbad reached into the turban and pulled out the bright object. Kar-Tyr winced by the sight of it, fretting it would burn his friend's hand. But the eerie radiance didn't char Sinbad's flesh. Not even when he put it around his neck.

"And I accept it as my own fate as well," he said, tying the medallion around his neck and donning his turban.

"Sinbad of Earth!" boomed a voice behind him.

He and Kar-Tyr whipped their heads around to discover the priest holding Qani by her hair, and there was a laser pistol in his hand. It was a frightening fact that caused Sinbad little alarm. Qani struggled violently to get free, but the more she fought the tighter the priest grip on her became. She squealed and kicked her feet in the air as he held his arm around her throat.

The unholy man was stronger than he looked. She felt that he could tear her scalp very easily. Behind them was small squad of his followers equipped with combat gear and armed with plasma rifles.

"False prophet!" the priest called out. "Outlander! Show yourself!"

Knowing they were outnumbered, there wasn't much for both Kar-Tyr and Sinbad to do than to admit defeat. They both raised their arms to the sky in a bitter surrender.

"Preacher," Sinbad began, keeping a close eye on Qani, "you are obviously a man of strong belief."

Distracted by Sinbad's plea, the priest found himself the victim of sneak counterattack where Qani flipped him over to the ground and grabbed the man's gun in midair.

"He believes in nothing, Sinbad," she said, placing him in a headlock and held him at gunpoint. "Just another Thulian demagogue preying on fear and ignorance."

Sinbad and Kar-Tyr ran toward them and faced down the security squad. Qani gave Kar-Tyr a spare laser pistol, while Sinbad drew his sword.

The squad raised their weapons at the interlopers, as Qani pressed the barrel of the gun against the priest round face.

"And what are you, child?" the priest gasped. "Some Azurian lover? Or are you some sort of misguided libertine? I serve the greater good—for all of Mars!"

Then a loud rumble shook the musty old temple. The vibrations gave off very fierce tremors to the very ground they were standing on. Everyone searched where the origin of where the seismic activity was coming from. At first, Kar-Tyr dreaded it was a horde of very angry giant spiders out to avenge the deaths of their brethren. But no spider, or an enormous group of spiders would cause this much trouble.

Sinbad, quite suddenly, had a very bad feeling about what was going to happen next.

He heard creaking sounds all round them. The priest's militia glanced about nervously.

The priest had the distinct pleasure of seeing Qani's jaw drop wide open.

He gave his female captor a very cruel smile. "You do nothing but anger the gods."

As Sinbad came forward, his eyes fixated on the motionless idol, the eyes of the thing opened suddenly! The outlander froze in his tracks. It was no image—it was a living thing!

That he did not instantly explode in a burst of murderous frenzy is a fact that measures his horror, which paralyzed him where he stood. A rational man in his position would have sought doubtful refuge in the conclusion that he was insane; it did not occur to Sinbad to doubt his senses. He knew he was face to face with a golem, and the realization robbed him of all his faculties except sight.

Sinbad gave a heaving sigh and rolled his eyes in revulsion.

"How did I know this was going to happen?" he said in disgust.

The six-armed chartreuse statue was climbing to its feet. Rising higher and higher above them. Stone cracked as it stood, like stiff, atrophied muscles angry at being forced into use again. It stood upright again, nearly fifty feet tall and surveyed the temple.

The thing looked limber enough as it strode down from its original position and in one smooth motion, bent at the waist, reached for, and uprooted the stalagmite arches with its first set of arms, and then slashed them at its enemies as if they were swords.

Its eyes settled on Sinbad. The head froze in place.

The giant Kali statue took its first step, and was now eye-to-eye with the intruders.

Sinbad thought a retreat was in order.

Then he heard the crack of stone echoed throughout the temple.

"What in Allah's name?" he said, stepping backwards.

The two legs strode right for him, the temple thundering with each step.

The Kali swung at Sinbad, who at the last possible second, ducked out of the way.

Qani released the mad priest in order to dodge the possessed statue's attack. The stone weapon came crashing down where she previously stood. The shock of the impact sent Sinbad off his feet. Kar-Tyr bucked up into the air, and struggled for his equilibrium.

Qani flung herself sideways out of the way, drawing her laser pistol, targeting the living statue, and firing as she fell. The plasma pulses hardly made a dent on the Kali's face.

The quake rocked the temple, while the ceiling began to cave in with debris falling all around them. People were trying to get as far away from the bizarre creature that was tearing through the hidden temple, with no other priority other than to create destruction. No one was paying attention to anyone else. Fear had affected them greatly, where they all had abandoned their concerns for their fellow man.

The jade Kali let out a roar that thundered all over the temple. Sinbad responded in kind, his eyes flared in recognition upon confronting the living monolith.

"Kill them!" the priest commanded, laughing madly at this ghastly sight. "Kill all those who would usurp your forbidden knowledge!"

Kar-Tyr and Qani began to fire at the statue's legs. Hoping they would be able to cripple it, so they could get an advantage over the green monstrosity. But to their dismay, the only thing they had accomplished was making it angrier. Sinbad watched the Kali carefully. Noticing the way it moved, fought, and thought. He had fought people and creatures that were bigger and stronger than he was, and succeeded.

He thought of what the priest had called him—a false prophet. Sinbad knew he was no such thing. He brought no enlightenment. He didn't offer any comfort. He only obeyed to the will of Allah. He was merely His tool. He was His sword. His hammer. And he shall open the way for His love. If this was the prophecy, then he is the prophet. But not the one the Azurians had prayed for.

Sinbad watched when the Kali placed its hand on the ground in an attempt to swat him like a fly. He zigzagged his way over collapsed chunks of masonry from the gallery above.

A fallen column, as thick around as a mighty oak tree, lay in his path. It was too high to jump, and much too thick to cut with his sword. He leaped down, onto the floor of the temple.

He made a mad dash and jumped onto the back of his gigantic hand, and then proceeded to climb up its arm like an ant on a tree. With his sword in the air, he leaped off the limb and cling onto the Kali's chest.

The priest laughed at Sinbad's ridiculous attempt. The false prophet was more foolish than he thought. He was saving the Kali a lot of trouble on trying to kill him.

"Ha-ha! You're a fool, outlander!" he cackled, as he watched the onslaught with childlike glee. "You will now feel the wrath of true power!"

As he climbed up the jade Kali, Sinbad was reminded of a song he once heard in the great Caliph's court. It was about a street rat that tamed a mighty djinn. He appealed to its vanity and its unquenched thirst for freedom. If such miracles happen on Earth, can they not happen here?

As the tentmaker once said, "The entire world shall be populous with that action which saves one soul from despair."

He looked up to the green giant and tried to talk some sense into it. "God of the red planet! Hear the words of a simple sailor. The people of this world do not need your jade fists in anger, but your compassion."

Down below on the floor, Kar-Tyr and Qani were still at work on trying to take out its legs. They tried their best to keep shooting at the same exact same spot. They figured the more they kept hitting it, the more the statue's legs would wear down.

Kar-Tyr fired another round into the Kali's shin. "We are barely scratching its surface!" he said to Qani, as he stepped away from the monolith's giant foot.

"Don't stop!" Qani replied, finally managing to get the stone to crackle. "We're almost there! Keep firing!"

Sinbad gave the Kali a soulful glance, trying to find any human reaction on the idol's face. But it was frozen on the same expression its creator had carved into its visage.

"I obviously don't have the words of a poet or the nature of a sultan," he said, scaling up to its shoulder. "Maybe you shall heed the force of a man. You are *no* god," he commented, feeling outraged on this abomination of all creation. "And like all pretenders Allah shall strike you down."

The Kali didn't show any stage of emotion. It wasn't truly alive. There was no spirit using this idol as a vessel. It was merely an automaton. No thoughts, feelings, remorse, and especially, not even a soul. It was only designed for one thing: to instill fear to the hearts of the unbelievers who wouldn't follow this cult's religion. And to punish those who would dare challenge its authority.

Kar-Tyr threw his pistol in frustration. "It's not working!" Then he reached for his kunai on his belt. "What we need is a change of tactics."

"What are you doing?" Qani asked, taking cover from the Kali's responding attack.

Kar-Tyr straightened his lariat and whipped it around the Kali's crackling femur. "My ancestors have a saying. The bigger they come, the harder they fall!"

"Daizha, help us!" Qani knew where this was going. She had to warn Sinbad. "Sinbad! Get off that thing right now!"

Sinbad heard Qani's warning, but there wasn't enough time for him to get to safety. He saw Kar-Tyr's kunai went taut around the Kali's right leg. The centaur pulled with all his might to send the living stone warrior face down to the ground. Sinbad scuttled around its neck and braced for impact, as the murderous jade statue shattered like a vinyl figurine.

CHAPTER TWENTY TWO
A LITTLE BODY DOTH OFTEN HARBOR A GREAT SOUL

The whole temple shook. Dust fell from the ceiling.

The priest watched in horror as his beloved holy idol went to pieces before him. Tears gushed like rapid streams down his cheeks, and he clenched his fists in rage.

"How dare you!" he cried in anguish. "Do you realize what you've done? A pox on your house, outlander! To you and your friends!"

Watching as Sinbad rose from the wreckage unscathed, still holding his sword in a very intimidating demeanor. The priest thought it was time for a hasty retreat.

"You shall rue this day, Sinbad of Earth!"

Kar-Tyr came to Sinbad's side. "Are you all right?"

"Yes, I am, my friend," Sinbad replied, giving out a quick sigh of relief. "Let's not do that again."

Then he heard the terrifying high pitch hum of plasma rifles being locked and loaded.

Sinbad slowly got up and discovered the mad priest's small militia group had surrounded him, Qani, and Kar-Tyr. A squad of four soldiers trained their guns on them at all flanks. None of them moved a muscle nor show any expression.

Sinbad looked at his two companions to see if either of them had any plans.

But sadly there isn't much left to do than to surrender.

Sinbad nodded to his comrades and they all lowered their weapons, dropping them to the ground. The soldiers began to close in, until the ground began to rumble.

"I heard your words, sailor," said a voice from the broken statue.

The militia commander turned around and aimed his gun into the unknown. The rest of his squad took a cue from this and also readied their weapons.

"They gave me strength to escape my prison," the voice added. It was soft, like a child. But it had a dignified tone, as if it belonged to a philosopher.

Out of the shattered jade skull came small Thulian child, wearing the royal robes of the Dozhakian Empire. The strangest part of all was, this boy wasn't walking—he was levitating through the air.

Sinbad was surprised that the prophet Ostath spoke of was so young. Muqari Dadgar might have been in his early teen years, but he was performing magical feats as if he were a well-seasoned arch mage. Sinbad had never seen such a powerful being of this size and caliber since the boy genie Barani, who was in the service of the dark magician Sokurah.

Muqari didn't even bat a single eyelash on subduing the attackers. With a casual wave of his tiny green hand, he yanked the plasma rifles from each of the soldiers' hands with just a mere thought.

They were all awestruck by the extraordinary sight of witnessing their own guns simply floating in front of them. Muqari focused carefully on all the weapons. With a slight jerk he turned the guns around on them and aimed straight for their heads.

He wanted to pull all the triggers and sent them all to Hell.

But he knew deep inside if he would go through with such a cold-blooded thing, he would be just like his wicked cousin Akhdar.

Cold.

Ruthless.

Unmerciful.

Evil.

With a flick of his wrist Muqari disassembled the rifles with his mind.

The pieces began to fly around in the air, and they were circling around each of the terrified soldiers. They all moved back in alarm, but they never let the mystic flowing debris out of their sight.

Then the parts came to a complete stop in front of them, and then they came falling down into a one neat pile on the floor.

The soldiers stared at the levitating lost prince, while being drenched in sweat. They were all waiting for his next move.

"You should be running," Muqari warned them.

Without any delay, the humiliated militia soldiers cowardly fled to join the priest, and begged Almighty Daizha to protect them.

Realizing they were in the clear, Sinbad and his friends collected their discard weapons. Sinbad was reminded of a proverb from his country, which stated, "A little body doth often a great soul." Muqari did not disappoint. He has all this power and he could easily kill those soldiers with a blink of an eye, but this young man had the self-discipline of a saint.

Kar-Tyr dropped his kunai in terror as the Muqari was making his way towards him. The frightened Kurwani warrior stared at the ascending child with an appalling familiarity. Qani shared her companion's feelings, but she was glad. Sinbad still remained wary of this little sorcerer.

The child looked at him with kindness in his eyes. "I see life in all things. And all things are connected. Both tangible and invisible."

"Do you mind explaining who you are?" Sinbad asked the strange flying child.

Qani nudged the Earthman in the ribs, and had an expression that was a mix of anger and anxiousness.

"He needs no introduction," she hissed at him, and then knelt before the boy, "he's Prince Muqari—the *rightful* heir to the Dozhakian throne."

Sinbad's eyes widened in discovery. "You're Akhdar's cousin?"

Prince Muqari somberly nodded his head in response and lowered himself onto the ground. He went over to Qani and placed his hand on her shoulder.

"Rise, milady," he said, helping Qani to her feet. He raised his head to look at Sinbad's puzzled face. "Unfortunately yes, sailor. Before my beloved father's untimely demise it was arranged I was going to be the new ruler of the empire. But to my people's disappointment, my cousin Akhdar who was consumed by jealously and greed decided to take matters into his own hands and sent me into exile."

Then he shifted his attention over to Kar-Tyr, who slowly backed away in fear.

"Yes, Kurwani," the lost prince addressed him. "I can feel the shadows of your thoughts. Akhdar is the source of our misery. I was not ready. My zhar was not yet awakened. Akhdar knew he needed to act before it did. And he did not bother with subtlety…or kindness," he said in repugnance, and pointed to the remains of the jade Kali. "He put me in the one place I could not escape." Then he directed himself to the rest of the party. "It is not his enemy or his foes that leave one to evil ways. It amused him that I would be the center of a cult, worshipping the Thulian God of War. Sailor, you are not the prophet. That is my burden."

"I am truly sorry," Kar-Tyr kneeled and began to sob.

"Kar-Tyr," Sinbad came to his friend's side, "what's wrong?"

"Do you remember what I told you back at the ship on how I did a great disservice on someone?"

Sinbad nodded.

"I am the one responsible for the prince's disappearance," Kar-Tyr confessed. "Akhdar told me if I didn't get rid of the young prince he would kill my wife…"

"But he killed her anyway," answered Sinbad.

Choking on sobs, Kar-Tyr nodded. "It is not about why I did it; it is all about that *I* did it. I know you cannot possibly forgive me, your majesty…"

"Enough, friend Kar-Tyr," said Muqari, placing his hand on his round shoulder. "I have a lot of time to think about the injustice my brother had done to me. There was a moment that I hated you with all my heart and soul.

But over time I realized I would have followed the same actions. Please, take my hand and arise."

Kar-Tyr took Prince Muqari's hand and rose up to his feet.

"I forgive you, Kar-Tyr of the Kurwani."

Drying his tears, Kar-Tyr said, "Thank you, my prince."

Sinbad felt relieved that the pressure of being this planet's savior had been lifted off his shoulders. But he had a feeling that his work wasn't done just yet. On what this young man—the true prophet—had said, he too had an axe to grind against Akhdar. Sinbad held on to every word this regal being had to say.

"But I ask you to bring Akhdar to heel," Prince Muqari declared. "To rid my planet of the disease that threatens to tear it apart. And reclaim Mars for all the Martians. What do you say, Sinbad of Earth?"

Qani rushed to Sinbad's side and took him by the hand. He lowered his sword and then looked at her with soulful eyes.

"You don't have to do this, Sinbad," she said, slowly shifting her gaze to the Thulian spacecraft. "As I told you before, you have no stake in this war. You have done more than enough for our cause, and for that I thank you."

Sinbad looked over to the huge ship. He thought the airship was impressive, but this was outstanding. Now he has the opportunity to sail through the stars.

"All we have to do is set a course for Earth and you will be on your way," Qani stated, leading him to the ship. "You will be back in the arms of your beloved Farah by dawn," she said softly.

Sinbad stopped Qani and then held her very closely. She was taken by surprise. She began to tremble and heave nervously as if she was swimming up to the surface for air. She thought he was going to kiss her, like he tried to do back on the deck of the airship the night before. But all she saw was a serious look that ran across Sinbad's face. He was a man who was in charge of his own destiny.

"I am afraid Farah will have to wait a little longer," he said to her.

Qani's face lit up with a friendly smile. *He IS the one.*

"There is much to be done," he continued. He gave Qani a heartwarming smile. "Besides I still owe you one, and I always pay my debts."

Qani laughed softly and embraced him. Suddenly she was transported back to the night before where he held her on the airship will all their secrets out in the open. She finally let go of him, and she was still smiling.

"Thank you, my friend," she said. "Prophet or not, you are what Mars needs right now. I believe in you, Sinbad."

"I will do whatever I can to live up to your expectations, Qani."

Sinbad looked over to Prince Muqari, who was waiting for an answer. Sinbad approached the missing heir and then lowered his eyes to meet the diminutive ones. Muqari stared at the Earth warrior for what seemed to be an eternity, and prepared for what he was going to say. He didn't need to use telepathy to know what was going to happen next. So he gave Sinbad a smile.

Sinbad ripped out a solemn oath and unsheathed his long blade quivered in his grip as the muscles rose in ridges on his brown arm.

He looked at Prince Muqari in the eye. "By Allah, I shall not leave until the prophecy is fulfilled."

EPILOGUE

Outside, the roar of a thousand armored soldiers shuddered up to the stars, which crusted the luminous moon, and the conch bellowed like a tortured animal.

In the courtyard of Akhdar's palace, the torches glinted on polished helmets and curved swords and gold-plated body armor. All the warriors in Akhdar's ranks were gathered in the great palace or about it, and each broad-arched gate and door fifty archers stood on guard, with bows in their hands.

A rough beast slowly moved forward, pitiless in his desire for revenge and domination, Emperor Akhdar made his slow and steady descent. It surveyed the expanse of his large army.

With a vision of the destruction to come, Akhdar uttered his first command to his legions.

They were walking, synchronized, remote-controlled drones. Experimental soldiers created by the disturbed Doctor Panhek from cadavers and traitors of the realm. They were all clad in metallic exo-skeletons and each of them was armed with large steam-powered rifles.

A new breed of soldier had arrived. A new world order was on the verge for the glory of Mars. Even the emperor seemed dwarfed by their surroundings.

Few things startled Aella, but standing over an army of undead soldiers who were no more machine than man, certainly did especially when she was in close presence of Doctor Panhek.

Much could be said about the man, but having an array of social skills was not among them still, Akhdar could not fault the heretic. To each their own.

Panhek took it all in. Only days ago, he was working in his very humble little dwelling in the outskirts of Dozhak, with illegally tapped power and access to the forbidden technology the elder Dadgar had outlawed. Now Panhek was operating in a very pristine place. There were more computers than he could image needing to use. He was in the possession of tools used for smelting, welding, wiring, plating, and most of all microwave circuit manufacture.

The lab was circular, with massive cylindrical columns supporting a large ring in the center. It was a surgical suite, and as Akhdar entered the room, he noticed the carts on which the Panhek's assistants had piled the necessary medical instruments. The usual collection of scalpels and hemostats, scissors and retractors and clamps, but that wasn't all, it wasn't even close. The more thought of them set an unaccustomed thrill of horror up his spine. Much of the lab's floor space was taken up with long rows of gleaming metal humanoid warriors. Most of which were not yet finished.

Akhdar was a man with practically unlimited resources and enough power to command an army. He took a step back and looked at the rows of Mortis Troopers.

His soldiers.

They are superior to any being on Mars in every way relevant to the battlefield. They were stronger than a Kurwani, more loyal than a Thulian, and better than an inferior Azurian.

That superiority, Akhdar was confident. He would use this to advantage over the people from other worlds as well.

"I cannot believe you authorized this, brother," said Aella, turning away from those god-awful things. "This goes against everything we have ever learned from our uncle."

"Aella," Akhdar said sternly, "must I remind you how senile our uncle was, and how his methods nearly destroyed Dozhak? The forbidden knowledge is the way of the future, and I will not let this Earthman and the rest of his fellow vermin come between me and my dream."

"Surely there must be some other way," Aella replied, feeling nauseated just by looking at the Mortis Troopers.

"No, dear sister," said Akhdar, "there isn't."

He had never heard a noise as loud as what came from the crowd and rebounded from the acoustically enhancing roof of the palace. Each group of drones was colored like the dress uniform of the service it represented. They were equipped to fly, with wing-like additions to every limb and active control surfaces along their backs. They were squat and loaded with heavy weaponry, as if each one was capable of maintaining an artillery barrage. For all he knew, they were.

The soldiers were lining up in some pre-programmed formation. The army broke into smaller battalions, and waited for their orders.

"Amazing," Akhdar said. "I couldn't imagine anything more from you, Doctor."

"There is so much more, sire," Doctor Panhek gestured nearly the holding area taken up by a group of twenty Mortis Troopers, reflecting various ethnicities, but all with formidable physical builds.

They all stood in attention, not a single-muscle moving among them, each with less expression than a statue.

"Significant improvements have been made. As you can see, we've been very busy before you gave me the order to carry out your request."

"But have you been *successful*?"

"We have made strides. Come with me, please."

Akhdar followed Panhek to the Troopers. All of them had incision scars on their foreheads.

"I installed command chips in each of their brains so they could follow a command without any question."

"Do they feel pain?"

"No," answered Panhek. "And they do not possess any fear. In addition, frontal-lobe concepts of morality are disengaged. And this, your highness, means *no* sense of remorse."

Akhdar stroked his chin with interest. "And these subjects are utterly obedient?"

"Of course," Panhek said causally. "You now have an army of invincible warriors in your possession, my liege."

Akhdar nodded, "I am favorably impressed, Doctor. Very favorably impressed."

"Nothing could please me more than having you say that."

With a curt nod of dismissal, Akhdar said, "Send a team of your Mortis Troopers to meet with Tarkhun."

"We already have the prototype unit in place," Panhek was saying, almost giddily. "We have a single subject who is *perfect*."

"You've done well, Doctor," Akhdar said, almost off-handedly. "You have done your kingdom such a great service."

"Thank you, sire," Panhek replied. "But there is so much more research that needs to be done. May I be so bold to ask you for a favor?"

Akhdar glanced at him, as if the good doctor was going to tell a joke.

"If I could get more assistants and a bigger laboratory—"

"I appreciate your thirst for knowledge, Doctor. It's certainly…admirable. But this is already going over several boundaries," he shook his head firmly. "What Mars needs right now, at this crucial moment in the Dozhakian Dynasty, is unification. Strong firm leadership. The world cries out to be taken out of chaos by someone willing to take *complete* control."

Panhek nodded in response, and then took one last look of his greatest creations.

"You may go back to your miniaturized dancing girls, Doctor," said Akhdar. "But before you do, I want you to see if the necromancer Sardeth Rex is ready for our contingency plan."

A sly smile reached across the corners of Panhek's mouth. "Very well, my lord; and thank you once again for giving me this opportunity."

Akhdar watched as the guards escorted Panhek back to his lab. Then the young emperor walked up to the head Mortis Trooper.

Behind all the bionic enhancements and all the other metal components was the face of the Azurian elder that once shared a cell with Sinbad. His pupils were dilated and his flesh was gaunt and there was a pale shade of faint blue on his complexion.

Akhdar was quite pleased with this model—the very successful prototype. The doctor said this new *improvement* wouldn't be a problem. The look of defiance in the old man's eyes vanished without a trace. Akhdar owned him now.

Right behind him were the automations of Rajia, Typhus, and Nukus. Typhus was heavily armored, but the new makeover didn't improve the hideous knife scars on his face. Nukus' enhancements covered most of his tattoos and all the accessories gave him a lot of bulk. Then there was Rajia without her signature battle helmet.

Akhdar was more interested in this model than all the others. Now his once favorite gladiator has the chance to redeem herself after her defeat by Sinbad in the arena. Akhdar noticed the whirring mechanical red glowing lens that replaced her missing left eye. The side of her hair was shaved so Panhek can install the new inhibitor chip to keep her under control.

"Listen up, Troopers," he announced, as the small squad turned their attention toward him. "My spy has informed me that our kingdom is in grave danger. For your first mission you must search and destroy my cousin Muqari. My sources say he has broken out of his prison and the rebels are protecting him. You can do what you want with them, but I have a special request for the rogue known as Sinbad the Sailor."

Then he stared at the old Azurian, giving him the unholy task.

"I want you rip his arms and legs out, and leave his head for last. Then I want you to bring it back to me so I can give it to my sister."

The Mortis Troopers raised their weapons upward, and expanded the glider wings in their backs getting ready for takeoff.

"Yes, my lord," said the old Azurian, speaking with no emotion or conscience whatsoever.

The night sky beckoned to them.

The Mortis Troopers fired up their jet packs and rose from the ground. They prepared to steady themselves and did so. Unfortunately they had not accounted for the accelerated strength that the new exo-armor provided them. Every moment was accentuated and heightened.

They rose slowly, taking their time, but quickly began to move faster. Even the smallest movements altered their trajectory in most unexpected ways. Eventually they discovered a combination of jet booster and well-balanced angularity that enabled them to fly straight and true. After executing that maneuver, they were all in complete control of their trajectory.

Akhdar looked on with a satisfying smirk as one by one of his deadly new Mortis Troopers flew out of the ceiling's skylight and took off to the air to do their master's bidding.

"Let's see how Sinbad fares with *these* monsters."

THE END